HARDWIRED

Meredith Wild

This book is a work of fiction. Names, characters, places, and incidents are the product of the author's imagination or are used fictitiously. Any resemblance to actual events, locales, or persons, living or dead, is coincidental.

Forever
Hachette Book Group
1290 Avenue of the Americas
New York, NY 10104
hachettebookgroup.com
twitter.com/foreverromance

Printed in the United States of America
RRD-C

First Forever Edition: May 2015
10 9 8 7 6 5 4 3 2 1

Forever is an imprint of Grand Central Publishing.
The Forever name and logo are trademarks of Hachette Book Group, Inc.

ISBN 978-1-4555-6513-9

For mom,
for begging me to write.

CHAPTER ONE

"What a perfect day," I said.

Winter had thawed in Boston and spring was upon us. The campus had come alive, buzzing with college students, tourists, and city natives.

Many still wore their graduation gowns from this afternoon's ceremony, the entirety of which I was still processing. Everything felt surreal, from saying bittersweet goodbyes to friends to the anticipation of facing real world problems in the days ahead. A blur of emotions whirled through me. Pride, relief, anxiety. But what I felt most was happiness. To be in this moment. To have Marie by my side.

"It is, and no one deserves it more than you, Erica." Marie Martelly, my mother's best friend and my own personal lifesaver, gave my hand a little squeeze and hooked her arm into mine.

Tall and slender, Marie towered over my petite frame. Her soft skin was the color of cocoa and her brown hair was twisted into dozens of short dreads, a style that expressed both her eternal youth and eclectic style. From the outside, no one would suspect that she was the only mother I'd had for nearly a decade.

I told myself over the years that not having parents was sometimes better than having the kinds of parents I heard about and occasionally met. My classmates' parents could be so overbearing. Physically there but emotionally absent, or old enough to be my grandparents and suffering from a serious generational gap. Excelling seemed vastly easier when I was the only person putting pressure on myself to succeed.

Marie was different. Over the years, she had always offered the perfect measure of support. She listened to my friend drama and my moaning about work and finals, but she never pushed me. She knew how hard I already pushed myself.

We walked down the tiny paths that wove through the Harvard campus. A soft breeze blew through the full leafy trees, rustling quietly above us.

"Thank you for being there for me today," I said.

"Don't be ridiculous, Erica! I wouldn't miss this for the world. You know that." She smiled down at me and winked. "Plus I always enjoy a little trip down memory lane. I can't remember the last time I was on campus. Makes me feel young again!"

I laughed at her enthusiasm. Only someone like Marie could visit her alma mater and feel younger, as if no time had passed.

"You're still young, Marie."

"Oh, I suppose. Life moves too fast though. You'll figure that out, soon enough." She sighed softly. "You ready to celebrate?"

I nodded. "Absolutely. Let's go."

We stepped outside the campus gates and hailed a cab that took us over the Charles River into Boston. A few minutes later we pushed through the heavy wooden doors of one of the best steakhouses in the city. Compared to the sunny streets, the restaurant was dark and cool, and a noticeable air of refinement floated over the quiet murmur of the evening's patrons.

We settled down with our menus and ordered dinner and drinks. The waiter promptly delivered two glasses of sixteen-year Scotch, on the rocks, a taste for which I had acquired from more than a few complementary dinners with Marie. After weeks of overdosing on coffee and late night take out, nothing said congratulations like a cool glass of Scotch and a steak dinner.

I traced lines into the sweat on my glass, wondering what today might have looked like if my mother was still alive. Maybe I'd still be at home in Chicago, living an entirely different life.

"What's on your mind, baby girl?" Marie's voice broke me from my thoughts.

"Nothing. I just wish Mom could have been here," I said quietly.

Marie took my hand in hers from across the table. "We both know Patricia would have been so proud of you today. Beyond words."

No one had known my mother better than Marie. Though distance had separated them for years after school, they remained close—all the way to the bitter end.

I avoided her eyes, unwilling to let myself succumb to the emotions that tended to rush over me like a goddamn flood every Hallmark holiday. I wouldn't cry today. Today was a happy day, no matter what. One I would never forget.

Marie released me and held up her glass, her eyes brightening. "How about a toast, to the next chapter?"

I raised my glass with hers and smiled through the sadness, letting relief and gratitude fill the empty place in my heart.

"Cheers." I tipped my glass to Marie's and took a healthy swallow, savoring the burn of the liquor on its way down.

"Speaking of, what's next for you, Erica?"

I let my thoughts drift back to my life and the real pressures I was still under. "Well, this week is the big pitch at Angelcom, and then at some point I need to figure out where to live."

"You can always stay with me for a while."

"I know, but I need to get set up on my own for once. I'm looking forward to it actually."

"Any ideas?"

"Not really, but I need a break from Cambridge." Harvard had been great, but academia and I needed to start seeing other people. I had spent the past year seriously overachieving, juggling a thesis, starting a new business, and managing the usual senior burnout moments. I was eager to start the next chapter of my life well away from campus.

"Not that I would ever want you to leave, but are you sure you want to stay in Boston?"

I nodded. "I'm sure. The business might take me to New York or California at some point, but for now I'm happy here."

Boston was a hard city sometimes. The winters were hell, but the people here were strong, passionate, and often painfully direct. Over time, I'd become one of them. I couldn't imagine calling anyplace else home on a whim. Plus, without parents to go home to, this had become my home.

"Do you ever think of going back to Chicago?"

"No." I chewed my salad in silence for a moment, trying not to think about all the people who might have been here for me today. "There's no one back home for me anymore. Elliot remarried and has kids now. And Mom's family has always been...you know, distant."

Ever since my mother had come home from college twenty-one years ago, newly pregnant with no plans to marry, her relationship with her parents had been strained, to say the least. Even as a child, what few memories I shared with my grandparents had felt uncomfortable and colored by how I had come into their lives. Mom never spoke of my father, but if the circumstances were upsetting enough for her to keep silent about them, I was probably better off not knowing. At least that's what I told myself when curiosity started to get the best of me.

The sadness in Marie's sympathetic eyes reflected my own. "Do you ever hear from Elliot?"

"Mostly around the holidays. He has his hands full with the two little ones now."

Elliot was the only father I had ever known. He'd married my mother when I was a toddler, and we shared many happy years together as a family. But no more than a year after my mother had passed, he became overwhelmed with the prospect of raising a teenager alone and enrolled me in boarding school out east with my inheritance.

"You miss him," she said quietly, as if reading my thoughts.

"Sometimes," I admitted. "We never had a chance to be a family without her." I remembered how lost and out of step we became when she died. Now we were bound to each other only through the memory of her love, a memory that faded a little more with each passing year.

"He meant well, Erica."

"I know he did. I don't blame him. We're both happy, so that's all that matters now." With a degree and a new business under my belt, I had no regrets about Elliot's choice. Ultimately it placed me on the path that had led me to where I was today, but nothing could change the fact that we'd grown further apart over the years.

"Enough about that, then. Let's talk about your love life." Marie shot me a warm smile, her beautiful almond eyes glittering in the dim light of the restaurant.

I laughed, knowing she would want every detail if I had anything at all to divulge. "Nothing new to report, sadly. How about we talk about yours instead?" I knew she would take the bait.

Her eyes lit up and she gushed about her newest love interest. Richard was a jet-setting journalist nearly a decade her junior, which was no surprise to me. Not only was she in great shape for her age, Marie was incredibly young at heart. I often had to remind myself that she was my mother's age.

While she reminisced, I enjoyed a short love affair with my food. Perfectly prepared and dripping with a red wine reduction, the bone-in filet nearly melted in my mouth. Deeply satisfying, the meal almost made up for the past several months of sexual deprivation. If it didn't, the plate of chocolate covered strawberries we finished our dinner with definitely did.

College had provided me with regular opportunities for short-term flings, but unlike Marie, I was never really looking for love. And now that I had a business to keep up with, I barely had time for a social life, let alone a sex life.

Instead I lived vicariously through Marie, genuinely happy she had a new man who kept a little pep in her step.

We finished and Marie agreed to meet me outside after she freshened up. I made my way toward the door, feeling happy and a little buzzed. I passed the host and turned back when he thanked me for coming. The next minute I ran straight into the man coming through the front door.

He caught me by the waist, pulling me up as I steadied myself.

"Sorry, I—" My apology fizzled when our eyes met. A mesmerizing tornado of hazel and green poured into me, obliterating my ability to speak. Gorgeous. The man was drop dead gorgeous.

"Are you all right?"

His voice vibrated through me. My knees weakened a little at the sensation. His arm tightened around my waist in response, bringing our bodies infinitely closer. The shift did little to help me regain my composure. My heartbeat quickened by the way he held me, possessive and confident, as if he had every right to keep me there as long as he liked.

A small part of me, the part that wasn't humming with desire for this strange man, wanted to protest his boldness, but all rational thought was clouded as I drank in his features. He couldn't have been much older than I. With the exception of his wayward dark brown hair, he appeared to be all business in a charcoal blazer over a white collared shirt with a couple buttons loose. He looked expensive. He even smelled expensive.

Out of your league, Erica, a little voice sang, reminding me it was my turn to speak.

"Yes, I'm fine. I'm sorry."

"Don't be," he murmured seductively, with a hint of a smile. His lips were etched and full of promise, impossible to ignore with my face just inches from his. He slid his tongue over his bottom lip, and my jaw dropped with a soundless sigh. God, the sexual energy rolled off the man like tidal waves.

"Mr. Landon, your party is here."

While the host waited for him to respond, I sobered enough to straighten, confident I could stand independently again. I leveraged the effort with my hands on his chest, hard and unforgiving even through his suit. He released his hold on me, his hands blazing a trail of fire over my hips as they left my body slowly. *Sweet Jesus.* Dessert had nothing on this man.

He nodded to the host but barely took his eyes from me, paralyzing me with that single thread connecting us. Irrationally, I wanted nothing more than his hands on me again, possessing me like they had so easily before. If he had my head swimming with a mere touch, there was no telling what he could do in the bedroom. I wondered if there might be a coat closet nearby. We could get to the bottom of this right now.

"Right this way, sir," the host said, waving my rescuer toward him.

He walked away with casual grace, leaving me tingling from head to toe in his absence. Marie joined me as I watched his retreat, a sight to behold.

I meant to be embarrassed, but in truth I was shamelessly satisfied with my inability to balance on four-inch heels. In lieu of a love life of my own, mystery man would become fodder for many fantasies to come.

★ ★ ★

I ascended the broad granite steps of the library building and traveled through the halls to Professor Quinlan's office. He was staring intently at his computer screen when I knocked at the door.

He swiveled in his chair. "Erica! My favorite Internet start-up girl."

His telltale Irish lilt had become less pronounced after living in America for so long. I still found it adorable and clung to every word.

"Tell me, how does freedom feel?"

I giggled a bit, warmed at his genuine enthusiasm to see me. Quinlan was an attractive man in his early fifties, with salt and pepper gray hair and kind pale blue eyes.

"Still getting used to it, to be honest. How about you? When does your sabbatical start?"

"I fly into Dublin in a few weeks. You must visit me if you find time this year."

"I would love to, of course," I said.

What would this year look like for me? Hopefully I'd be nursing my business through early growing pains, but in truth, I had no idea what to expect.

"For some reason I feel like it would be strange seeing you outside of campus, Professor."

"I'm not your professor anymore, Erica. Call me Brendan, please. I'm now your friend and your mentor, and I certainly hope we'll see plenty more of each other beyond these walls."

The professor's words hit me hard, and my throat tingled a bit. Sentimental moments were plaguing me this week, damn it all. Quinlan had been incredibly supportive these past few years, guiding me through my major and making connections for me to push the business forward. The tireless cheerleader every time I needed a boost.

"I can't thank you enough. I want you to know that."

"Helping people like you, Erica, is what gets me up in the morning. And it keeps me out of the pub." He gave me a crooked smile, revealing a lone dimple.

"And Max?"

"Well, unfortunately Max's ambition for drink and women far exceeded his ambition for success in business, but it seems like he turned it around after all. I'm not sure if I was any help there, but perhaps. They can't all be like you, dear."

"I'm so worried things with the business won't work out in the long run," I admitted, hoping he had some clairvoyance that I lacked.

"There's no doubt in my mind that you will be successful, one way or the other. If not with this, there will be something else. None of us know where life will take us, but you're making sacrifices and working hard for your dreams. As long as you stay true to those dreams, keep them at the forefront of your mind, you're moving in the right direction. At least that's what I tell myself."

"Sounds right to me." My nerves were strung tight in anticipation of tomorrow's meeting, which would be a make it or break it moment for the business, and for me. I needed all the encouragement I could get.

"I'll let you know when I figure it all out anyway," he promised.

I didn't know whether to be inspired or discouraged, knowing he sometimes felt as aimless as I felt right now.

"In the meantime, let's see what you've got for our friend Max tomorrow." He motioned toward the folder on my lap and cleared a path on his desk.

"Definitely." I laid out the business plan and my notes, and we set to work.

CHAPTER TWO

The receptionist at Angelcom Venture Group gave me a questioning glance before leading me into the conference room at the end of the hall. I checked myself over, making sure nothing was grossly out of place. So far so good.

"Make yourself comfortable, Miss Hathaway. The rest of the group should be arriving shortly."

"Thank you," I said politely, grateful the room was momentarily empty. I took a deep breath, trailing my fingers along the edge of the conference table until I reached a wall of windows overlooking Boston Harbor. Awe mingled with my growing anxiety. In a moment I would be face-to-face with a handful of the city's most wealthy and influential investors. I felt so far out of my comfort zone, it just wasn't funny. I took a deep breath and shook out my hands anxiously, wishing my body would relax a little.

"Erica?"

I spun around. A young man about my age, with blond hair parted neatly to the side, dark blue eyes, and wearing an impressive three-piece suit, approached me. We shook hands.

"You must be Maxwell."

"Please, call me Max."

"Professor Quinlan has told me a lot about you, Max."

"Don't believe a word of it." He laughed, revealing a set

of perfectly white teeth contrasting with a tan that made me wonder how much time he actually spent in New England.

"All good things, I promise," I lied.

"That's good of him. I owe him one. This must be your first pitch?"

"Unmistakably."

"You'll do fine. Just remember, most of us were in your shoes at some point."

I smiled and nodded, knowing the chances of Max Pope, heir to shipping magnate Michael Pope, pitching to anyone other than his father for a measly two million dollars were slim to none. Regardless, he was the reason I was here this morning, and I was thankful. Quinlan had known just the favor to pull.

"Help yourself. The pastries are amazing." He gestured to the plentiful breakfast buffet along the wall.

The knot in my stomach disagreed. I needed to get a handle on my nerves. I couldn't even stomach coffee this morning. "Thank you, I'm fine though."

As the other investors trickled in, Max introduced me, and I did my best to make small talk, silently cursing Alli, my best friend, absentee business partner, and marketing go-to. She could make entertaining small talk with a can of soup, where I had little else on my mind beyond the facts and figures I was prepared to present, which wasn't ideal for idle conversation with people I'd never met.

When people began to settle at the conference table, I positioned myself on the opposite side, organizing and scanning over my paperwork for the twentieth time. I located the clock on the wall across from me. I had less than twenty minutes to convince this small group of strangers that I was worth investing in.

The rumble of voices quieted, but when I looked to Max for the cue to start, he gestured to the empty center chair across from me. "We're waiting for Landon."

Landon?

The door swung open. *Holy shit.* I forgot how to breathe.

In walked my mystery man—six feet of masculine glory—looking nothing like his suited colleagues. His black V-neck highlighted his sculpted shoulders and chest, and his worn out jeans fit his physique like a dream. My skin grew tight at the thought of having those arms around me again, accidentally or otherwise.

Armed with a jumbo iced coffee, he dropped into the seat in front of me, seemingly unaware of his lateness or lack of formality, and flashed me a knowing smile. He was an entirely different person from the dapper professional I'd so luckily fallen into the other night. He suffered from a gorgeous case of bedhead, his dark brown hair spiking every which way, begging for my fingers. I bit my lip in an effort to hide my raw appreciation for the man's body.

"This is Blake Landon," Max said. "Blake, Erica Hathaway. She's here to present on her fashion social network, Clozpin."

He stilled for a moment. "Clever name. You brought her in?"

"Yes, we have a mutual friend at Harvard."

Blake nodded, locking me in a penetrating stare that had me instantly flushed. He licked his lips. The simple motion had no less effect on me than it had the night we first saw each other.

I drew in a deep breath and crossed my legs, acutely aware of the sensations he inspired between them. *Get it together, Erica.* The ball of nervous energy that had resided in my stomach mere seconds ago had exploded into a blinding sexual energy that had me pulsing from my fingertips to my nethers.

I blew out a slow breath and smoothed the lapels on my black suit coat, silently scolding myself for swooning at an incredibly inconvenient time. I stuttered into the presentation. I explained the premise of the website and moved into a brief outline of our year of bare bones marketing and the resulting exponential growth, trying desperately to stay focused. Every time Blake and I made eye contact, my brain started short-circuiting.

Eventually he interrupted me. "Who developed the site?"

"My co-founder, Sid Kumar."

"And where is he?"

"Unfortunately, my co-founders were unable to attend today, though they very much wanted to."

"So you're the only one on your team dedicated to the project right now?"

He arched a brow and leaned back casually into the seat, giving me a better view of his torso. I forced myself not to stare.

"No, I—" I struggled to formulate an honest answer. "We've just graduated, so our level of involvement in the coming months depends heavily on the project's financial stability."

"In other words, their dedication is dependent on funding."

"Somewhat."

"Is yours?"

"No," I said sharply, immediately defensive at the implication. I had dedicated my life to this project for months, thinking of nothing else.

"Continue." He waved me on.

I took a deep breath and glanced at my notes to get back on track. "At this juncture, we are seeking an injection of capital for marketing to enhance growth and revenue."

"What's your conversion rate?"

"From visitors to registered users, about twenty percent—"

"Okay, but what about paid users?" he interrupted.

"About five percent of our users upgrade to pro accounts."

"How do you plan to improve that?"

I tapped my fingers impatiently on the table, trying to keep my scattered thoughts on track. Every question he posed sounded like a challenge or an insult, effectively squashing every confidence-inspiring pep talk I had given myself leading up to this meeting. Teetering on the edge of panic, I looked to Max for a sign of hope. He seemed mildly amused by what I imagined was par for the course for Mr. Landon. The others stared blankly between their notepads and me, showing no indication of their interest either way.

For a split second I had thought last night's run-in meant he might go easy on me, but apparently not. Mystery man was turning out to be a bit of a jerk.

"We've been focused on building and maintaining the

basic membership, which as I mentioned, is growing virally. With a solid base of potential consumers, we are hoping to attract more retailers and brands in the industry and increase our paid memberships."

I paused, bracing myself for another interruption, but Blake's phone silently lit up, mercifully distracting him. Relieved to finally be out from under his microscope, I concluded with the competitor analysis and financial projections before my time was up.

An awkward silence descended upon the room. Blake took a sip of his coffee, closed out the screen on his phone, and set it back on the table. "Are you seeing anyone?"

My heart pounded in my chest and my face heated, as if I'd been unexpectedly called on in class. *Was I seeing anyone?* I stared at him in shock, unsure if I fully understood the implication of his question. "Excuse me?"

"Relationships can be distracting. If you were to get the funds you need from this group, it could be a factor that affects your ability to grow."

I hadn't misunderstood him. As if being the only woman in the room wasn't enough pressure, I had him shining a spotlight on my relationship status. *Misogynist prick.* I clenched my teeth, this time to keep myself from hurling a string of expletives at him. I couldn't lose my cool, but I wasn't about to smile away his inappropriate behavior.

"I can assure you, Mr. Landon, that I am one hundred percent committed to this project," I said, my voice slow and steady. I met his gaze, doing my best to communicate how unimpressed I was with his approach. "Do you have any other questions pertaining to my personal life that will influence your decision today?"

"No, I don't think so. Max?"

"Um, no, I think we've covered quite a bit. Gentlemen, are you ready to decide on this?" Max grinned and gestured to the others.

The other three men in suits nodded, and one after the next, they voiced their commendation of my efforts and subsequent decision to pass on the project.

Blake looked me in the eye, pausing for a moment before delivering his verdict as casually as he'd devastated my morning. "I'll pass."

Panic alarms went off and tears threatened, quickly followed by my inner voice. She was crafting a farewell speech for Mr. Landon that included telling him where to go and how to get there. I looked to Max, waiting for the final blow.

"Well, Erica, I think you've created a really great community with this, and I would certainly like to hear more. Let's schedule a time in the next couple weeks for a follow up, and we can get into more of the logistics. After that, we'll decide if we want to offer you a deal. How does that sound?"

Sweet relief. I wanted to jump over the table and hug Max. "That would be wonderful. I will look forward to it."

"Great. I think we're done here then."

Max rose to chat with the other men before they headed out, leaving me face to face with Blake, who was now smirking at me with that gorgeous smug face. I didn't know whether to smack him or fix his hair. I had a few other things in mind too. Feeling so conflicted about someone in such a short period of time made me question my own sanity.

"You did well," he said, leaning in closer.

His voice was low and raspy, making my skin tingle.

"Really?" I countered unsteadily.

"Really," he reassured me. "Can I take you to breakfast?" His eyes softened, as if we hadn't spent the past twenty minutes at odds with one another.

Confused, I stuffed my notes back into my bag. Blake was beautiful, but he grossly overestimated his assets if he thought I was going to let him pick me up after that show.

"There's this great little pub across the street. They do a full Irish breakfast."

I stood and met his gaze, thrilled by the opportunity to serve him up a little slice of rejection. "It's been a pleasure, Mr. Landon, but some of us have work to do."

★★★

"He asked you out?" Alli gushed into the phone. New York City hustled and bustled in the background as she spoke.

"I guess so." I was still reeling from the morning events.

"Did you wear your power suit? With the teal blouse?"

"Yes, of course," I said, stripping the very garment off of me and collapsing onto our futon back at the dorm.

"Well, no wonder. You look amazing in that. Was he hot?"

Blake Landon was one of the sexiest men I had ever shared airspace with, but he had no respect for women in business, which put a serious damper on my attraction to him. Unfortunately, he was perilously close to being in my top ten of people I most despised.

"It doesn't matter, Alli. I've never been so humiliated." I winced, reliving his challenges and the subsequent rejection.

"You're right. I'm sorry, I wish I could have been there to help."

"Me too. Anyway, how was the interview?"

Alli paused. "It was good."

"Yeah?"

"Really good, actually. I don't want to jinx myself, but it sounds pretty promising."

"That's great." I tried to hide my disappointment, knowing she was excited about this one. She would be working under the marketing director at one of the biggest labels in fashion. I had known for months that Alli would be looking for a full-time gig after graduation, but the thought of running the site without her depressed me. Unless we could afford to hire a new marketing director, I would become the new voice of the company, and networking had never been my forte.

"Nothing is set in stone though. We'll see."

"We should celebrate," I said. Heaven knew I needed some sort of reward for surviving my hellish morning.

"We should celebrate our new best friend, Max!" she squealed.

I laughed, knowing Max was just her type too, if she only knew. She fell apart over three-piece suits. "Hopefully he isn't just extending his favor to Quinlan by hearing me out for this follow up."

"People don't dangle two million dollar carrots in front of people as a favor."

"True, but I don't want him to invest unless he's actually interested."

"Erica, you're overanalyzing, as usual."

I blew out a slow breath. "Maybe." I hoped she was right, but I couldn't help running every possible scenario through my mind in an attempt to plan and prepare for all of them. My brain never stopped these days with so much on the line.

"I'm getting on the Acela in an hour. I'll be back before dinner and then we can grab drinks."

"All right, see you then." I hung up and forced myself to get up so I could locate my comfy sweat pants, the ones I reserved for breakups and hangovers. Today had drained me beyond belief.

I stopped to appraise myself in the full-length mirror in the room Alli and I shared. I loosened my French twist and my wavy blond hair fell down my back. I was thinner than usual, thanks to the past few weeks of stress, but my matching bra and panties still clung to my subtle curves.

I ran my hands over the soft lace hugging my hips, wishing someone else's hands were there to make me forget all about today. I wasn't expecting to go weak in the knees over some cocky investor at my first boardroom pitch, but my physical reaction to Blake was a serious indicator that I needed to revive my social life. I needed to get out and meet more people. Get away from my computer, at least on Saturday nights. That was usually when we did maintenance on the site because the traffic was slow, but at this rate I wouldn't have another relationship in my twenties.

I shook off the worry, got dressed, and shot off an email to Sid with the news. He wouldn't be awake for another few hours. In addition to being nocturnal, as many programmers were, he had come down with the flu the day before the meeting. He wasn't much of a public speaker either, but strength existed in numbers and I could have used his support.

The business kept Alli, Sid, and me afloat, covering costs and our modest expenses as college students, but there were high expectations for where our Ivy League educations would land us fresh out of school. While Sid and Alli had been job hunting like any responsible college senior, I had gone all in on Clozpin, convinced after our initial success that I could turn it into something far better than a nine to five job for all of us.

Getting Max to invest might be my last hope before I had to sideline that dream and get a normal job. In the meantime, I had less than a week to move out of the dorms and find a place to live.

★ ★ ★

I woke to the smell of coffee quickly followed by a dull throbbing in my head. "Damn the wine." I rubbed my temples and willed the pain away.

I sat up on the futon, wrapped myself in my comforter, and thanked the gods for the precious gift of coffee as Alli handed me a steaming cup and ibuprofen on cue.

"Whatever, we had a blast." She sidled up next to me with her cup of joe. Her long brown hair was pulled up into a messy bun and she looked effortlessly cute in an oversized off the shoulder top and black leggings. "I haven't seen you have so much fun in ages. You deserved a little break."

"That meeting put me over the edge," I said, thankful despite the headache that my nerves were no longer as frayed as they were yesterday.

"So tell me more about Max, and when can I meet him? According to drunk Erica, we're soul mates."

I laughed as details of the night came back to me. No night of dinner and drinks was complete without girl talk.

"I pretty much only know what Professor Quinlan told me. He's smart but always ended up digging himself out of some trouble at school. I don't think he would have graduated without Quinlan's help, and a degree was one thing his daddy couldn't buy." I shrugged, wanting to give Max the benefit of the doubt now that he'd saved me from total humiliation. "I'm sure it's not easy to fly straight with a billionaire father though. Some people can't handle that much freedom."

"Well it just so happens I'm in the market for taming billionaire playboys." She gave me a sassy smirk over her shoulder.

"I have little doubt you are." I rolled my eyes.

"So he just does this investing thing now?"

"I'm not really sure what he does now outside of Angelcom. With that much money, he's probably into all sorts of things."

"Okay, the Internet search begins." Alli bounced up and settled back with her laptop, narrating Max's benign resume of charity associations and Internet investments. "Let's see what we can dig up about Blake Landon."

I fisted my hand around the mug handle, vaguely remembering my drunken rant about what an offensive ass Blake had been at the meeting. That he assumed he could derail my presentation and take me out after was unbelievable, but with looks like his, he probably had most women eating out of his palm with very little effort. Unfortunately for him, I wasn't most women. The seething rage I felt toward the man was tempered only by the unholy way I felt under his gaze.

"Please, I could care less." Of the warring emotions, I tried to focus on my anger, but in truth, I was secretly curious about what Alli might find. Until yesterday I hadn't heard of Blake, but judging by the way they let him run the show at Angelcom, he must have some influence. Alli stared intently at the screen, reading with obvious interest. I finally caved. "Well, what does it say?"

"He's a hacker."

"What?" She must have had the wrong Blake Landon, though he'd hardly looked like an upstanding corporate citizen that morning.

"Well, he used to be anyway. He has rumored connections to M89, a U.S.-based hacker group that compromised over two hundred high-profile bank accounts about fifteen years ago. It doesn't say anything else about it though. Officially, he's the founding developer of Banksoft, which was acquired for twelve billion dollars. He's the executive director of Angelcom and is an active investor in a number of early-stage Internet companies."

"Self-made billionaire, then."

"Sounds like it. He's only twenty-seven. Says his parents were teachers."

The information did little to diminish the anger I felt toward him sabotaging my pitch, but it did fill in some of the blanks. I had to admit, I respected him more knowing he wasn't handed his fortune, but between him and Max, he still acted like the privileged brat of the two.

"Well, I don't suppose it matters much now. If I'm lucky, we'll never cross paths again anyway."

CHAPTER THREE

It had been drizzling rain for hours. Streams coursed down the windowsill beside my desk overlooking one of the many courtyards on campus. The dorms were quiet as most of the students had already left for the term, so I decided to catch up on work. I was checking the statistics on Clozpin when a new mail alert popped up on my screen from a name I didn't recognize. The subject line read, "TechLabs Conference Panelist." A thrill of excitement coursed through me as I read the message. It was a request to fill in for a last minute cancellation at TechLabs, the biggest tech conference of the year.

"Alli..."

She grumbled something from under her blanket where she had been napping.

"Do you want to go to Vegas?"

"I thought you were hung over."

"I am, but I just got invited to speak at the TechLabs Conference this weekend."

Alli threw the cover off and sat up. "Are you serious?"

"Very. They had someone cancel on their social network CEO panel, and they want me to fill in."

"We should do it. No question. This could be an amazing marketing opportunity." She clapped her hands excitedly.

The trip would be expensive, but how could I pass up an opportunity to potentially launch us into the spotlight? *What the hell.* I couldn't justify going half way at this point.

"Let's do it," I said, immediately giddy at the thought. Sure, networking could be great, but the idea of going to Vegas was pretty exciting all by itself. If I stayed away from the casinos, we'd be fine.

"Awesome, we need to start packing now," Alli said.

"You're kidding me, right?"

"Erica Hathaway, you're the CEO of a fashion social network, representing your company in Las Vegas, the capital of glitz and glamour. We have serious work to do."

I laughed as Alli snapped into action, losing herself in our miniscule closet, throwing what looked to be every mini dress she owned onto the bed.

"I'm going for the CEO look, not the call girl look, okay, Alli?"

"You've never been to Vegas, sweetie. Trust me."

We spent the next few hours negotiating outfits while I booked flights and prepped material for the conference. In a little more than twenty-four hours, we would be in Vegas.

The next day around noon, I started across campus to meet with Sid. It was about time for his wake up call.

Not surprisingly, Sid and I met online first. I had the concept, the designs, and a small investment for start up costs, so after mulling over my original idea for a few weeks, I put out the call to the student body for a programmer to help build the site. Sid had been the first to reply. After a couple meetings, we decided to partner on the project.

I banged on his door for a few minutes before he finally opened it. Sid was tall, well over six feet, and literally the skinniest human being I had ever known. With his dark skin and big brown puppy dog eyes, he was adorable in his own special way, but he'd been painfully single ever since I'd met him. I wasn't the only one who needed to get out more.

This morning his eyes were bloodshot and tired, and I silently wondered if a new video game had come out. That usually had an effect on his already erratic sleep schedule.

"Here, I brought breakfast." I tossed him an energy drink, and he grumbled a response before heading back into the cave—a messy suite he shared with a handful of other hermits. I followed him in and sat down on the couch.

"What's up?" He cracked open the can and settled in at his desk covered in empty cans and pop tart wrappers. I resisted the urge to start cleaning.

"I'm going to Vegas to speak at the TechLabs conference, so I wanted to touch base with you before I left tonight. We might get a spike in traffic from the exposure. I just want to make sure we're prepared for that."

"How big of a spike?"

"I have no idea, but there are forty-five thousand people attending the conference. Alli is coming, so she'll be doing PR too."

"Okay, I'll monitor the stats and have some load bearing servers set up for overflow." He scribbled something into his notebook and booted up his machine.

"Do we have those already, or do we need to buy more?" I asked, hoping that we could avoid downtime with minimal funds.

"We can always use more. Is it in the budget?"

"Uh, not really. This trip is going to be a stretch."

"How long until this money with Angelcom comes through?"

"*If* it does at all, I have no idea. I'm hoping to get a better sense of that when I meet with Max in a couple weeks. I think it usually takes a few months, but I have a feeling he might be able to get it pushed through more quickly if he's really interested."

"Okay, we'll figure it out, I guess. I have a few old machines around here I can put together in a pinch. Let's just hope the college network doesn't go down."

"Work your magic."

I only understood about twenty percent of what Sid actually said, but I had no doubt he was a genius in his own right, so I trusted he would figure it out. He couldn't wake up before noon, ever, but the man could build a computer out of ram chips and motherboards in a few hours. Plus, Clozpin had become his baby too, and like me, he worked on little else these days. I was thankful for his dedication, even if it meant working around his quirks.

"How's the job hunt?" I asked, hoping he was as uninspired as I was to enter the real world.

"Uneventful. I haven't been devoting much time to it."

Silently relieved, I left it at that and got up to start cleaning.

"Erica, you don't have to do that. I'll clean today, I promise."

"Don't worry about it. Make sure we don't go offline in the next forty-eight hours, and we'll call it even."

"Deal."

★★★

As soon as we entered the Wynn, I knew Alli was right. It was barely past ten o'clock on a Friday night, and the casino was crawling with sexy women wearing the tiniest dresses I had ever seen. I looked like a nun by comparison. Back at the room, Alli dolled me up before we would head out to explore the hotel. I settled on a tight black panel dress with nude pumps, and I let my hair go a little wild and curly.

"Girls here probably go to church in this dress, Alli."

"No kidding. Hike it up a bit." She coaxed some cleavage out of her tiny neon dress.

Mine easily busted out of the scoop neck of my dress. Stress hadn't made my tits any smaller apparently. "No, thanks. I'd like to leave a few things to the imagination. You should too."

"Whatever. It's not like we know anyone here." She shrugged.

I couldn't disagree. This might be a chance to let loose a bit, but that could be dangerous too. Thanks to Blake, my skin was already crawling with an almost painful craving to be touched, everywhere. My vibrator wasn't staving off the need he'd inspired and I was dangerously close to taking home the first Blake look-alike I could get my hands on.

Every time I recalled the pitch meeting, my thoughts drifted to different ways the morning could have played out, all ending with me flat on my back on the conference table screaming his name. *Jesus Christ*. I forced him from my thoughts. He was on my shit list, *not* my to-do list.

Alli distracted me, primping and fussing over my accessories. No one loved fashion more than Alli. At first I couldn't understand how she could spend so much energy on her appearance, but eventually I came to realize that fashion had a lot more to do with feeling good on the inside than impressing anyone else on the outside, though it certainly helped with that too.

It was past midnight when we stepped onto the casino floor as a throughway to our destination, a bar on the other side. The place was mobbed, and Alli grabbed my hand to navigate us through the crowd of loud and boisterous people.

"Erica!"

I slowed, certain I'd heard my name over the noise. I couldn't be the only Erica here, but when I heard it again, I turned toward the sound and recognized a familiar face. Blake was standing at a nearby roulette table staring directly at me.

"Oh, shit. Let's get out of here." I looked away and took the lead with Alli trailing behind me.

"Wait, who is that?" Alli stopped me, causing a small traffic jam behind us.

"*That* is Blake Landon."

"Whoa, what is he doing here?"

"I don't care. I just want to be as far away from that man as possible."

"He's looking right at you, Erica. Let's just go say hi."

Alli waved at him and dragged me toward the table where he was playing. By some miracle, he'd become more handsome than I remembered. In a black collared shirt and gray suit, he was flawless. Intimidating. Sexy as hell. I took a deep breath and tucked a strand of hair behind my ear nervously, praying he couldn't sense the sexual tension that was palpable at this point.

We would make this quick and be on our way.

"Erica." He greeted me with those penetrating eyes. "What a surprise."

I did my best to appear unaffected but found myself holding my breath as his gaze traveled the length of me. I crossed my arms, immediately regretting my wardrobe choice, but the effort to conceal my cleavage only enhanced it.

His lips parted slightly when his stare fixed there a second too long. I straightened and broke away from his stare, noticing the almost equally gorgeous man next to him. He looked like Blake's slightly shorter twin, his hair a few shades lighter and his eyes a darker hazel, almost brown. He gave us a little wave.

"Erica, I'm Heath, Blake's brother."

He shot Alli a heart-stopping smile. She squeezed my hand slightly.

"Nice to meet you, Heath. This is Alli Malloy, one of my co-founders," I said, silently hoping the introduction went absolutely nowhere.

Alli tore her gaze away from Heath to greet Blake. "I've heard a lot about you, Mr. Landon." She smiled at him, and then me, raising her eyebrow a hair.

Now that she'd seen him in the flesh, she knew what I was up against, but her expression held no hint of sympathy. I could tell she was already crushing on his brother, and any chance I had of her going to bat for me had just gone out the window.

"Place your bets!" The croupier released the ball onto the wheel.

"Do you play roulette?" Blake asked.

"I do, but I'm not gambling tonight." Gambling was off limits on this trip. Not to mention the minimum bet at this table was $1,000.

"Well, I am. What numbers do you play?"

The ball slowed down on the wheel, and I felt an unnatural sense of urgency for him to bet while he still could. "Um, nine and one." I blurted out my birthday, numbers that had served me well in the past.

Blake placed $10,000 chips on both numbers and a few others, seconds before the ball dropped into the number nine slot. Alli and I screamed in unison. My heart beat wildly as I tried to do the math.

"Number nine!" The croupier handed Blake five colorful chips.

Blake gave one back to the man as his tip and tossed the rest into his pocket. He caught my hand and the contact shot through me. Between his touch and the recent win, my body was buzzing with pent-up energy. I pulled back defensively, startled by how much I craved his touch.

My gaze fell to the $10,000 chip that sat in my palm, amounting to more than all my historical roulette winnings combined.

"What's this for?"

"For being my lucky charm. I wouldn't have won without you."

He gave me a playful smile that, combined with the thrill of having seen him win, almost made me forget how angry I still was. This might work with other girls, but I wasn't about to be paid off.

"I can't keep this." I handed it back to him.

"I insist. Come on, let's get out of here before another number drops."

Reluctantly, I put the chip in my clutch, and we walked away without looking back.

★ ★ ★

"You look different. I barely recognized you." Blake leaned in close so only I could hear him.

Alli and Heath were deciding what tapas to order while we waited for our tequila flights to arrive. We had wandered into a cantina with Vegas flair bordering the casino floor to celebrate, and Heath was already charming the hell out of Alli, leaving me to contend with Blake. His warm breath drifted over my neck, giving me instant chills. I tried not to imagine what his lips would feel like there instead. His proximity bordered on unacceptable, and he smelled amazing—like clean, spicy, sexy male. Someone could bottle that and make millions.

"Yeah, not exactly boardroom attire..." I tugged down the hem of my dress, which barely covered the essentials now that I was sitting. If he looked me over one more time I might burst into flames right here.

"I prefer it."

There were hundreds of beautiful women in the bar, and plenty of them were eyeing Blake. What luck, to not only run into him, but to also be trapped in his crosshairs while Alli flirted shamelessly with his brother.

"Are you here for the conference?" I asked, eager to change the subject.

"Mostly," he replied.

"Blake's here for business. I, however, am here for pleasure." Heath winked at Alli.

He was laying it on thick, and Alli was eating it up. I couldn't tell if she was genuinely interested or just doing really good PR. I hoped it was the latter.

"Actually, Heath is my VP of business development. Technically he's here for the conference too."

Heath laughed. "Whenever Blake's work takes him to Vegas, my involvement in the company becomes suddenly very important. We have very important titles, but most of us just sort of orbit around Blake here. He does all the real work."

I waited for Blake to reply but his jaw only twitched. He seemed different somehow, more serious than I'd seen him before. He appeared relaxed, controlled, but I sensed tension beneath the calm countenance.

Alli broke the silence. "Sounds like Erica. She's our fearless leader."

Blake was about to speak when the waiter arrived with enough tequila shots to guarantee some seriously poor decision-making later in the evening. I picked mine up tentatively, making an agreement with myself and the tequila that this would be my first and my last. I couldn't trust myself around Blake as it was, and tequila made me do crazy things.

Heath raised his in the air to toast.

"What shall we toast to?" I asked.

"To winning," he said, and our glasses clinked.

I could drink to that. I tossed mine back, grabbed a lime, and sucked it hard to salve the burn of the liquor.

For the next hour or so, Heath regaled us with his stories—adventures in Sin City, backpacking in Europe, and the opulence of living in Dubai. Charismatic and funny, Heath was a magnetic force of his own. Alli asked him questions and kept him talking, which was almost a relief. I was still pissed at Blake and didn't feel up for sharing any tidbits of my personal life with him.

"Can I get you another drink? Something different?"

I shivered at the depth of Blake's voice, effectively distracted from the show of Alli's and Heath's interactions.

"I have to speak on a panel in the morning," I said. "I should actually call it a night." It was almost two a.m. local time. The long day was starting to catch up with me, but I wasn't so sure about Alli. "Do you want to head up, Alli?"

"Um..." She looked to Heath.

"Hang out with us for a while," he said softly.

She looked back at me, saying yes with her eyes, which were lit up like Christmas.

"Are you sure, Alli?"

"Yeah, I'll be up in a bit. Don't worry about me." Alli glowed. The tequila was already winning.

"We'll make sure she gets home in one piece," Heath promised.

I almost believed him. Normally I would have guilted her into leaving for her own sake, but I didn't want to spoil her fun tonight.

Blake stood up with me. "Let me walk you up."

"No, thank you. I'm fine."

"I'm heading back too. We can walk together."

I relented, fairly confident I could survive the next ten minutes alone with him.

We made our way to the elevators and Blake ushered

me into an empty car, his hand resting on the small of my back. The unexpected contact warmed me through to my core. We stood side by side as the doors closed. My fingers drummed the railing anxiously.

"They seem to be hitting it off," he said, breaking the silence.

"I noticed. Your brother is very charming."

"He's a handful." He shook his head and ran his fingers through his hair.

"Alli can be too. Maybe they'll keep each other out of trouble."

Blake raised an eyebrow, looking doubtful.

Silence descended again. The hum of the elevator seemed to amplify the energy between us, as if my attraction to Blake had somehow become audible and now radiated in the silence. Clearly I had underestimated how long ten minutes with him could be.

When the elevator stopped at my floor, Blake walked me out and escorted me down the hallway to my door.

"Here we are," I said, hoping our goodbyes would be brief.

Instead his hand trailed from my back to my elbow and down my arm until we were hand in hand. He traced tiny circles in my palm with the pad of his thumb, and I was uncertain in that moment if the sensation had caused actual pain. It was an undeniable shock to my system, almost electric, traveling to my fingertips and other areas.

"Blake, I—"

My body was rioting against the tyrannical misgivings of my brain. His face was mere inches from mine, intoxicating me with his scent once more, reminding me of the first moment we met.

"Aren't you going to invite me in for a drink?" he murmured. His tongue traced his lower lip and his teeth caught it. The way he looked at me was anything innocent.

But who could say no to him?

I swallowed hard and stepped back a little, disconnecting from the electricity of his grasp. I shook my head and twisted my hair nervously, trying to concentrate on anything other than his lips. "I have to get up in a few hours."

"Me too."

This was the same Blake Landon who had nearly destroyed my chances for funding my company only a few days prior. I wasn't about to lie down with the man. *Right?*

I took a deep breath and looked him straight in the eye. "Blake, I'm sure you're not used to hearing this, but I'm really not interested. We had fun tonight, but I'm here for work."

"You don't look like you're here for work."

I narrowed my eyes at him, but he only grinned.

"Seriously, Erica, are you saying that you aren't attracted to me, at all?" His arm slid up the wall as his body circled mine.

Determined to keep distance between us, I pressed myself against the door. Meanwhile my heart was ready to beat out of my chest. Were those last few inches that separated us the last bastion between me and...*a night of a lifetime?*

No, between me and a very big mistake.

"If you're fishing for a compliment, you're not getting

one from me," I said. "And even if I were attracted to you, I would not be acting on that for a number of reasons, not the least of which is keeping my relationship with Angelcom as uncomplicated as possible."

"I'm not investing in your project, so it's not complicated."

"I disagree."

"How could I persuade you?" He smirked, challenging me.

The fabric of his suit strained a little against his arms and thighs. Jesus, techies weren't supposed to be this sexy. All I wanted to do was unwrap him like a present. How could I possibly resist him if he touched me again, or God forbid, kissed me?

I wanted nothing more than to drag Blake into my room and fuck him senseless, but I knew better.

"It's quite simple. You can't."

I turned away and fumbled in my purse for the key. The next minute his body was behind me, and a warm and possessive arm circled my waist. I closed my eyes and sucked in a sharp breath, reeling at the sudden contact.

"You sure?"

I struggled for my next breath, trying desperately to ignore the way his body felt pressed against the back of my mine. My lips wouldn't form the words I needed to say, so I simply nodded, praying he'd leave me be.

His arm slid from my front, pausing with a firm grasp at my hip. There he went touching me like he owned me again. Damn if it didn't thrill me more than it should have offended me. Still, I couldn't go down this road with him.

"I'm sure." My voice wavered, betraying the doubt I felt.

His hand slid up my arm to my shoulder where he swept the hair away from my neck. He brushed a soft kiss there, his lips lingering on the skin until I was tingling again. My vision went white, and I pressed my hands against the door for balance.

"See you tomorrow," he whispered.

When I turned, he was gone. He'd disappeared down the hall and into the elevator. I leaned into the door, cursing myself and wishing he had stayed as much as I needed him to go. My fingers trembled but I finally found the key…and the chip next to it.

CHAPTER FOUR

The door latched closed, and my eyes shot open. The room was pitch black, but the big digital clock on the end table read eight o'clock. The faint outline of a woman inched quietly toward the adjacent bed. Her neon dress nearly glowed in the dark.

"Alli?"

"It's me."

"Are you just getting in?" I rubbed my eyes, and slowly the details of my current reality were dawning.

"Yes, Mother," she whispered sarcastically.

I switched on the bedside lamp, bringing her into focus. "Well, look what the cat dragged in." I leaned back on my elbows and smiled. She looked like she hadn't slept in days, which was almost true. Her mascara was smudged and her hair was in a state I'd never seen in public—only a few degrees below perfect.

"Ugh, I can feel you judging me." She kicked off her heels and collapsed onto the bed still dressed.

"So are you going to tell me what happened?" I was now fully awake, which surprised me considering the current hour and my minimal R.E.M. sleep.

"What do you want to know?" she mumbled into the bedspread.

"Every sordid detail, obviously."

Alli flipped herself over and stared listlessly at the ceiling. "I really like him."

I thought I heard a sigh. *Oh no.*

"Jesus, Alli, please tell me you didn't sleep with him."

"What the hell do you care?" She slapped her hands down to her sides.

I bolted out of bed and met her glare. "I care, Alli, because I'm trying to project a professional image with our company, and I didn't expect you to screw Blake's brother. Now he'll tell Blake, and oh shit..." I calculated all the possible implications of this indiscretion.

She shot up straight. "Stop right there. I told him you would freak out if Blake knew, so he gave me his word."

"Unbelievable." I walked over to open the shades to our room.

Alli cringed as light poured in.

"Well, what about you? I half expected to walk in on you two, the way he was eye-fucking you all night."

"Alli, seriously. There is absolutely nothing between Blake and me."

"Bullshit."

"I'm serious. I can't screw up this deal. I told him last night that I wasn't interested. End of story."

"Blake doesn't strike me as the type who hears the word 'no' frequently. Also, you didn't tell me he was drop-dead gorgeous."

"Gorgeous or not, I'm here to work."

"Erica, are you really mad at me about this?" She pouted her bottom lip a little.

Here came the guilt, but I couldn't let her off the hook

completely. "It'll be fine. Just get some sleep. It'd be great if you could do a little networking today since we're flying out tomorrow."

I escaped to the bathroom where I silently fumed under the steady pressure of the shower. I wanted to be angry with Alli, but in truth, I was mostly worried for her. I'd given her the opportunity to let her guard down around Heath, who was likely a master womanizer. This was as much my fault as hers.

When I returned, Alli was fast asleep under the duvet. I dressed in our pre-approved outfit, a stylish black patterned blouse and bright white blazer with dark straight jeans. I slipped into the black pumps Alli had left at the foot of the bed and grabbed my bag. Time to work. *Without any back up, again*, I thought. *I might as well get used to this.*

Fifteen minutes later I'd found my way to the function room where I would be presenting. Stepping up onto the empty platform, I read the name cards set out for the panelists.

You're not supposed to be here, Erica.

Sometimes I really hated the little voice in my head, but now my anxiety was shooting into overdrive. I would be shoulder-to-shoulder with a star-studded cast of tech CEOs, veritable celebrities in the technology world.

Reeling, I dropped into my assigned seat and surveyed the room, which was already filling with hundreds of eager conference attendees.

My mind raced as I fumbled for my notes, wishing I could be anywhere else. Just as full panic was setting in, Blake took a seat next to me, looking delicious in a gray V-neck shirt and jeans.

"What are you doing here?" I sounded more exasperated than I meant to.

"Good morning to you too."

He gave me a smile, and my body relaxed a little, maybe from the sheer relief of seeing a familiar face in this crowd. Plus his mouth on me last night was not nearly a distant memory yet.

Everything about this trip so far had been unexpected—running into Blake last night and Alli's understandable but problematic fascination with his brother. Now here I was with Blake again, sitting in the presence of geeky greatness.

After letting my wheels turn a bit he finally responded. "I'm moderating the panel."

My mouth opened, but the questions of how and why stuck in my throat. There was only one logical reason why.

"You did this."

"Did what?"

I glared, wishing I could level him with my stare.

"You had me invited here, to speak on this panel."

He smirked. "I don't think I can take all the credit. You're a significant competitor in the social space. That's what you told us at the meeting, right?" He leaned back into his seat the same way he had at the pitch, eyeing me cautiously.

"Yes, that *is* what I said." I swallowed hard, no less incensed.

"Well, then, you shouldn't be worried about sitting up here with the big boys. You'll do fine." He turned to his smart phone.

Shit. I had caught Blake's eye, and now he had drawn

me into this game of professional cat and mouse. How long would this go on? Until I slept with him? In the meantime, how the hell was I going to get through this panel where I was completely out of my league?

The room was filled and the other panelists sat down around us. I squeezed my eyes shut, rubbing my temples to stave off the tension headache coming on.

"You don't like being challenged?"

I opened my eyes to find him staring at me, his beautiful green eyes appraising me cautiously. He was pushing me and something snapped.

"I like being challenged, Blake. I don't like being sabotaged." I strained to keep our conversation audible only to us. Maybe in his mind, Blake was challenging me, but it didn't feel like that on my end. I had plenty of self-doubt, but when someone obviously underestimated me, the gloves came off. I had worked tirelessly and given him no reason to doubt me or my abilities.

"Trust me. If I wanted to humiliate you, you wouldn't be here."

"You have real fucking nerve." My voice echoed through the room. The emcee had turned the microphone system on, and all eyes were on me. *Shit.* I sat all the way back in my seat, wishing I could disappear into the floor. Apparently I didn't need Blake to humiliate me. I could do that fine on my own.

The emcee quickly recovered the moment and proceeded to introduce the panelists and the moderator, the esteemed Blake Landon. I cringed at the sound of his name and the applause that followed, but I needed to pull myself together. Shooting daggers at Blake would not get me through this panel. He would be guiding the conversation, and I had just very publicly cursed him out.

I straightened in my seat and steeled myself with a few deep breaths, willing myself to relax and focus. The panel started with introductions, which went well since I had practiced mine no less than fifty times on the flight here. From there, Blake asked a handful of prepared questions, directing them to the appropriate panelists. Nothing was far, if at all, out of my depth and my anxiety soon faded. I even mustered the courage to chime in where others left off on their questions, though I was careful to avoid eye contact with Blake. He could throw off my momentum with a well-timed smirk. His face had proven seriously distracting in the professional setting.

After a short round of questions from the audience, we wrapped up. I let out a sigh of relief, grateful that I had survived. I scolded myself for freaking out at what had turned out to be a totally manageable public speaking engagement. Crisis averted.

"Not bad at all," Blake said.

Too paranoid about the microphones, I shot him a glare. I pulled together my things and stood up, suddenly anxious to leave and regain some distance from Blake.

He quickly rose with me. "Hey, don't run off just yet." He stopped one of the other panelists on his way off the stage.

"Hey, Alex," he said, getting the man's attention.

He turned back and caught me by the elbow. I resisted, and then realized he was introducing me to Alex Hutchinson, CEO of one of the largest e-commerce websites in the U.S.

"Erica, Alex. Alex, we've been working with Erica at Angelcom, and I thought it'd be good for you to connect. There might be some mutual interest with her focus on women's apparel."

"Nice to meet you, Erica. I'm looking forward to checking out the site."

Alex had at least fifteen years on me and looked more like one of the suits I'd pitched to back in Boston, but he gave me his full attention.

"Thank you, I'd love to get your input."

"Sure, when did you launch?"

"About a year ago."

"Excellent, I'll check it out. Here's my card, and my cell is on the back. Let's stay in touch, and let me know if I can help with anything, all right?"

"I definitely will. Thank you so much."

As Alex headed off, two others approached us, both men around our age. One headed up a popular virtual game development shop, and another had founded a burgeoning music network for discovering new artists not long before Clozpin launched, which made me feel a little bit better about being there.

We made small talk, and Blake gracefully guided the conversation back to me at all the appropriate times. Giddy excitement washed over me. I'd have been too petrified to seek any of these people out on my own. The reception overall was very positive, and I felt validated that I could hold my own, that we had built something worth using.

Eventually the crowd and the rest of the panelists dispersed, leaving me alone with Blake again.

"Wow," I said, still reeling from it all.

"Was that so bad?"

"No, it was awesome actually. I wasn't expecting any of this."

"Maybe that's a good thing."

He was right. The anticipation of knowing the caliber of people I would be presenting with and subsequently meeting would have been unbearable. My panic this morning had been mercifully short-lived, and aside from the microphone incident, all had gone exceptionally well. Even so, I wasn't about to give him any satisfaction by admitting that.

"This was great, but I don't need your charity, Blake." The meddling needed to stop.

He frowned slightly. "You think this was charity?"

"Well, it's either that or an overelaborate ploy to get me into bed."

The corner of his mouth lifted as he threaded his fingers with mine.

"I'd be lying if I said it wasn't."

His other arm slipped under my blazer and pulled me up to him. His embrace was gentle but firm, giving me a taste of the strength of his body. I sighed softly, reveling in the warmth of his body against mine and the relief that always seemed to follow.

"Not going to happen." The protest sounded as weak as my resolve. My free hand found a place on his chest, contoured over the curve of his pectoral. His heart beat strong and steady under my palm, mimicking my own as my body melted into him. *The things we could do...*

He pulled me closer, the semblance of complete self-control in his expression betrayed by the heat in his eyes.

"I disagree."

He angled his face above me, his lips a hair's breadth from my own. I inched my fingers around his nape and drove them through the silky strands of his hair. My heart beat madly, silencing any lingering thoughts of protest. I couldn't outrun this desire.

Yes.

Answering him, I pushed up to my toes. Our lips met—warm, soft. *Perfect.* I drank in his scent. In an instant his hand was tangled in my hair, keeping me in the kiss I had no wish to escape from. I leaned into him, moaning softly, surrendering to the onslaught of sensations that having his mouth on me conjured.

The tip of his tongue grazed my lips, coaxing them open to his. I parted for him on demand, eager to know if he tasted as good as he smelled. His tongue darted in and found mine, taunting me with tiny licks that gave way to deeper strokes. He swallowed my small gasps, kissing me deeper, pulling me closer.

The hand that wasn't guiding our kiss teased the exposed flesh between my blouse and my jeans, roaming over the jut of my hipbone. Mine stayed fisted in his hair and splayed over his chest. I was paralyzed with the fear that if I moved an inch, I'd lose control completely and climb him right here on the stage.

Reality began to break through when whispers and the clicks from camera phones carried through the room. A small group of attendees were huddled at the back entrance, their faces hidden by their phones, which were pointed directly at us. *Bloody hell.*

I pushed away from Blake, who didn't seem fazed by

the paparazzi nerd crew. Flustered and panicked, I grabbed my things and hurried off the stage, making my way to the nearest elevator. Against my better judgment, I had lost control with Blake and now I was humiliating both of us.

"Erica!" Blake rushed up behind me. "Wait up. Are you okay?"

His hair was mussed to hell, but I resisted the urge to fix it. I was too tightly wound, and a touch, however innocent, could annihilate my already perilously weak commitment not to sleep with him.

"Yes, I genuinely can't wait to become the laughing stock of the conference." I shook my head in disbelief, cursing myself for being so reckless.

"Hey, any publicity is good publicity, right?" He smiled and reached for me, but I stepped back out of his grasp.

"Blake, you don't get it! Everything is on the line for me right now," I snapped. I was shaking now. Too many emotions surged through me—exhilaration, blinding lust, and utter embarrassment.

"Shh, relax." He put his hands on my shoulders. "I'm sure those kids don't even know who we are, and if they do, it'll just be a blip."

Those kids, who were my age, very likely didn't know me, but I couldn't say the same about Blake.

I shrugged. My exhaustion was bone-deep now. I leaned back into the wall, feeling more depleted by the minute. "Whatever…I guess there's not much I can do about it now."

Blake took a small step forward and tucked a strand of hair behind my ear. "Listen, I've got a few meetings this afternoon, but I want to take you out tonight."

I sighed. The man was persistent.

"I'll be the perfect gentleman," he promised, but a dangerous flash of hunger clouded his eyes.

"You have a habit of offending me indiscriminately. Don't make promises you can't keep."

The bell dinged and the doors opened. I retreated to the empty elevator, and miraculously, Blake didn't follow me.

Just before the doors closed, he said, "I'll pick you up at eight."

★ ★ ★

I nursed a glass of wine and Alli started on her second espresso martini at one of the award-winning Italian restaurants in the casino. I filled her in on the details of the morning, including the highs of connecting with a handful of high-powered executives in the industry, and the subsequent lows of potentially discrediting myself by being caught in Blake's arms, on camera, only moments later.

"He's persistent. But that doesn't really surprise me," Alli said.

"I can't help but feel like I'm losing the war with him." I picked at my pasta *fra diavolo*, torn by the way I felt around Blake. One minute I was cursing him out, and the next I had to harness every ounce of self-control not to give in to him.

"Erica, I know you're hyper-focused on the business right now, but if you're attracted to him, and he's obviously super attracted to you, why not just go for it?"

"I've been to hell and back, Alli. You know this. The

business is the first thing I've cared about in a long time. It's kept me grounded, and if I screw this up because I can't get a handle on my hormones, I don't know what I'll do."

While getting a more traditional job was a remote possibility, I refused to accept failure as an option. Sure, I periodically experienced the-sky-is-falling moments, but I always pulled through stronger, giving more of myself and pushing us further than we ever expected to be. Under normal circumstances, I could juggle casual sex and work or school, but this wasn't one of those moments. I needed to stay focused or risk losing everything.

"You've already proven yourself to him professionally. Do you really think he won't respect you if you sleep with him?"

"Maybe. It's not a chance I'm willing to take."

Blake was unpredictable. He had been both devastating and extremely helpful to the cause, so I had no idea what to expect from him, especially if we complicated the relationship with sex.

"When you play by those rules, Erica, you give them credence. Guys fuck around all the time, and no one thinks twice about it. Just because you're a woman doesn't mean you're not entitled to a night of hot sex."

"Says the girl who rolled in at eight o'clock this morning." I pointed my fork at her. "Seriously though, the business is more important to me than any fling right now."

Alli paused for moment. "Maybe Blake isn't fling-material."

"I highly doubt that."

"Blake isn't some asshole frat boy. Maybe you should give him a chance."

I winced. "You're right, he's an asshole billionaire. I'm not sure what's worse."

Alli sagged her shoulders, a sadness reflecting in her eyes. We both knew what was worse.

"So have you heard from Heath since…you know?" I asked, hoping to steer the subject away from Blake and my past.

"Yeah, he texted me this morning." A slow smile spread across her face.

She was already smitten. Heaven help us all.

"Thanks for the memories?" I joked, and we both laughed. "Do you think it'll go anywhere?"

"I'm not sure. He lives in New York, so who knows? We're going to grab dinner tonight." She looked up. "I mean, if you don't mind. We can hang out if you really want to ditch Blake."

I knew she was lying, like any decent friend would.

CHAPTER FIVE

Not surprisingly, Alli and I battled over my attire. We settled on a peach strapless high low dress, which we agreed was date appropriate but didn't scream, "Let's skip dessert." I repurposed my nude pumps and fluffed my hair nervously in the mirror.

Blake knocked on the door at eight o'clock on the dot.

"Hi." I held onto my clutch like a life preserver.

"Erica." A hint of a smirk curved his lips.

He wore a simple white collared shirt rolled up at the sleeves and dark blue jeans. His normally wayward hair was smoothed carefully to the side, though it rebelled here and there in a way that was still sexy and fashionable. I'd spent the past several hours trying to predict what the night would bring, and now I couldn't keep my thoughts remotely clean.

After a few moments of shameless ogling, I found his gaze trained on me, a mirrored reflection of raw appreciation. A rush of emotion hit me—butterflies, carnal desire, and an unsettling premonition that I could be getting in way over my head with Blake Landon. The man was sexy, rich, and confident, and my hormones had absolutely no willpower in his presence.

"Blake!" Alli joined me at the door, giving Blake the once-over. "You guys look so cute!"

"We're not going to the prom, Alli," I mumbled, though it felt that way a little bit. Except the hottest boy in school was at my doorstep, and that didn't seem quite right. Sure, I cleaned up nice and attracted my fair share of hot guys, but I'd taken myself off the market months ago to focus on work. I'd forgotten what it felt like to be physically appreciated like this. In fact, I wasn't sure if anyone had ever really made me feel like this, and all Blake and I had done was kiss.

Blake offered his arm to me and motioned for our retreat. I hooked mine in his, and he led us down the hall.

"You kids have fun!" Alli called after us.

"I'll have her home by morning," Blake said, winking back at her.

I rolled my eyes, feeling my face heat at the idea of being with Blake all night. Was I really doing this?

Once in the elevator, Blake hit the number forty-five, the highest number on the grid, and we began our ascent.

Confused, I asked, "Where are we going?"

"The top floor."

"What's up there?"

"My room, actually."

My earlier excitement wilted. "Subtle, Blake." I yanked away and crossed my arms. Perfect gentleman, my foot. *God, I'm so naïve.*

Blake laughed. "It's not what you think. Trust me."

I raised an eyebrow. "You've given me no reason to trust you."

"I've heard that takes time, so maybe there's hope yet."

The elevator doors opened, and he led me to the end of the long hallway where he slid his key to gain entrance to the room. I followed him in, awestruck by the sprawling suite that could only be described as a modest palace.

We walked through an ornate entryway, and before us,

a floor-to-ceiling wall of windows showcased the Las Vegas skyline. The sun had set moments earlier behind the silhouette of the barren mountains, imbuing the sky with gradients of gold and amber, while every major landmark on the manmade strip before us mimicked nature's brilliance. A million little lights brought the night to life in this wild, addictive city.

"I thought this might be a better view than the restaurant," he said quietly.

"It's breathtaking." My eyes scanned the horizon, thrilled by his choice. For the second time today, a giddy excitement bubbled inside me thanks to Blake. Still, I tempered my outward display, unwilling to give him the satisfaction of wowing me so easily.

"I'm glad you think so." He guided me toward our table for two by the windows.

The two-story suite was draped in luxury and elegance. The motif featured warm washed-out tones among a variety of textures, from upholstered mohair walls to cool cream marble surfaces that contrasted with the sleek and tastefully integrated modern electronics.

I coolly catalogued the suite's amenities until a server delivered a champagne bucket from one of the adjoining rooms.

"Madam?" The server offered up a chilled bottle of Cristal Rosé.

"Please," I replied.

He expertly filled our flutes to the brim.

"I took the liberty of ordering for us." Blake tipped his glass to meet mine. "I hope you don't mind."

"I'll let it slide," I joked, but in truth, I was relieved.

I couldn't think straight around Blake let alone figure out what kind of food I could eat gracefully in his presence.

"So, tell me more about Erica Hathaway."

"What do you want to know?"

"What do you do for fun?" The question was innocent enough but his eyes betrayed a darker meaning.

My body clenched, my fingertips gripping the chair's edge. My defenses were wearing dangerously thin around Blake. Why had I ever agreed to this? Well, I hadn't, but I hadn't exactly refused either. Regardless, here we were, and thus far everyone was on their best behavior except my libido.

"To be honest, not much, at least lately."

"So you're a workaholic?"

"You could say that."

"Well, we have that in common." He leaned back into his chair and gazed out into the horizon.

"It seems like you do well enough these days to take a more relaxed approach to life."

"My life is hardly a vacation, if that's what you're implying."

"I see no reason why it shouldn't be."

"Then I suppose you don't know me very well."

"Enlighten me," I said. "A little bird told me you used to be a hacker."

Over the rim of my nearly empty champagne flute, a grimace flashed across his face, then disappeared.

"You shouldn't believe everything you read online."

"No?"

The server brought our meals, two perfectly cooked rib eye steaks atop a bed of asparagus and sautéed mushrooms.

My heart sang for a moment and I thanked the server, who disappeared as quickly as he'd arrived, leaving us alone once more.

Famished from the intense day, I ate, enjoying each divine bite. "You aren't interested in sharing your life story, I take it?"

He paused before answering, intently focused on his meal and avoiding eye contact. "You've read the cliff notes already. What more is there to tell?"

"How else will I know how to become insanely successful unless you tell me all your secrets?" I searched his eyes, wishing he would tell me more, something I couldn't find online.

He sighed and ran a hand through his hair. "I developed banking software, sold it, and now I invest in other, mostly successful, ventures to kill time. Satisfied?"

"Not really," I said truthfully.

"So how involved is Alli in your business?"

I wanted to know more about Blake's infamous history, but I decided to circle back to it later since it seemed to be a touchy subject, and he hadn't really started grinding my gears yet.

"She was my inspiration for the site actually. After three years I think I've finally completed my fashion education with her, even though she still insists on dressing me half the time. Anyway, now she does our marketing. She's responsible for making the connections that have resulted in most of our paid accounts."

"You said her involvement was dependent on financing though."

"Alli's parents are expecting her to get a job that pays

more than we can right now, so she doesn't have much choice until we get financing or grow more quickly. She's been interviewing in New York, so I imagine that's where she'll end up eventually if things don't work out here."

"How are you financing the site right now?"

"Honestly?"

He shook his head slightly. "You're not pitching me. I'm just curious."

"We supplement the site income with my inheritance, which, thanks to all this wonderful education, is finally dwindling."

"I'm sure you're not the first one to leverage your personal finances to follow a dream."

The champagne warmed me, a welcome relaxation in the presence of someone who had a habit of winding me up. He was being surprisingly sweet, though. At least when we weren't talking about him.

When we finished, Blake tossed his napkin on the table and topped off our glasses, emptying the pricey bottle of pink bubbly. He grabbed his glass, stood, and reached for my hand.

"Come with me."

Tentatively, I accepted it, and he led us to the bright white leather couches at the other end of the expansive main area. I sat, and he took a seat next to me, sliding his knee alongside my leg to face me.

"So you've graduated and now you're talking to Max. What's next?"

"That's the million dollar question."

"Or the two million dollar question, in this case," he said.

"Right. I don't exactly know. I have to move out of the dorms next week, so I suppose I have to figure out my next move pretty quick."

"You strike me as someone who will make it work, one way or the other." He tucked a strand of hair behind my ear, fingering my dangle earring before dropping his hand onto the back of the couch.

My inhaled a shaky breath, and I felt certain he'd noticed.

"What do you want to do tonight?" he asked quietly, his gaze traveling over me.

As if the gauge of his stare had direct control over my body temperature, I flushed, my skin becoming unbearably heated. I wasn't so naïve to believe that the night wouldn't end in Blake's bed, but I was losing the battle a little faster than I'd planned to. I'd wanted other men before and had them. Detached and focused on the physical, I could almost always keep things on my own terms. But nothing about being with Blake felt detached now.

"How about another drink?"

He hesitated, his fingertips grazing my bare shoulder. "Sure, but if you can't walk by the end of the night, I'd rather that be because of me."

Oh God. The visions that his words invoked overtook my better judgment. I closed my eyes a moment, silently coming to terms with where the night was taking me.

"How about a tour then?" I said, barely able to utter the words.

He raised his eyebrows. "Of Las Vegas?"

I laughed. "How about we start with the suite."

His eyes darkened, an intense shade of green, traveling

down my body and back to my eyes. His teeth caught his lip briefly before it released. "Is that what you want?"

Something shifted in the air between us. My breath caught when I saw the hunger burning in his eyes. My need to have his hands and mouth on me had become singular and overpowering. I cared less about the repercussions of acting on that need with each passing moment.

I nodded silently. He stood, and I rose with him as he caught my hand.

"A tour it is, then."

One by one, he guided us through the massage rooms, butler pantries, and guest bathrooms. Every room's opulence was as obscene as the price he must be paying for this place.

We wandered up a gold-railed staircase to the second floor and into the master bedroom, another corner room with floor-to-ceiling windows. He stopped at the doorway. I left him there, lured toward the skyline I was still in awe of.

"I could get used to this view."

"Me too," he murmured.

He was close enough to touch me now, but he didn't, playing this gentleman promise out to a maddening degree maybe. In this tense middle ground, I waited for him, wanting him to set things in motion, but with each passing second the tension and the sexual energy between us became increasingly palpable.

I let out the breath I had been holding in.

Fuck it.

Emboldened by the champagne, I found the sheer hem of my dress. Collecting the layers in a bunch, I pulled it over my head. I stood there, bare-chested, clad only in my panties, heels, and liquid confidence. The wall of glass cast my reflection back, and Blake came into view behind me. The heat of his body radiated onto mine, my skin already aflame, as much from my own self-consciousness as my growing need.

He touched me then, his thumb blazing a trail down my spine to the waistline of my panties. He skirted the edge of the lace to my side where he seized my hip in a firm grasp, pulling us together suddenly. I gasped at the sudden contact, a thread of panic lacing the desire.

My head rolled back onto his shoulder, and I could feel desire winning. His lips began a path of sweet torment, tasting and nibbling my over-sensitive skin from my ear down my shoulder. One hand flexed at my hip while the other caught my breast. My flesh overflowed from his grasp, and my nipple hardened under his touch. I was on fire for him. My senses inflamed, lust coursed through me until I was nearly blind with need.

"Tell me what you want, Erica," he murmured against my neck.

My mind rambled a string of silent pleas. I arched slightly, feeling his hard length straining against his jeans and into my backside. I covered his hands with my own and turned to face him, shameless and weak under his gaze. Now solidly green, his eyes smoldered, melting me from the inside out. Our bodies barely touched as I ran a hand down his chest, slowing above his belt. God, he felt amazing, hard and warm. I lifted on my toes and pressed a shaky kiss to his lips, my mouth opening to his.

"I want you, Blake," I whispered.

He kissed me back eagerly. His body tensed with restraint, barely reined in. "You have no fucking idea how much I want you right now."

My knees weakened a little. He caught me up to him, stealing my breath with another urgent kiss. Reveling in the velvet strokes of his tongue, I blindly made my way down the buttons of his shirt, the hard curves of his abdomen tense beneath my fingers. I reached for the button of his jeans and unhooked it.

"I want this too." I smirked.

Blake's eyes widened a fraction. I gave his bottom lip a playful bite before kissing my way down his torso. His olive skin stretched tight over his muscles. Crisp brown hairs dusted across his chest and down the center of his well-defined abs.

On my knees, I stared up at him. He was all I'd imagined the first night we'd met, and so much more. Beautiful. A prime specimen of a man.

I traced the impressive outline of his erection before tugging his jeans and boxer briefs down just enough to release him. When he sprang free, I held him in my hands. His flesh was hot on my own, burning with primal need. He sucked in a sharp breath as I circled him gently.

I was wet with anticipation, but as much as I ached for him, I needed to taste him first. To relish a moment of control over this man who'd had my whole world spinning in a matter of days.

Starting shallow and soft, I worked him over. Then I took him farther and with more pressure. He cursed, driving his fingers through his hair. I pumped him with my hand while the other lay flat on his stomach, moving in time with his labored breaths.

"Erica, Christ. Come here, wait—"

He became inexorably harder, thicker. After a few deep

strokes that hit the back of my throat, he cursed again, and I knew he was close.

Before I could finish him off, he hauled me to my feet. His eyes were wild and intense, as if he'd passed the limits of his control.

"My turn," he said, his voice so raspy and raw it almost sounded like a threat. He scooped me up into his arms and effortlessly tossed me onto the bed.

He stripped me of my lace panties and set his hands on my knees, coaxing them apart. Embarrassed and emboldened at once, I felt my cheeks heat. I was exposed completely, but when he lowered to me, the sensation of his mouth between my legs overwhelmed everything.

I sucked in a sharp breath, his name on my lips.

He tongued my wet, quivering sex with the expert skill that he'd used on my mouth, flicking and taunting and sucking. Sweet Jesus, he had a gifted mouth.

He moaned, vibrating my clit as he sucked me. My walls clenched deliciously and I clutched at the silken fabrics beneath us. The energy in my core climbed with an alarming speed.

"You taste so good."

The feeling of his breath on the sensitive tissues followed by the determined strokes of his tongue over the tight bundle of nerves pushed me over the edge. My mind left me.

"Oh God!" I came hard, letting the orgasm ripple through me.

My breathing was ragged as I tried to regain my senses. Under heavy eyelids, I watched him undress fully before me. Despite my very recent orgasm, my desire for Blake had barely waned. I ached for him, to have him inside me, finishing what we'd begun.

He leveled me with a look so intense and determined that I almost came again on the spot. His cock bobbed gently, long, broad, and hard as stone as he rolled on a condom.

"You ready for me, baby?"

I nodded quickly. Ready as I was ever going to be.

"Thank God, because I'm not sure if I could stop now if I wanted to."

He climbed onto the bed over me, and I panted softly, scorchingly aware of his approach. The thick tight muscles of his thighs parted my legs around him. I hitched my leg high over his hip and arched, urging him into me eagerly.

He grasped me by the hip and stilled my effort. We were barely connected, the head of his penis notched at my entrance.

"Blake," I said, my voice breathy and desperate.

He bent to find my mouth, and our tastes mingled with the scent of my arousal. The act seemed too intimate, too raw under the circumstances, but heightened my already blinding need for him.

I struggled against his grasp, wild to have all of him. He loosened his hold and pushed inside. I uttered a small cry into his mouth, shocked at how completely he filled me. I relished the deliciousness of the sensation. Nothing felt more right than the achingly slow drive of his body into mine. My body stretched to accommodate him, and the bite of his entry soon gave way to a deeper hunger.

"Perfect," he said, thrusting again.

I closed my eyes and held him tighter to me, letting that single world rule the moment. He moved with deliberate and measured strokes, filling me and holding back with painstaking pauses. Rotating satisfaction with an impossible longing. Each movement bringing me closer to the edge.

The promise of release beckoned, but he kept me wanting more while he took my mouth in slow, deep kisses. The rhythm was driving me crazy with the need to orgasm.

"Blake, please." My voice cracked.

He slowed his pace until I thought I would die of frustration. "Trust me," he whispered into my ear.

Then without warning, he grabbed my ass and drove hard into me. By the second punishing thrust I found my voice, though I barely recognized it when I screamed. Relentlessly he claimed new depths of my body, giving me everything I had damn near begged him for. And I took it all.

"God…fuck…Blake!" A storm raged inside of me, my body responding uncontrollably to his. I gripped his hair by the root and clung to him.

"That's it, baby. Come hard for me," he rasped.

My climax pulsed through me. I clenched around him, my whole body shuddering as he became impossibly bigger, pounding out his own release in time with mine.

He groaned, stilling inside me, pulsing deeply.

Eyes closed, he collapsed onto his elbows above me. Gradually our breathing slowed, our bodies cooled, and we began to return to ourselves. He brushed soft kisses over my cheek and neck while my arms and legs tangled around him.

I sighed. "I didn't know…"

He smiled and kissed me. "Know what?"

"That…it could be like that."

His smile faded and his lips parted slightly as he ran his

thumb over the curve of my cheekbone. My chest ached at his closeness and the wonder I thought I saw in his half-lidded eyes.

He gave me a chaste kiss and pulled away.

"I'm going to wash up. I'll be right back. Unless you want to join me."

I shook my head slightly. "I'm not sure if my legs work right now."

He laughed a little as he stood. "I did warn you."

As he disappeared into the en suite bathroom, I got a little thrill worshiping the back of him. His ass was perfectly sculpted like every other delicious inch of him. Everything about Blake had become too much, an onslaught to my senses, a train barreling through my better judgment.

And I was loving every minute of it.

★ ★ ★

I woke up abruptly, disoriented until I recognized the hand-painted gold butterflies on the ceiling. Blake lay on his stomach next to me, snoring quietly into the pillow. His body was soft and relaxed, a different picture from the muscle-bound animal who had quite recently blown my mind. I must have dozed off while he showered. He hadn't bothered to wake me and send me on my way.

Still, I couldn't be here when he woke up. I was completely blissed out, but the idea of facing the walk of shame in the daylight hours sobered me into action.

Ambient light filled the room but the desert sky before us was pitch black, save the frenetic city lights, with no hint of the impending dawn. I slid quietly out of the bed and dressed, though despite my best efforts, I could not find my panties anywhere. I put on my heels and stopped at the writing desk. I scribbled a note, setting the $10,000 chip on top of it.

What happens in Vegas…
x, E

I took in the skyline a minute longer, then left Blake's suite without a sound.

Moments later I crept into our hotel room with impressive stealth, but Alli was propped up on a pillow watching TV when I entered.

"Hey, what are you doing up?" It was nearly two a.m.

"What are *you* doing up?" She pursed her lips.

"Uh, nothing."

"You little slut. Tell me everything." She muted the TV and sat up cross-legged on the edge of the bed.

"Not much to tell." I shrugged and slipped out of my dress in favor of a robe.

"Don't even start with me, Erica. Dish, now." She pointed her manicured little finger at me.

I sighed and sat on the edge of the bed facing her. This morning I had berated her for the same thing. What a hypocrite.

"I'll just say, if Heath is anything like his brother, um, in bed"—I stumbled over the words—"I forgive you, all right?"

"Shut up! Was it amazing?"

"There are no words. Now I just have to figure out how to stay the hell away from him."

"Why? What do you mean?" A frown marred her brow at the mere suggestion.

"We had our moment, but I'm really hoping this is once and done for him, because ..." I let my face fall into my hands, which still smelled like him. I breathed in his scent and let the memory of our night settle over me.

"Erica, what?"

I sat up abruptly, as if I'd been caught doing something I wasn't supposed to.

"You were telling me why you want this to stay a one-night-stand," she reminded me.

"I don't know!" I twisted my fingers in my lap. "I just know I could get addicted to that. To him. I'm here for work and basically he's all I can think about already."

I gestured to the ceiling, his general direction. I shook off the memories that felt too new, knowing Blake was still perfectly naked, slumbering a few floors away.

"I don't know. I'm a mess. I need to sleep."

Alli nodded, but I caught a coy smile before she switched off the TV and turned over under her duvet.

Grateful for the reprieve, I retreated to the bathroom to shower. The intoxication of being with Blake tapered as the water thrummed my already weak muscles, draining the last of my waning energy. Already he meant too much.

CHAPTER SIX

A few days had gone by since Alli and I returned from Vegas. I wanted to believe that life would return to normal, but nothing was normal about my life right now. I was on the verge of not having a place to live, starting down a road of running my business full time, and now I couldn't get Blake out of my head.

For all my wishing our one night together stayed that way, the little voice in my head wanted him to reach out to me somehow. I silently berated myself for foolishly longing for something—someone—I'd never have. Just like our rather public embrace at the conference, I was a blip. A passing interest for a cocky billionaire who had no reason to linger too long on anyone.

I shuffled through my mail, reminding myself that I'd gotten exactly what I'd asked for. When I stepped out of the campus center, I heard my name. A girl with cropped blond hair ascended the steps to meet me. She looked like a teen model. Tan, tall, and impeccably dressed in a tank top and a linen skirt.

"Liz," I said. "How are you?"

She smiled broadly. "Great. I can't believe we're finally done!"

"I know, time flies." I shook my head in shared disbelief. "Do you want to grab a coffee? I'd love to catch up."

Her warm brown eyes seemed genuine, but I had always

avoided these moments. Our friendship had fizzled when I moved across campus after our freshman year together, and we had never really addressed it. I hesitated. School was over, no homework, no plans. I had no excuses.

I shrugged. "Sure."

We walked a short distance to the closest cafe where some moody hipsters made us delicious overpriced cappuccinos. We sat at a table for two, the chaos of the cafe filling the silence between us. I'd seen Liz around campus here and again, but we hadn't really *talked* in years. We barely knew each other anymore.

"Do you have any plans for the summer?" I asked.

"I'm going to Barcelona with my parents for a few weeks, and then I start work in July."

"Where are you working?"

"At an investment firm here in the city, crunching numbers or whatever." She blew steam off her cup. "What about you?"

"I actually started a fashion social network last summer and it's been going pretty well, so I'm going to be running that for a while. We'll see where it goes."

"That's amazing. I would have never expected that."

I raised my eyebrows. What *would* you expect, I wondered, picking at the flaky crust of my chocolate croissant.

"How are Lauren and everyone else at the house?" I asked, referring to the girls who'd shared a floor with us.

"Really good." She paused before continuing, "We've missed you though."

I took a long sip of my cappuccino, sensing where the conversation was heading. College was over, and a new chapter was beginning. Maybe it was finally time to clear the air, especially if I might be running into her in the city now. Boston was still small enough for chance meetings.

"I'm sorry I didn't give you a heads up about moving out at the end of the year. I was going through a lot at the time." That was an understatement, but I didn't really want to get into it with her right now. The last thing I needed was to dredge up painful memories.

"I realize that. I just thought we were friends, you know?"

"We were," I said. "We still can be. I just needed a fresh start after everything that happened."

She nodded and gave me a weak smile.

I sighed, resigned to the fact that I wouldn't be getting around this topic no matter how hard I dodged it. "Nothing was the same after that night. You and everyone else were the same, but I wasn't. I couldn't go out partying with all of you like nothing happened."

I took a breath, trying to push the painful memories back down. I pushed my plate away, a twinge of nausea taking root in my gut.

"It had nothing to do with our friendship, or you. I just couldn't stand that look on everyone's faces. Plus, what if I ran into him again, you know? I don't know what I would have done."

Dealing with what happened to me had been difficult enough. At the time, the thought of reliving it in any way had terrified me. The only thing that kept me from constantly looking over my shoulder today was the fact that I'd buried the memories so deep I scarcely believed the man who'd hurt me existed anymore.

When I looked up at her, the pity in her eyes made

me even more sick to my stomach. I eyed my purse and searched for a believable excuse to leave.

"I wanted to talk with you about it, but you never really gave me a chance," she said.

"Believe it or not, I don't really like talking about it." I pressed my lips into a firm line. I never wanted to talk about it—or think about it—ever again. But that wasn't Liz's fault. None of this really was.

Her eyes were bright and innocent, reminding me of the many nights we'd spent foraging her parents' gift boxes of junk food, sharing stories and dreams in our freshman naïveté.

I sat back in my chair, drawing in a deep breath. "I needed to work things out on my own, and for whatever reason, I couldn't do that at the house."

She nodded. "I understand."

She didn't, but I gave her credit for trying, even though she was dragging me through memories I'd long buried.

"Maybe we can get together when I get back from Spain and catch up a bit," she said. "We don't have to talk about that stuff, obviously. I know it's upsetting for you."

"Sure." I forced a smile. I couldn't change the past, but maybe we could salvage some of what was lost.

"Let's stay in touch."

We talked about professors and housing in the city while Liz finished her muffin. Afterwards we exchanged numbers and said our goodbyes. As I turned toward the campus again, my phone dinged with a text. It was Alli.

Need to talk. I have news.

My stomach sank. I called her as I walked.

"What's up?"

"I have news."

"So you said. What is it?"

She paused a moment. "I got the job."

"Great," I blurted, disappointment clear in my tone of voice. I couldn't help it. This was terrible news.

"Erica?"

"What do you want me to say?"

I stepped out of the way of foot traffic as people passed me on the street. Seeing Liz had put me on edge, and now I was losing Alli—my best friend, roommate, and business partner. I refused to count this as a high point in my day.

"Congratulations, Alli. I know you wanted this. Unfortunately I didn't."

Alli was silent on the phone for a few seconds. "We talked about this, and now you seem surprised."

She was right, but it didn't offset the sting. Things were in motion now, just shy of Max's potential decision to fund us.

"When do you leave?"

"In a few days. I can crash with a friend in the city until I get a place."

My phone started buzzing with another call. I didn't recognize the number but needed an excuse to get out of this conversation before I said something I didn't mean. "Someone's calling me, Alli. I gotta go."

She sighed. "Okay, bye."

I registered a pang of guilt as I switched over to the other line.

"Hello?

"Erica, it's Blake."

I cursed under my breath. Of all the times I'd wanted him to call. "This isn't a great time."

"Are you okay?"

"I'm fine." I sounded anything but fine.

"Where are you? I'm in the neighborhood."

I glanced around for the nearest recognizable landmark. "Near Campbell Square."

"I'll pick you up in five minutes." He ended the call before I could argue.

I sat on a park bench, idly checking email on my phone to distract me from the bomb Alli had dropped on me. In one, Sid reported a decent influx of new users since the conference, which was welcome news since I had wondered if the entire effort had amounted to an expensive 3,000-mile booty call for Blake. My thoughts drifted back to Alli and Liz and how utterly alone I had become in the past hour. My eyes burned with emotion, and I wiped away a tear that fell.

A car horn broke the moment. Blake sat in the driver's seat of a sleek black sports car waiting at the curb. I approached and was momentarily confused by the lack of door handles until one glided out of its hidden pocket in the passenger door. I got in, instantly mesmerized by the enormous LCD screen situated between the driver and passenger seats.

"What the hell is this?" I asked, instantly overwhelmed by all the gadgets and gizmos.

"It's a Tesla."

I stared out to the road ahead, waiting for the car to move.

"Hey," he said softly, brushing his thumb against my cheek.

He looked fresh and cute, but his smile soon faded. My throat tightened as if I could cry again. I swallowed against the sensation, my body stiffening in an act of self-defense.

"I'm fine, seriously." I turned my face and wiped away any errant mascara that might clue him in to my recent meltdown. I didn't know if I could bear being any more vulnerable to this man than I already was and still maintain a shred of professional integrity. "What do you want?"

"I wanted to see you. Are you hungry?"

"Sure." I wasn't, but I wanted to be anywhere but here. I let Blake take us away in what I now recalled was an extremely expensive high-tech car whose stock had just skyrocketed.

"How much Tesla stock do you own?" I asked as the city blocks sped past us.

"I got in on the second round of funding, so quite a bit."

"Of course you did," I mumbled.

Blake made his way into the city in record time and with little regard for pedestrians and traffic laws, but somehow I still felt safe and relieved to have the campus in the rearview. We rode the rest of the way in silence until Blake pulled into a reserved parking space across from the clock tower.

The Black Rose was an Irish pub in the heart of Boston, a few steps away from the famous Faneuil Hall and Quincy Market. Inside, a dark wood bar lined one end of the restaurant and coats of arms from the motherland covered the walls. Blake and I settled into a quiet corner of the restaurant where we could watch the people outside going about their day, including tourists, bankers, and men driving horse-drawn carriages.

The cute young waitress was cheery and asked for our order with an Irish lilt that made me think of my favorite professor who was *also* leaving in a few short weeks.

"Two Irish breakfasts and two Guinnesses," Blake said, handing her our menus and promptly returning his attention back to me.

"Do you always order for other people?"

"I didn't want you to battle with yourself over ordering a pint so early in the day."

He leaned in, the motion showcasing his biceps that were peeking out of the sleeves of his T-shirt that featured the Initech logo from *Office Space*. He had no business looking so unprofessional on a workday.

"Do you want to tell me why you were crying a minute ago?"

I shook my head, emotionally drained and unprepared to be with Blake at this moment in time. "Maybe this was a bad idea."

Blake took my hand as I reached for my purse. "Hey, I'm sorry."

I closed my eyes, wanting desperately to be falling apart somewhere where Blake wasn't in the audience.

"Stay," he said softly.

I sat back, letting my hand stay in his, my anger melting away. His touch had a calming effect that I both resented and was beginning to appreciate.

"Why did you want to see me?"

"Well, for one, you didn't give me a chance to say goodbye. Do you always run off like that?"

"I didn't think you'd care," I said, embarrassed about the whole affair, even though I'd thought of almost nothing else since I left his suite two days ago. "Anyway, I had an early flight home."

"Have you heard from Max?"

I took a deep breath, relieved to be talking business again. "Yes, we're meeting next week."

"How's the housing hunt going?"

I rolled my eyes and groaned. "Now that Alli is officially moving to New York, I suppose it just got simpler."

"That doesn't sound like good news."

"Yeah, I'll have to start dressing myself again, which will be tough," I joked.

I wasn't lying, but obviously her fashion sense wouldn't be the only thing I'd miss. Alli was my best friend, my confidante, my wing-woman. I still couldn't believe my roomy wouldn't be my roomy anymore. We'd only be an hour's flight away, but I held onto an irrational fear that our lives would begin moving in different directions that would eventually take their toll on the friendship we'd worked so hard to build. Only time would tell.

"I have a good broker." Blake fished a business card out of his wallet and handed it to me. *Fiona Landon, Licensed Real Estate Broker.*

"If she's related to you, I doubt she'd have anything in my price range."

"She's my little sister, and you never know. She's known for digging up good finds. Just tell her I sent you."

I sighed. "I told you about my situation to make conversation. It wasn't a cry for help. I'm perfectly capable of figuring this out on my own."

"I know you are," he said quietly, rubbing his thumbs over my knuckles. "Give her a call," he urged.

I slipped from his grasp and stuffed the card into my purse, knowing I'd call her for the simple reason that Blake wanted me to and he wouldn't let it go until I did.

The waitress brought our breakfast, which was delicious and fattening, two requirements for comfort food that I thoroughly appreciated at the moment. Washing it down with a few sips of Guinness wasn't too bad either. Blake and I made small talk and chatted about sports, one topic any two Bostonians could agree on. When I wasn't in emotional turmoil and when he wasn't throwing me headfirst onto a professional roller coaster, I did enjoy his company. Little by little, he coaxed me out of my grim mood.

Outside the sun warmed the cobblestone streets as we walked back to the car. After all these years, Boston still dazzled me. The streets had history and its people had a kind of character that always made it feel like home. It was impossible to live here and not feel a passion and possessiveness about it.

Blake laced his fingers into mine, and my heart beat a little faster.

"Where to now?" he asked.

I wanted to believe the question was innocent, but I saw the asking in his eyes. I wouldn't have minded answering with *Back to your place*, but I wasn't about to make a habit of sleeping with Blake whenever he gave me that look.

I looked down, trying to ignore how much I still

wanted to be with him. "I should head back home. I have a lot of work to do," I said, hoping he'd believe me.

He regarded me silently for a moment. "Fair enough. Let me give you a ride."

I agreed and Blake led us back to the car.

On the way home, Blake's phone rang. A casual photo of a beautiful brunette showed up on the LCD panel next to the name Sophia. He ignored the call and stared straight ahead at the road, showing no emotion. I had no right to ask who she was. We were hardly in a relationship, and the idea that someone as rich and gorgeous as Blake wouldn't be playing the field was pretty unrealistic. Still, the thought of other women in his life stung me.

We pulled up to the house, and Blake circled the car to let me out. Walking up the steps up to the entrance, I fumbled with my keys. I turned to say goodbye, and Blake pulled me close. The breath rushed out of me.

"You owe me a goodnight kiss, Miss Hathaway."

Before I could respond, he covered my mouth with his own. I melted into the kiss and the warmth of his body. Mercy, his lips. The stress of the morning became a distant memory, replaced with a hunger that neither of us was in a position to satisfy at the moment.

"Invite me up."

I pulled back breathless and shook my head.

"Then come home with me." His voice was raw.

Somewhere in the distance, I started psychoanalyzing everything, pulling myself out of the moment.

"I can't."

Technically, I could. In fact, I wanted nothing more than a repeat of my night in Blake's Vegas pad, but I had no idea what I might be getting myself into. A string of hook-ups? Standing in line with any number of other women who caught his eye? Beyond that, I needed to focus on work now more than ever. Getting screwed to oblivion by Blake on a regular basis probably wasn't going to help me in that department.

"Dinner, then."

"No," I insisted. "Besides, you were hardly the perfect gentlemen last time."

"Wasn't I? As I recall, you were the one who asked for the tour of the bedrooms."

He pressed his growing erection against me, eliciting a whimper. I tried to care that we were in plain view of anyone passing by, but I worried more that I was slipping further away from myself and deeper into a dangerous attraction that already had its hooks in me.

"Blake, seriously, Vegas was...really great." I paused, desperately trying to pull myself together. "I'm just not in a good place for this—whatever this is with us."

I kissed him gently, breathing him in one last time before slipping from his grasp. He released me, but by the wanting in his eyes, I could tell he wasn't happy about it.

"Goodbye, Blake."

CHAPTER SEVEN

With only a few days left before the dorms closed, I was running short on time and options to find a new place to live. I couldn't believe how far behind I'd fallen with this, but life was throwing me curve balls lately so I decided to reach out to Blake's sister and hope for some quick results.

Fiona Landon was stunning. Her light brown hair curled under into a stylish simple bob. Young, professional, and elegant, she was dressed in a navy blue polka dot dress when we met to begin the quest for my first apartment.

The first few places she showed me were in line with what I expected—on budget, smallish, and fair location, but a decent hike to any public transportation. I quickly realized that I'd either have to make some concessions or come up with a more realistic budget.

We stopped for a quick lunch at a little deli near the public gardens to regroup.

After making some calls to set up a last minute showing, Fiona joined me at the table. "So how do you know Blake?"

I choked a little on my lemonade. God, if she only knew.

"I'm in talks with Angelcom to invest in my business."

"Oh wow, that's great. I hope it works out."

"Me too."

"Blake gets so involved in his investments. I've seen some of those companies really take off."

I nodded and spared her the fact that he had "passed" on me. Well, he'd passed on the business anyway. He was pursuing me physically with a single-minded determination that one might expect from a ruthless businessman.

"What about you? Do you do this full-time?"

"Blake has several real estate holdings, so I mostly stay busy managing those, but I dabble with other listings in town."

"I guess it's good to keep it in the family."

"Definitely. Blake keeps us busy with all his projects."

"I met Heath recently too actually," I said, conveniently leaving out the details of our Las Vegas rendezvous.

"Oh, yeah?"

"He's a character," I continued, hoping to glean a little bit more about her charismatic brother and whatever issues Blake had with him, if only for Alli's sake.

"You could say that. I have no idea how Blake keeps up with him." She looked past me, her face carefully void of emotion. "Do you have any siblings?"

"No, it's just me." For years it had literally been just me. I often imagined what life might be like with a sibling or two. Someone to share the emotional burden with after my mother died or to make light of our hardships with and carry on together. The closest person to know what I'd been through was Elliott, but like me, he'd moved on.

Fiona and I finished our lunch and she drove us to the last apartment of the day, which she promised would be more in line with what I was looking for. She pulled in front of a picturesque brownstone on Commonwealth Ave. The street was tree-lined from one end to the other, with walking paths and beautifully manicured commons separating the two sides of the street. The location was address to many of the who's who of the city, and while I enjoyed the change of scenery from the lackluster places I'd seen so far, I worried how far out of the budget this would fall.

Nonetheless, I followed her up a flight of stairs. We entered a light and spacious two-bedroom apartment.

"Wow."

"This just came onto the market," Fiona said.

The appliances were new, the walls had a fresh coat of paint, and the dark wood floors were impeccable.

"This is perfect, Fiona, but I doubt I could afford something this nice."

"The owner is listing it at the right price for the right renter. It's above your budget, but it's such a great find, I had to show you." She handed me the listing sheet with the asking rent, a figure over budget, but well worth the extra features it offered.

I blew out a slow breath and did some mental math.

"You could always pick up a roommate with the extra room. It won't stay listed long, Erica, so if you think you might want it, I can make a call right now."

I'd have bay windows, a bathtub, and a second room to do with what I wanted. I was flying by the seat of my pants lately, so why stop now?

"Where do I sign?"

★ ★ ★

I stuffed the last of my clothes into a black trash bag and tossed it next to the others. Alli and I had barely spoken all day except to negotiate who would claim joint purchases. It felt strangely like a breakup, and in much the same way wreaked havoc on my already frayed nerves. Both finished, we each settled on the bare dorm mattresses, the springs squeaking below us. I wouldn't miss these.

"Have you heard from Heath?" I asked, anxious to break the silence and the tension between us.

She raised her eyebrows slightly and nodded. Great, I was getting the silent treatment.

"And?"

"And what?" she snapped. "It's not like you care, Erica."

"Listen, I'm sorry. You caught me at a bad time, and I just—" A tear slid down my face and I immediately wiped it away. "I wish you didn't have to go, but I want you to know that I understand why you do. I—"

She crossed the distance between us and hugged me hard.

"I want you to be happy, and I know you will be," I whispered.

She pulled away and held my face in her hands. "You're my best friend, Erica. A couple hundred miles isn't going to change that. And don't think for a minute that you can't rock this business without me. This is your baby. There isn't anything holding you back now."

"You make it sound like it's going to be so easy."

"You've made this whole thing look easy from day one. I have no idea how we pulled it off, but I know we couldn't have without you leading the way."

I wanted to believe her, but now that her leaving was a reality, the weight of my responsibilities hit me hard. Thankfully I had a lot more time to manage them, but I started to question my decision to stay in Boston when it seemed like everyone who mattered to me was leaving.

Early the next day, Fiona met me at the door looking as polished as she had before in a colorful sundress.

"Congrats!" She smiled and gave me a quick hug.

"Thank you for finding me such an amazing place."

"Anytime."

When she glanced over at the SUV that had delivered me, her smile faded a bit. Brad stepped out and joined me on the sidewalk in front of the building. Brad was a friend of a friend. I didn't know him really well, but he was nice enough and clearly he spent some time in the gym, so I didn't feel too bad asking him to move my futon up a flight of stairs to the new place.

He did so with expert grace, leaving the immaculate walls of the stairwell unscathed. Fiona seemed nervous when she handed me the keys to open the door. After I did, Brad passed through the threshold toward the room that would be my bedroom. Before I could follow him in, someone came down the stairs.

Oh, a neighbor! I thought excitedly, until Blake Fucking Landon turned the corner and faced me with a heart-melting smile.

"What are you doing here?" The tone of my voice revealed more panic than I wanted it to. I'd just gone through three regretful days believing I'd be rid of him for good, while simultaneously questioning why I had permanently sworn off the best sex of my life.

"I live here."

I shifted my glare to Fiona who visibly cringed, revealing that she was in on this the entire time.

"Sorry," she mouthed before turning to leave us.

"You live here." It wasn't a question, but more of a confirmation of the worst-case scenario.

"Well, actually I own the building, but yeah, I live here too."

I crossed my arms and my foot started tapping. How could I best articulate the absolute rage I felt toward this excruciatingly sexy man who could not keep himself from interfering with my affairs?

"You look angry. What can I do?"

He had the decency to look a little tentative, which was wise because I was considering physical violence to make my point. Words were wasted on him.

"For starters, you can stop meddling in my goddamn life, Blake!" I poked my finger into his rock hard pectorals. "What makes you think you can swoop in here and conveniently plant me in your downstairs apartment and think that's totally fucking normal?"

"For a Harvard girl, you've got quite the potty mouth."

"Cut the shit, Blake."

"Did you really want to live in one of those fleabag apartments?"

"You are completely missing the point."

Exasperated, I turned into the apartment and slammed the door behind me. He followed me in, coming face to face with Brad, who looked surprised to say the least. Blake was leaner and generally less beefy, but he had some height on Brad. Blake's wide-eyed gaze narrowed at the sight of him, and his hands fisted at his sides.

"Uh, hey?" Brad looked uncomfortable.

I grabbed my wallet from my purse and pulled out

the fifty bucks I owed him. "Thanks so much, Brad. I think we're good. Just throw the rest of the bags in the entryway, and I can bring them up."

"Are you sure?"

"Yes," Blake and I said in unison.

Somehow in the process of fighting with me over the privilege of hauling my bags into the apartment, Blake talked me into having dinner at his place upstairs. I was starving and emotionally wiped out, so I reluctantly agreed.

We walked through the entryway and into an open room with a designer kitchen to the right and large sitting and dining areas to the left. The apartment, for the most part, was every bit what I would expect. Light and modern, the main room was filled with contemporary furnishings, cream microfiber couches, dark hard woods, and pops of ocean blue in the paintings and accents. I guessed someone else, likely a woman, had helped him decorate the space.

What surprised me most, especially after getting a load of his high-tech Tesla, was the complete lack of visible electronics, but perhaps he was simply so high-tech they were camouflaged into the room somehow.

"No gadgets and gizmos?" I asked.

"Not really. If I need to be wired in, I go to my office."

"That surprises me."

"Why?"

"Well you can probably orchestrate a small conference from your car's touch screen. I didn't figure your living space would be any different."

"I've been staring at screens for fifteen years. Eventually it occurred to me that I get some of my best ideas when I'm offline for extended periods of time."

"I guess I can see that," I said, not quite able to come to grips with my own technology obsession. I needed to be accessible at all times, just in case. The thought of being off the grid for more than an hour, especially for someone like Blake who must be in much higher demand, was unthinkable.

"Wine?"

Today had been hot, exhausting, and stressful. I wanted nothing more than to end it with a cool glass of white wine, but that was a one-track journey into Blake's bedroom—a place I was determined to avoid, especially under these new living circumstances. Now that we were neighbors, thanks to the one-year lease I'd very recently signed, I had to enforce new boundaries.

"Water," I said. "So what's for dinner? Can I help with anything?"

"Uh—" He hesitated, and then opened a drawer and pulled out a stack of take out menus. "Take your pick. I highly recommend the Thai place down the street. The best you'll ever have."

I shook my head, a little amazed that he'd made such an effort to invite me up for dinner without having a game plan. For him, that seemed unusual. He was always five steps ahead of me, a quality I'd never underestimate again.

"Let me guess. You don't cook?"

"I have many talents, but cooking isn't one of them, no."

"Have you ever tried?"

"Not really." He shrugged.

"Okay, where's the nearest market?"

He raised his eyebrows. "A couple blocks away."

"Okay, I've got an empty fridge and I'm guessing you do too. How about we go pick up some things, and I'll show you how to make a proper meal for the next time you invite a girl over to your place."

He paused. I wasn't sure if he was annoyed or considering my offer. Regardless, he'd crossed the line with me too many times. I refused to walk on eggshells around Blake, billionaire or not.

"Fine, let's go," he finally said.

Blake was completely out of his element in the market. I felt him out for likes and dislikes, and then collected all the ingredients for one of my specialties, linguine and clams, one of the first dishes my mother had taught me to make.

Since I still lacked basic household items, like pots and pans, I set to work preparing the meal in Blake's gourmet kitchen, while he stood on the sidelines. I felt out of practice, but gradually I found my bearings. After four years of communal living with bare bones kitchenettes, I missed being in a real kitchen, and Blake's lacked for nothing.

"Are you just going to stand there, or are you going to help me?" I asked, only half serious.

He joined me at the counter, and I gave him his first task.

"Here, dice this." I handed him an onion. I watched him out of the corner of my eye, pretending not to notice as he blinked away the tears.

I made myself at home, narrating along the way for his sake. Though mostly silent, Blake was an attentive student. A little too attentive at times—I caught him staring at my ass when I went hunting for a strainer in his cabinets. I took full advantage of the power swap, schooling him on a few pasta cooking basics, like identifying al dente pasta and the critical difference between freshly grated versus jarred parmesan cheese.

Once finished, I prepared two plates, and Blake carried them into the dining area. We sat at the distressed wood farmhouse table, a beautiful and expensive piece of furniture. Admittedly, I was beginning to get used to the finer things when in Blake's presence.

We dove in and were silent for a few moments.

"I approve." He nodded and twisted some more pasta onto his fork.

"Thanks. The good news is that the leftovers will be even better."

"How can leftovers be better than this?"

"The pasta absorbs all the clam juice. It's divine."

He moaned an affirmative as he finished another mouthful.

I smiled, content and maybe a little empowered.

"Are you all set for your meeting with Max?" he asked. His plate was nearly clear while I had barely made a dent in mine.

"Not entirely. I've been running around with the move and tying up loose ends. I plan to work through the details this week though."

"He'll want to know more about your conversion statistics."

"Okay." I nodded, making a mental note to try to flesh that out more.

"And you'll need a specific breakdown of your expenses now, and what you expect them to be after funding. With Alli out of the picture and your personal expenses changing, you need to start thinking about what the financial landscape will look like if you get funding."

"Okay, thanks."

"Do you have any stats on your marketing efforts? What's working, what's not?"

"Um, a little bit," I said. "I have analytics, but I haven't really crunched those numbers in a while."

He leaned forward, resting his elbows on the table. "What are you doing tomorrow?"

"Sounds like I'll be doing my homework."

"Why don't you stop by my office for a bit, and I can help you break down some of this. You'll get funding faster if you can answer all of these questions right off the bat. Otherwise it'll just lead to more meetings. There are only a few questions you need to answer to get a deal, but you need to know every angle of the answer."

If anyone could nurse me through this process, Blake could. Turning him down would be rude, not to mention downright foolish. Still, I was dubious about further involving him in my affairs, not that he'd given me much choice.

"Is that a conflict of interest?" I asked, trying to think of any legitimate reason to refuse his help. I hated that I needed him right now.

"No, Erica. I already told you, I'm not investing in your project."

"I appreciate the offer, Blake. I really do, but I don't want to put you out."

"You won't. My office is right across from the clock tower." He pulled his card out of his wallet. "Meet me there after lunch and we can go over figures." He picked up his empty plate and headed into the kitchen.

"When's the last time you ate?" I asked when he returned with another heaping plate and a frosty bottle of a local microbrew.

"I'm a sucker for a home cooked meal." He grinned and took a swig from the bottle. "What's on the menu for tomorrow night? Let me know and I'll stock the kitchen."

I rolled my eyes. "I didn't realize I'd need to subsidize my rent with cooking services."

"I think I'd be content to let you live here rent free if you fed me like this every night."

"Tempting," I teased, though I would never consider it. Blake had obviously taken extreme measures to position me here in his building, available at his leisure so it would seem. Sweetening the deal with gourmet cooking was probably counter-intuitive. Perhaps I could stave him off with food in lieu of sex though. Could be a good plan, though I had an even better one.

CHAPTER EIGHT

We cleaned up from dinner and settled next to each other on the couch facing out the bay windows, much the same way we had in Vegas. Committed to a very different outcome for the evening, I was not so subtle when I shimmied away a few inches, making his physical proximity slightly more bearable.

"Where did you learn to cook like that?" Blake asked.

I paused before answering to carefully consider how much of my personal life I really wished to share. Talking about my mother invariably introduced the mystery of my father, a difficult concept for people to grasp. The fact that I didn't know my father's identity elicited a range of reactions from others, from shock to judgment to pity. Despite my misgivings about bearing all to Blake, dodging his questions would only delay the truth. No doubt he would pester and pry it out of me, bit by bit.

"My mother was a phenomenal cook. She taught me everything I know about food."

"Was?" he said gently.

"She passed away when I was twelve." I swallowed against the twinge of sadness that surfaced every time I spoke of her. "She started getting sick, and by the time they found out what it was, the cancer had spread aggressively. She was gone a few months later."

"I'm sorry," he said.

"Thank you." Saddened by the memory, I picked at the rip in my jeans. "So much time has passed, I have a hard time remembering everything about her. I feel like food is one of the ways I can keep her memory alive. That sounds strange, doesn't it?"

"I don't think so." He turned toward me and took my free hand. "So your father raised you?"

He drew slow circles into the back of my hand, simultaneously distracting and calming me.

"My stepfather did for about a year. When I was thirteen, I came east for boarding school. I spent one summer back in Chicago, and the rest with my mother's best friend, Marie, who lives just outside the city. I've pretty much been on my own since then though."

"That's a long time to be on your own."

I nodded slowly. "That's true, but I don't really have anything else to compare it to. It is what it is, I suppose."

"You must miss them."

I hardly knew what it was like to have a father, but I'm sure I would have enjoyed having one under the right circumstances.

"I miss my mother every day," I said. "But this is my life and everything that has made me who I am, so I can't dwell on what might have been."

I'd always be out of step with most people my age who'd been given many more chances to get it right, whose parents were there to scoop them up when they faltered and to point them in the right direction when indecisions were met.

I had quickly learned that my own safety net had sizeable gaping holes in it, which likely explained why lately I felt like I was at sea without a life preserver. Now my new weakness for Blake added a level of difficulty to the already risky endeavor of taking on the business full time. Yet here I was, giving him another opportunity to wear me down.

"It's late. I should go."

"You don't have to." His voice was serious, but not suggestive.

I searched his eyes for clues, hoping what I saw in them wasn't pity. Mine wasn't the happiest of stories, but feeling sorry for myself had gotten me nowhere.

"I know, but I have a million things to do before we meet up tomorrow." I stood. "Enjoy the leftovers."

He rose. "I eagerly await the hour when I can consider them leftovers."

He was close enough that his breath drifted across my lips. The sexual tension crackled between us. A couple hours ago I was piping mad, but since then he'd devoured my favorite pasta and had been incredibly sweet. Still, being neighbors now required careful consideration about how best to move forward. Unfortunately he hadn't given me much of a chance to consider anything, and my emotions were jumbled and confused.

I stuffed my hands in my pockets, resisting the urge to touch him. I looked down, wondering if this was the right time to talk about it.

"What's wrong?" Concern etched the sharp lines of his face and he cupped my cheek in his palm. I leaned into the simple touch.

"Well for one, I'm still mad at you."

A hint of a smile curved his mouth as he traced my lip with the pad of his thumb. He licked his lips, and mine parted at the gesture, tingling with the promise of his kiss.

"I like when you're mad," he murmured.

"Are you always this persistent?"

"Only when I see something I want."

"How did *I* get so lucky?" I couldn't hide my smile.

"Are you fishing for compliments?"

"No, but I'm hoping you have a good reason for turning my life upside down."

He stepped back and ran a hand through his hair, the absence leaving me momentarily bereft. I wanted him back, touching me.

"You're different."

I frowned a little. "Okay."

"I wanted to see you again, and you weren't really giving me that option." He arched his eyebrows. "Can that be enough?"

I sighed and moved to him. "I guess we'll see." I pressed a swift kiss to his cheek and left him before I could talk myself into staying.

I walked back into my apartment, which was too bright and bare compared to Blake's. This was my new home, but I had a long way to go before the place would feel like my own. I eyed the mountain of bags and boxes that I needed to organize before getting back to work tomorrow. Then I remembered something.

I grabbed my phone and pulled up Sid's number. He picked up on the second ring.

"What's up?" he said.

"A few things. Alli got a job in New York."

"Bummer," he said without emotion.

"Also, someone at Angelcom is prepping me for my next meeting with Max, which bodes well for the financing."

"Cool."

"Lastly, where are you staying when the dorms close?"

"I was just going to crash with some friends around here until something came through."

"I've got an extra room at my new place, and I could use the company. Are you interested?"

He paused a moment. "Are you sure?"

"Yeah, definitely."

"All right, sounds good to me."

I smiled and gave him the address before we hung up.

★ ★ ★

The signage on the frosted glass double doors read, *Landon Group*, in bold serif font. I crossed the threshold into a landscape of high tech workstations that filled the long room. I spotted Blake leaning on the windowsill talking to a young man whose headphones were hanging around his neck. A smattering of Trekkie memorabilia decorated the desk. *Sid would love it here*, I thought. Blake looked up and muttered something before crossing over to me.

"Hey." He flashed me a boyish smile and took my hand to lead me through the wide center aisle of the room to an enclosed office at the far end.

The gesture caught me off guard, but to my surprise, everyone seemed completely focused, as if no life existed beyond the stream of data feeding the machines. I was dressed all wrong too. In a white pencil skirt and a sleeveless black collared shirt with respectable black pumps, I stuck out in a sea of T-shirts, hoodies, and Hawaiian shirts. Apparently I had a lot to learn about tech start-up culture.

Just outside what I assumed was Blake's personal office, a punky petite woman sat at an L desk, zeroed in on her computer screen. She looked up when we approached.

"Erica, this is Cady."

She jumped up and shook my hand. Cady was dressed as casually as everyone else in jeans and a simple white T-shirt. Her left arm was sleeved in colorful tattoos that blended together as one expansive work of body art, but what stood out most was her short bleached-out mohawk frosted with hot pink tips. Her ears were decorated with shiny metal gauges that matched her spiked belt.

"Hi, Erica. It's good to meet you." She took my hand, revealing a beautiful smile that lit up her gray eyes. Even with all her decorations, she was very attractive.

"Likewise."

"Erica, Cady is my personal assistant. She's also your neighbor."

My eyes shot to him. I didn't realize he had a roommate.

"I live downstairs from you. I think we just keep missing each other," she said.

I breathed out with relief, surprised by my own reaction. "Oh, wow. Okay." What the hell? I shouldn't care if he had a roommate. After all, I was about to have one.

"Let me know if you ever have any questions about the place or the neighborhood. I'm kind of Blake's unofficial property manager too."

"Right, thanks."

She gave a little wave as Blake pulled us into his office, shutting the door behind us.

His office was more typical of what I expected from his apartment, though it still impressed me. Three oversized monitors lined one of his two desks. Two displayed dozens of lines of code and the last was filled with spreadsheets. Heath's assertion that Blake did all the work seemed valid. Even I wasn't sure I could wear that many hats at once.

In another corner of the office, an enormous television hung on the wall, connected to what appeared to be every video game console one could imagine. He led me to a large frosted conference table facing a glass writeboard.

"Very *Mission Impossible*," I said, secretly hoping for an excuse to write on it. Maybe I could illustrate the boundaries that needed to exist with our relationship.

He laughed and sat down at the table beside me. "Okay, show me what you've got."

I flipped a switch and my business brain took over, shifting my priorities and focus for the next two hours while we worked diligently, outlining a plan for the second phase of the presentation to Max. We hashed out numbers and I explained more about the business. I scribbled notes down, mapping out the points that I would organize back at the apartment tonight, trying not to be distracted by his proximity.

Even under these circumstances, I couldn't stop remembering that Blake and I had once shared a night of unbridled passion. People avoided workplace affairs for this very reason. When I wasn't looking directly at him, I could pretend I wasn't unbearably attracted to him, but not without concerted effort.

"Have I earned my dinner, yet?" He was leaning back in his chair, a pen tucked behind his ear and a wicked smile on his face that just wasn't fair. Women had to work so hard to achieve "effortless" beauty, but Blake could make my heart skip a beat with a well-timed smile and a pair of well-worn blue jeans.

"Do you always wear T-shirts to work?" I asked, ignoring his question.

"Usually." He shrugged.

"But you wear suits to casinos?"

"I wasn't at work."

"Your wardrobe metric seems to be a bit skewed, Blake." I turned back to my notes even though I had completely lost my train of thought. Visions of him in that gray suit propped up against my hotel door kept clouding my mind. *He should wear suits more often*, I thought. *No. No, he shouldn't.* I shook my head at my notes, thankful Blake wasn't tuned into my internal dialogue.

"If I wore a suit here, there'd be a mutiny. I have a reputation to maintain after all."

Sid wouldn't be caught dead in a suit, so he might be right.

We spent the rest of the afternoon at Blake's office. I toiled away on my presentation while he tapped at his keyboard, making magic happen between his three monitors. I had made considerable progress and felt confident I could satisfy whatever questions Max might have for me in our follow up and fill in the blanks left by my brief pitch earlier. I closed my laptop and stood to go when Blake spun around in his chair.

"What's the plan?" he said.

He sized me up with a wolfish grin that looked anything but innocent.

"I'm not your private chef. You realize that, right?"

"Perhaps we could negotiate." He rose and leaned against the desk in front me. "What could I do for you?"

I shivered at the low rasp in his voice. Why did he have to be so damned sexy? Maybe we could skip dinner and go right to dessert. Chocolate mousse sounded good. Licking chocolate mousse off his rock hard abs came to mind. Every delicious ridge...all the way down. Oh God. I licked my dry lips. I hadn't spent nearly enough time worshiping his body the last and only time I'd had him naked.

"Do you have something in mind, Erica?" Blake left his post at the desk and stalked closer.

I had reached the cut off for the amount of time I could safely spend alone with him. Like a drug, his presence was potent. I bit my lip at the fantasy of him being my living, breathing dessert plate.

Get a grip, Erica.

I snapped out of my reverie and straightened. "Do you have your fancy car here?"

"I do. And no, you can't drive it," he teased.

"I need to grab some household things for the apartment. Give me a ride, and I'll make you chicken parm tonight."

"I'm ready when you are."

We spent the next hour in a large department store, filling the cart with kitchenware, towels, and bedding. I grabbed the cheapest sheet set I could find in a color I liked, but Blake wordlessly put them back and replaced them with a 400-thread count set at thrice the price.

"I'm not made of money, you know."

The corner of his mouth turned up. "I'll buy those. And I promise, you'll thank me later."

I ignored the flush that worked its way through me at everything that promise implied. Still, I didn't argue the point any further since I was relying on him for transportation.

At the checkout, I was so busy organizing bags in the heaping cart that I didn't notice Blake slide his credit card through before it was too late.

"What the hell, Blake?" I protested.

"Call it your housewarming present."

"Absolutely not. You're being ridiculous."

"It's the least I can do. I did basically force you into living next door to me."

"Below you," I corrected.

"That's how I like you," he murmured, his eyes darkening.

Those few little words rendered me speechless and I heated from head to toe. My hands trembled a bit as I stuffed the receipt into my purse.

Blake insisted I wait in the car while he loaded the bags. We rode back to the apartment in relative silence. I stared at the screen between us and remembered the call that had come in the last time I was with him here.

"So who's Sophia," I asked. I feigned disinterest, looking out the window as buildings sped by us.

"She owns a company I invest in," he said. "Why do you ask?"

"I was just curious."

I shrugged and spotted our brownstone. So far Blake hadn't blatantly lied to me about anything, but he had a penchant for misleading me. For now I decided to believe him and put the subject out of my mind.

Blake brought everything upstairs for me. He ascended

the steps, his arms lined with about ten bags each while I hurried to unlock the door.

Just as we started putting things away, Sid walked in. Blake straightened immediately from his task of folding towels, which he was doing all wrong but I didn't have the heart to tell him.

"Sid, hey. This is Blake. Blake, you remember me talking about Sid, our developer."

Blake visibly relaxed and the twitch in his jaw disappeared. What was with him and staking his claim in my apartment? Sid could be easily agitated, so the last thing I needed was for Blake to make him uncomfortable on day one.

"Sure," he said, walking over to shake Sid's hand. "Nice to meet you."

Sid towered over him but his arms were about half the diameter of Blake's. The two men could not have been more different, in physicality or temperament.

"You too. And you are?"

"I'm Erica's neighbor," Blake said quickly.

A pang of disappointment shot through me. What had I expected him to say?

"I guess you're my neighbor too then." Sid shrugged out of his enormous hiking backpack.

The taut line of Blake's jaw made me question my grand plan.

"Great," he said.

I walked over quickly, hoping to neutralize the situation that Sid had no idea he'd just walked into. "Yeah, Sid is going to crash here until we figure out the financing thing. Dorms close this week, you know."

"Right," Blake said, running his hand through his hair.

I'd fill Sid in on Blake's association with Angelcom later. In the meantime, I had a kitchen to organize, a meal to cook, and an awkward dinner to host.

I showed Sid his room. All I had was the blow up mattress and bedding that would have to do until we got some real furniture. He didn't seem to care much, so I returned to the kitchen and started prepping the meal. Before I knew it, Blake was behind me. He spun me around.

"You never told me about the roommate."

His voice was low and serious enough to set my heart beating a mile a minute. Was he angry? I couldn't really tell, but I felt like a child about to go to time-out.

Inviting Sid to be my roommate had been a rash decision, granted. I knew how he lived, typically in a pile of pop tart wrapper rubble, and it worried me a bit. But in truth, I wasn't ready to live solo anyway, and I could use his presence at the apartment to deter Blake's advances, though it wasn't working at present.

I swallowed hard before replying. "You haven't exactly been straightforward with me either, Blake. I don't know what you expect."

"It's a complication. I suppose we'll have to work around it."

"Oh?"

"We'll just be spending a lot more time upstairs is all."

He stepped between my legs and lifted my knee over his thigh with a single fluid motion. My breath rushed out of me, and I gripped the edge of the counter as he pinned me to it. He pressed a hot kiss on my neck before taking my earlobe between his teeth.

I gasped at the sensation and held on tight. Squeezing my eyes shut, I reminded myself of every good reason not to give in to him. There was a line with Blake. On one side of it, I wanted him desperately, but somehow I could muster the willpower to refuse him. We were on the other side of that line, where I was completely at his mercy, helpless against his determination to have me.

His hands crept under my shirt and stroked the bare skin of my back, the contact sending me into orbit. My nipples hardened and brushed against his chest as I arched into him.

"I need you, Erica. Tonight." He pressed the evidence of his desire into me.

His mouth was on mine before I could say no, obliterating any remote ideas about putting him off again. He kissed me hard and deep, sucking and licking with an urgency I fully met. I finally released my hands and raked my fingers through his hair, urging him closer. He pulled back to catch his breath, and I gripped him tighter, willing him back to me.

There we were, Blake's hands on their way up my skirt, each of us on fire for the other, when Sid shuffled out of his bedroom and stopped short in the living room.

I froze, petrified by being caught in the act. With Sid entirely out of his view, Blake slowly retreated. He gave me a little smirk, letting me know our little show had gone according to his plan. He adjusted himself before turning around and busying himself with something at the island.

Flustered by my desire and newfound irritation, I channeled my emotions into the food, ignoring Blake's requests to help. We were obviously playing a game, but I was already growing tired of it. The only move I could think up was to ignore him, to not give him what we both wanted even though I was ready to combust with sexual frustration. If I could get a handle on that, maybe he'd learn I wasn't someone to toy with.

Somehow we all made it through dinner. I ate at the counter. Both Sid and Blake devoured my mother's chicken parmesan at the breakfast bar. We needed real furniture at some point. Buying furniture worthy of the space while on a budget would be a challenge, but not impossible. I resolved to do a little bargain shopping after I finalized my presentation notes in the morning.

Now more than ever, I needed this to feel like home, a safe place away from the rest of the world. Right now the apartment was barren and strange. Between that, Alli being out of my immediate life, and Blake's mission to turn my world upside down, I felt as if I were dangling precariously, hanging on for dear life to any semblance of normalcy.

Blake must have picked up on my withdrawal, because when we finished cleaning up, he let me know he was taking off. I walked him to the door, and Sid disappeared on cue.

"Are you okay?" Blake's eyes, not so long ago clouded with the heat of lust, were now filled with concern.

"I'm fine, just tired. It's been a long day." It was only half of the truth, but I didn't have the energy to talk it out or bicker with him.

"Do you want a ride to the office tomorrow?"

"No, thanks. I'd rather just finish up here. I have some errands to run."

He nodded, and when he leaned in for a kiss, I turned

my head, narrowly escaping his lips on my own. I closed my eyes. As much as I wanted to make a point, I dreaded the look in his eyes. When I opened them, he had disappeared up the stairs.

I shut the door and leaned against it. My face fell into my hands. How the hell had I gotten into this mess?

CHAPTER NINE

I spent the morning shopping online and picked out a bedroom set, figuring I would donate my futon to Sid eventually. I also ordered a small dining room table and matching chairs, and a few other odds and ends. I scoured the classifieds and found a decent used couch that someone could deliver for an extra few bucks. Sid had already moved in his television and gaming systems, which sat in the otherwise bare living area.

This apartment might be the closest thing to a real home that I'd had since my mother passed. Of course now I was sharing it with Sid, but who knew how long that would last? I clung to the thought of this being home, my home, giving the word new meaning with this new chapter of my life that was filled with so many unknowns.

For the past four years, more even, I'd had everything planned out. Now I had no idea what to expect from my future. I had only my intuition to guide me. Unfortunately Blake was marching all over my intuition. I wasn't expecting a man like him—and everything that came with him—in my life.

Unable to concentrate on work, I slapped down the screen of my laptop. I needed some fresh air. Thanks to Blake's chauffeuring me around and the new living situation, I'd been cooped up inside most of the day.

I stepped outside and walked the length of the street

until the grass-lined walking path ended. There I settled on an empty bench and let the sun warm my skin. The day was mild, still too cool for the beach but perfect for being outside comfortably.

I decided to call Alli. I missed her too much already. After several rings she picked up.

"Hello?" she answered, her voice hoarse.

"Are you okay? You sound sick."

"I'm fine. Long night."

"Who are these friends you're staying with?" I asked, suddenly concerned.

"I was with Heath."

"Oh."

"What can I say? He parties like a rockstar." She let out a weak laugh.

"On a Thursday night? When do you start work?"

"Monday, and you can stop worrying now. We're just having fun. Plus I'm meeting some new people here. Making connections for us."

"Okay." Though what great connection partied all night on a Thursday?

"So how are things with you?"

"Pretty good. The new apartment is great."

"Ugh, I'm so jealous. The apartments here are ridiculous. I feel like I'm shopping for closets."

"If it makes you feel any better, I could end up on one of those hoarder shows in a few months. I invited Sid to come stay with me. The new can collection has begun."

She laughed. "Oh shit. Okay, I'm not jealous anymore. At least I won't have to share my closet, if I'm lucky."

I laughed and agreed.

"What's new with Blake?"

I told her about the housing situation, which didn't surprise her as much as I thought it would. Maybe Heath had already clued her in to Blake's over-controlling tendencies. Thankfully she didn't grill me on whether I intended to keep our one-nighter just that, because I was still trying to figure it out myself.

"So when are you going to come visit me?" she asked.

"I guess when we both get settled. We'll see how things go with Max. I should be able to visit after that."

Alli filled me in on all the fun spots she was discovering in the city that we'd go to eventually. In the middle of our conversation, Blake beeped in. I promised to call her later and answered Blake's call.

"Hey, the site went offline a few minutes ago."

My stomach fell. "What? How do you know?" The site had gone down before, which obviously wasn't good, but I needed everything to be perfect for my meeting with Max tomorrow.

"I set up a program to ping me if the site went down."

"Why?"

"Erica, can we focus on the issue at hand?" He sounded more irritated than I should have been, considering it was my website we were talking about. "Can you put Sid on?"

I didn't like being pushed to the side, but this was not my department.

"I'm out right now, but I can be home in a few minutes."

"Give me his number, I'll call him."

"Don't bother. I'll call you back in a bit."

Back at the apartment, I knocked quietly on Sid's door,

then louder. He was never up this early. Eventually I walked in, determined to wake him from his sleep coma. He was fully dressed and passed out face down on the sheetless air mattress.

"Sid!" I yelled, breaking the silence of an otherwise quiet and peaceful morning.

He groaned and rolled over. "What?"

"The site's down."

"Oh," he said, unmoving.

"Blake called. He wants to talk to you."

"I need caffeine," he grumbled.

I huffed, in no mood for his pissy morning routine. "I'll be back with some energy drinks. Get up and figure out what is going on please." I left my phone on his desk with Blake's number up and walked down the street to the convenience store.

A few minutes later, I returned to find Sid frowning at his computer screen, analyzing what, from past experience, looked like the server logs. These held answers about the site's activity that I had no idea how to interpret. I heard clicking noises coming out of my phone, which was set on speaker.

"It looks like they're attacking the log in script and bombarding the server with requests so the host shut us down," Sid said.

"Sounds like it's just script kiddies then," Blake's voice said.

"What are script kiddies?" I asked almost in a whisper, not wanting to be the ignorant one. Still, I needed to know.

"Amateur hackers with too much free time," Sid answered.

"Oh." Compared to skilled hackers on a schedule? A hacker was a hacker, as far as I was concerned. An enemy threatening my business. Hopefully Sid and Blake could craft a defense plan soon.

"Do you have a redundant server?" Blake asked.

"Obviously," Sid replied flatly.

"Get that going, and let's see how persistent they are. Can you give me access to the server?"

Sid looked at me for the okay, and I nodded.

"I'll send it over now."

"I can set up an IP blocker, if you want to work on patching vulnerabilities," Blake said.

"Sounds good."

"Do I need to call the host?" I asked Sid quietly.

"No, I'll reboot the server, and we'll be back up in a few minutes."

I took a deep breath. "Do you need anything from me?"

Sid turned his head, fixing on the bag of cans I held. I fished one out for him and put the rest in the fridge, feeling a bit useless.

I pulled out my laptop at the island and refreshed the website repeatedly until the site came back up, while Blake and Sid continued their unintelligible tech speak in the other room.

The fact that we had been hacked concerned me, especially since I hoped to finalize a deal with Max within a matter of weeks. Blake and Sid didn't seem overly concerned about the nature of the threat, but I had an unsettled feeling. Why were we being targeted all of a sudden? Who hated fashion so much that they needed to take us offline?

Once we were on the other side of this minor setback, I hoped to have more answers from Sid.

I spent the rest of the day monitoring the site and testing Sid's patches as he rolled them out. We ate leftovers and went over statistics for me to reference in the morning. As the night rolled on, I didn't hear from Blake. At the very least, I expected him to come raid the fridge. After all, we'd seen each other every day since I moved in, and he seemed to have a growing dependency on my Italian cooking.

I peeked out to the street for his car. Not seeing it, I considered texting him, but what would I say? I missed him, but I wasn't about to tell him that.

★ ★ ★

I arrived at Angelcom a few minutes ahead of schedule. I entered the reception area and the same frumpy brunette greeted me with a tight smile and walked me down the hall into Max's personal office. Like the conference room, it featured a wall of windows with a view of the Harbor and the skyline to the north. Dressed in an impeccable black suit, Max pored over some paperwork at his desk. He stood up when he saw me, circling the desk to shake my hand and give me a polite kiss on the cheek.

"Erica, you look beautiful."

"Thank you." I didn't know what else to say, but I self-consciously smoothed back my hair, already tucked tightly into a twist. I tried to appear unaffected by Max's new level of comfort with me. He motioned to a small round table in his office.

He peppered me with all the right questions, ones I had expected thanks to Blake. I answered them expertly, painting an accurate and hopefully attractive picture of the venture. After about an hour, he paused and looked at me for a moment.

"What?" Was this the end of the meeting? A ball of nervous energy formed in my stomach.

"I'm very impressed, Erica. You've covered all the bases. I really don't think I can come up with anything more."

I clicked my pen nervously. Fessing up about Blake's involvement now would be better than Max getting wind of it later. "Blake's been really helpful, actually. He worked through a lot of this with me, so I suppose I can't take all the credit."

He paused, staring silently at me. "Is that right?"

"I can see why his businesses do so well. He's extremely thorough."

A frown marred Max's brow. "He's not as perfect as you might think."

"Well, no one's perfect."

"Agreed, but Blake's lucky he's not rotting in a jail cell right now. Every success he's had is because of the opportunities my father gave him. He'd do well to remember that."

A new brand of anxiety coursed through me with this information. What trouble could have landed Blake in jail? My mind raced through the possibilities. Clearly the two had history, and Blake, not surprisingly, had kept me in the dark despite all our discussions about investing with Max.

I had always thought of Max as Blake's peer, a colleague. With this bad blood between them, why did they share a place on the board of the company?

"In any case, he missed his chance on this one, I suppose." He changed again, back to calm, charming Max.

The transformation gave me an eerie feeling, but I tried to ignore it.

"That's true," I said. Admittedly, I was confused by Blake's active interest in not only me, but my company, especially after such a dramatic review and refusal at the start.

"Let's make this happen, Erica," Max said abruptly. "I think there's real potential here, and I'd like to be part of it."

The ball of nervous energy dissipated as relief and happiness flowed through me. "Wonderful. Where do we go from here?"

"Let me draw up the paperwork. There are legalities we'll need to work through, but I should be able to have a term sheet ready to review in a week or two. Hopefully we can get this off the ground quickly. If it ends up taking longer, I can arrange for rolling funds in the interim so you guys aren't in a pinch."

I smiled broadly. "That sounds great. I'll follow your lead then."

"Perfect. Keep doing what you're doing, and I'll be in touch."

We rose and shook hands, and I left the building wanting to shout the good news off the rooftops. *We did it!* All the work, the stress, and the multitasking. God, the multitasking. Being able to juggle school and not give up on Clozpin as a side project had been a miracle in itself. I pulled out my phone and scrolled through my numbers, trying to decide who to call.

One name stood out.

I'd been hard on Blake. But would this have gone so

smoothly without his help? I called him and it went to voicemail.

"Hey, Blake. I just wanted you to be the first to know that Max is moving forward with the deal. He's drawing up the paperwork next week. So, great news. Thank you. For everything."

I hung up and rang Alli next, but the call went to voicemail too. I checked the time. It was nearly eleven a.m., and I couldn't fight the feeling that Heath was becoming a less than healthy influence on my best friend. Something was off with him, but I needed to get to the bottom of it before I could pass judgment. In the meantime, I would figure out a way to visit sooner rather than later.

I switched out of my heels into some flats and walked home, wanting to get some exercise and take advantage of the mild morning that was growing hotter by the hour. Finally, summer had arrived.

★ ★ ★

The apartment was silent all the next morning. Maybe this cohabitation with Sid could work after all. We were on totally different schedules, which made it seem like I had the place to myself most of the time.

I wrote up an organizational chart for positions that we might want to fill in the next six months. A marketing director was a top priority. Getting out of my shell and networking was important and something I fully intended to continue, but I needed to be running the site and overseeing all operations. I couldn't be responsible for pulling in all the paid accounts, keeping track of finances, maintenance, and now reporting back to Max with our periodic progress. Losing Alli from the team was a setback, but there were hundreds of eager professionals in the city waiting for an opportunity like this. I set to work drafting roles and responsibilities for the job when Blake texted me.

Congrats. Top of the Hub tonight to celebrate. Be ready at 7.

His communication threw me for a loop. Why didn't he just call me? He was being distant for some reason, but apparently he was still in the mood to celebrate. At one of the best restaurants in the city no less, but not seeing him for a while made me worry about what he was actually thinking. Was it the good night kiss snub? Did he think I was being a tease because I couldn't stop melting around him and then pushing him away?

See you at seven, I replied.

My focus immediately shifted from ideal marketing director qualities to what I would wear tonight. The irony of Blake implying that seeing someone would be distracting for the venture, when he was now in the very position to be that distraction, was not lost on me. Still, I rifled through the contents of my closet for something suitable to wear. I huffed, empty-handed. I missed Alli's fashion sense and her ample wardrobe.

I called Marie, hoping she was nearby.

"Help!" I said with mock panic.

"What's up, baby girl?"

"I got the funding, and I'm going out tonight to celebrate."

"I knew it. Congratulations!"

"But I have nothing to wear."

She laughed, a throaty sound that made me smile.

"Honey, that's a problem we can fix. Do you want to grab some lunch before we hit the stores?"

"Absolutely. Thank you."

After days with techies and suits, I needed girl time. A couple hours later we were seated at The Vine. The beautiful little Mediterranean open air restaurant was tucked in the basement floor of a brownstone on Newbury Street, one of the most exclusive and expensive shopping districts in the city. Not surprisingly, it was only a few short blocks away from the new apartment. Marie and I sipped iced tea and shared calamari while we caught up.

"So tell me about your date," Marie said.

I paused, contemplating how to bring her up to speed on everything Blake had thrown at me lately. "You don't happen to remember that guy I literally ran into at the restaurant the other night?" Butterflies danced in my belly at the thought of my first chance meeting with Blake.

She stilled, and her beautiful brown eyes widened. "You're kidding me."

"Not kidding. He's the executive director for the angel investment group who is giving us the funding." I skipped the part about him seducing me in Las Vegas and luring me to live in his apartment building. Marie wasn't my mother, but she did get protective at times.

"Wow, that sounds right up your alley."

"Hardly. He's so out of my league. It's actually incredibly intimidating."

"I don't suppose a busy guy like that would spend time with you if he thought you were out of his league."

I sighed. I wished I knew what Blake was thinking, but he had me too busy sorting out my business to pry much.

"I guess not. It's been a bit of a whirlwind so I don't really know what to think." I poked at my salad. "To be honest, Marie, I don't know up from down right now."

"That's how love goes, baby." She shook her head with a smile.

Love? Leave it to Marie, the hopeless romantic, to even think it. Blake was a magnificent distraction, but that had nothing to do with love.

"I'm not sure we're there, or if we'll ever be."

She cocked her head, a half smile curling her lip. "You never know. Love can sneak up on you in a heartbeat, even when you aren't looking for it."

I nodded with a nervous smile.

"Suppose so. What's new with Richard anyway?"

Her soft smile transformed into a full one as she launched into the details of their last date. I settled back into my seat, trying to listen, but all I could think about was that four letter word. Except I had no room in my life for love right now.

CHAPTER TEN

I pretended to work the rest of the afternoon, but really I was silently counting down the minutes until I would see Blake. I was eager to celebrate the deal with Max, but I had missed seeing Blake lately. Now I felt as if I owed this milestone of success in large part to his support. Even if that support came with all the sexual tension that I was trying to make sense of between us, I was grateful for it all the same.

As the hour grew closer, I slipped into the sexy, overpriced cocktail dress Marie had helped me pick out. Solid black, with a thin white strip along the tulip hem, the garment was dressy but still suited the hot day with tiny spaghetti straps and light layers of chiffon. I paired the outfit with some strappy heels and silver dangle earrings, and I pinned my hair up in a loose bun.

We would see what Blake had to say about all this, I thought. I touched up my smoky gray eye shadow. With or without Blake, I felt like a million bucks and I wanted to look great tonight. Alli would be proud.

Sid was rummaging through the fridge when I emerged from my bedroom, my heels clicking loudly across the floor. I stopped at the breakfast bar to wait for Blake. Sid turned and saw me, his eyes wide.

"What?" I said, suddenly concerned that I didn't look nearly as good as I thought I did.

"Uh—" He blinked. "Nothing. You look really nice."

He smiled and disappeared back to his bedroom in time for Blake to knock on the door.

After another second he let himself in and slowed as I circled the island to greet him. He wore the same charcoal gray suit from Vegas, with a freshly pressed white shirt. A bit of stubble offset the formality of his attire. *Damn.* I sauntered over, trying like hell to stay steady on my heels, savoring the look of pure carnal appreciation that swept his face.

"Hey," I said.

"You're killing me in that dress."

I bit my lip, never knowing what he might do when we were alone like this. With a feather-light touch, he traced a line from my cheek to my chin, tipping my face toward him before giving me a slow, sweet kiss that had me breathless at the finish.

We walked into the busy restaurant, and the maître d' escorted us without delay to a table for two that seemed private by way of the wall of wine separating us from the main dining area. Through the huge windows, Boston sprawled. Below, dozens of tiny white sails dotted the Charles River and the sunset reflected off its meandering path through the city.

"You know how I love a good view," I murmured. I loved that we were ending this perfect day here, and I'm sure it showed.

"I do, and now that I know you're a food connoisseur, I'm going to change things up and let you order for the both of us."

I laughed. "That *is* a change."

"Everything here is incredible, so you can't go wrong."

"I don't doubt it." I perused the menu.

When the server arrived, I ordered. Duck confit for him and haddock for myself.

After the server left, I asked, "Is it difficult for you to not be in control?"

He paused a moment. "Yes, but I've been trying it in small doses lately."

"How's that going for you?"

"It's…not always easy."

"Seems like it might be liberating. I think sometimes it would be nice to take a break, to be able to defer to someone else completely. If only for a little while."

"You can defer to me whenever you'd like."

He pulled his bottom lip between his teeth, twisting his mouth up into a devious smile. I narrowed my eyes at him playfully, feeling my skin tingle. I was enjoying our pseudo-sexual banter more than I expected, but I needed to move the conversation away from the topic of sex. Blake could take my mind from zero to filthy with a few choice words.

"You've been making yourself scarce. Anything new?"

His eyes met mine with a penetrating gaze. "Just putting out fires at work."

"You haven't asked me about the meeting with Max."

"What's to tell? I knew Max was going to invest from the moment I saw you in that boardroom."

I wish I had known, I thought, *if only to save myself a fair measure of stress and anxiety.* "How did you know that?"

"Well for one, you're beautiful."

I warmed at the compliment, though coming from someone who defined physical perfection, I had a difficult time truly accepting it.

"I'm not sure what looks have to do with it." I fidgeted with my napkin.

"Looks can be persuasive, especially to a guy like Max. Secondly, you have a good concept."

I frowned, confused as to why Blake's glowing opinion of me this evening ran in such stark contrast to his brutal line of questioning at the pitch. "If you thought I had a good concept, then I'm not sure why you felt the need to humiliate me at the pitch and shoot me down."

I had come to know Blake better these past couple weeks, but the tirade of emotions I felt that first day were not easily forgotten. My hand fisted as I remembered the experience, his simple and easy rejection stamped on my memory. I riled again, my skin prickling with anger now.

"I wanted to see how you'd perform under pressure. Plus, how else was I supposed to find out if you were available? Two birds with one stone." He shrugged, as if it were nothing.

To him, it probably was. To me, it was a life-changing event, the culmination of months of hard work. If we were going to move any further together he needed to know that.

"Blake, I worked really hard for the opportunity to pitch your group, and you completely disrespected me. It's hard for me to imagine how I would have felt if I hadn't gotten the second meeting because of you. The word devastated comes to mind."

I looked out at the skyline to avoid his gaze, afraid my anger might fade when I genuinely wanted him to know what an ass he'd been that day. I'd been holding that thought to myself for weeks now, and I was suddenly ashamed that

I'd actually slept with Blake before calling him out on his behavior. All my pride at having accomplished what I had at my age, and I was hardly a beacon of feminism.

"You're right," he said quietly.

My anger slipped at the shock of hearing his words.

"You didn't deserve that."

His eyes were disarmingly serious as I processed his almost-apology. The server came with our food, and we ate in silence for a few moments.

"Max seemed upset that you helped me," I said.

His hand came down on the table hard enough to startle me. "You told him I helped you?"

My eyes went wide. "I assumed he would know eventually. I thought you were friends."

"We're colleagues, not friends, Erica." He forked his duck aggressively and sliced off a bite before popping it into his perfect mouth.

"How do you know his dad?"

He raised his eyebrows, his patience with this line of conversation clearly thinning. I worried that my perfect day was being threatened, but we'd come this far already.

"Blake, you know all kinds of things about me, and I feel like I don't know anything about you. Tell me something. Anything!" I waved my hand in frustration, needing him to know how difficult this inequity was becoming for me.

His jaw twitched as he continued with his entree. My appetite waned despite the mouth-watering fillet in front of me. Food this divine should never go to waste. I poked at the seasoned couscous around the fish when Blake began to speak.

"When I was fifteen, I got into some trouble."

"What kind of trouble?"

"Hacker stuff."

"What kind of hacker stuff?" I pressed.

"It's not important."

I settled back into my chair, pouting a little.

"At the time, Michael, Max's father, wanted to diversify, so he started to invest heavily in computer software. He knew my story and sought me out. I was at a low point in my life, but he gave me an opportunity. I was able to build out the banking software on my own terms, the way it needed to be built. Obviously, it paid off for both of us, doubling his portfolio and setting me up to be able to do what I do now."

"How does Max play into this?"

"Max is a few years younger than me. He watched Michael invest in me. Not just professionally, but as a mentor and a friend. He resented it, and when the software sold, he knew at that point he'd never be able to catch up to me. It's been chafing his ass ever since."

"Oh."

"Are you happy now, boss?" he asked, pointing his fork at me.

He was kind of cute when he was annoyed and confessional.

"Well I'm not happy to hear that in particular, but I'm happy you told me."

I replayed the two meetings at Angelcom through my mind with the new knowledge that Max was in constant competition with Blake, eager for any opportunity to overtake him. My business was about to become irrevocably tied to Max. I now harbored very rational fears that my association with Blake could become problematic at some point, but Max wouldn't have known about our relationship if I hadn't told him.

When the check came, Blake handed the server his card before I could reach for my purse. I let it go and excused myself to freshen up.

When I emerged, I made my way toward Blake, who waited at the elevators. He stood with casual grace, his hands in his pockets, his suit straining in all the right ways, reminding me of the rock hard body beneath it. I could focus on almost nothing else as I passed by the long elegant bar and its patrons, but a face along the way caught my attention.

I stopped in place, suddenly gripped with an all-consuming panic that drowned out the noise of the crowded restaurant. My heart beat ratcheted out of control. An icy pain rushed through me, seizing my body from my lungs to my fingertips.

I steadied myself on the wall beside me, seemingly unable to move forward another inch while the face of the man I recognized turned in my direction, as if he sensed me watching him.

Dressed in a tailored pinstriped suit, he looked like anyone else at the bar having a drink after a long day, but I knew better. After a few seconds, his face twisted into a smile as recognition dawned.

He remembered me.

After three years of looking over my shoulder, never knowing when I might see him again, I had come to believe I never would. Without a name, he was a ghost, a memory so excruciating that I'd spent years trying to convince myself he'd never existed at all. Yet here he was, a living nightmare come back to haunt me. I cursed myself as the irrational thought struck me that talking with Liz had somehow conjured him back to life.

I vaguely remembered hearing Blake call my name before he was at my side, taking me by the arm to break me out of my trance. He came into focus, and I tried in vain to mask the fear that plagued me.

"What's wrong?" he asked, his face lined with concern.

"Nothing." I caught his hand and pulled him toward the elevators.

After a few attempts to get me talking in the car, Blake seemed to give up. We stepped into the cool air of his apartment and I made myself at home at the wet bar in the living room. I filled a cut glass lowball to the brim with ice and some smoky amber liquor from one of the many bottles in his collection.

I sank into the couch and pressed the cool glass against my forehead, willing away the frenzied thoughts that had taken over. I wanted to banish each and every one of them. Tuck them away where they no longer felt like my own, or better yet, where I might forget them entirely. I took a healthy gulp from my glass to hasten their journey.

I shouldn't be here, but I couldn't be alone right now, and sharing square footage with Sid didn't count. I needed a powerful distraction, and Blake had always been supremely helpful in that department. He sat on the coffee table across from me, holding my legs between his. He stroked the sensitive skin above my knees, but my body was numb, unable to process even the most basic desires that Blake inspired in me.

"Talk to me, please," Blake said evenly.

I stared past him, giving him nothing. Sharing my past with Blake seemed impossible, but something sparked to life. A little part of me wanted to break down the wall that kept my past safely hidden from the present.

"There's nothing to talk about," I said, unsure how I could even begin to tell him, even if I wanted to. I could barely handle the onslaught of emotions that had been terrorizing me since leaving the restaurant.

"That's bullshit. You looked like you'd witnessed a crime scene in there."

"I was remembering one." I regretted the words as soon as I uttered them. My body tensed with a different kind of fear. Blake would never look at me the same again. He would know someone had taken his pleasure from me, and that in my stupid, young ignorance, I let him.

Silent, he waited for me to continue. I forced the rest of the drink down, waiting for the relief it promised. If I told Blake now, he'd either head for the hills, or maybe he'd care, though I couldn't imagine why. It dawned on me that if we had any chance for a future, he'd have to know.

"We were freshmen. I went with some friends off campus for a weekend party, and we ended up at a frat house. The place was mobbed. We danced, we drank too much punch. I barely ever drank, so I was obliterated by the time I got to the bottom of my cup. I wandered away from the group. A guy there, he ..." I trailed off, lost in the memory I'd so carefully buried.

How could I possibly explain how naïve I had been, to follow a friendly stranger to the bar that we never found, like a child being lured with candy? Then to be so intoxicated that I could barely fight him off, my refusals lost in the chaos of the party that raged inside.

The man I saw tonight was the man who had taken my innocence, leaving me violated and sick in the bushes where Liz finally found me. Years of preserving myself for a first love, or at the very least, a buzzed night of mutual consent, had all been for naught, and the shame had kept me silent.

"I tried to fight him off," I whispered. This time, I couldn't swallow away the tears that fell free down my face. My limbs felt weak and heavy, weighed down by my past and the reality that losing whatever I had with Blake to it would be a crushing blow.

Blake's jaw clenched, and he sat back, raking his hands through his hair. The momentary separation from his touch physically hurt, the places where our skin had met ached for his return. I needed the contact as an affirmation that this new knowledge wouldn't color how he felt about me. A sickness twisted inside me at the thought.

"Are you happy now?" I laughed weakly through my tears, wishing Blake would respond.

His expression was frozen with a nameless emotion.

"I'm damaged goods."

"Stop." The authoritative bite to his voice gave me pause.

"Stop what?"

"You're not damaged, Erica."

I swallowed hard, wishing I could believe him. "I'm simply stating the obvious. It doesn't make sense for you to want to be with someone like me anyway. You should be dating socialites, models, not someone like…me." My voice caught as the words left me.

"I'm not interested in dating models."

"Well, that makes no fucking sense, you realize that? I'm a mess. I mean, just look at me."

"I do. Frequently, in fact. You've been driving me crazy for days. I can barely sleep at night."

"And now?"

"Now, I have you. No roommates, no crowds, and you're trying to come up with every reason to scare me off. If you think this changes things, you're wrong."

I looked away, helplessly fighting the tears that just kept coming. When he sat next to me and pulled me onto his lap, I went willingly, wanting to feel him close again. How he could still want me, I would never know. He wrapped me tight in his arms, cocooning me to his chest until my tears ran dry.

"You're stunning," he said.

Nuzzled into his shoulder, I shook my head. "How can you say that after what I just told you?"

"Because it's true. Erica, one horrible experience doesn't define you. If it did, I doubt you'd want to be with me either."

"But I do," I said.

My hand slid over his shirt to feel his heart beating a slow and steady rhythm. I knew nothing about his heart, but something inside of me wanted to deserve it then. What would it be like to have his desire, and his love? Suddenly my feelings for Blake began to overwhelm the painful memories he'd coaxed out of me moments earlier.

He lifted my hand and brushed his lips softly over my fingertips. "I want to be with you too, baby."

In that moment I felt like we had been together and

known each other far longer than we had. I had shown him a part of me, and he was still here with me despite all of it. Inch by inch, he caressed me, claiming every expanse of bare skin with a quiet tenderness I'd never known, healing me with his hands and lips. The pain and the numbness gave way to relief, and then, to a familiar warmth that simmered below the surface.

I tipped my head back, a silent plea for his kiss. Somehow, he'd broken through my walls, overwhelming my senses with the pressing need to be possessed. His smell, his taste, and his primal hunger—I craved them all. His lips met mine. Tentative at first, then more sure. I explored the depths of his mouth, tangling my tongue with his, ravenous for him. He met me with equal intensity. He shifted me so I was straddling him, pressing our bodies together so they were flush. A soft cry escaped my lips at the sudden contact and the fervency of his movements. Then he stopped, fisting his hands to his sides.

"What's wrong?"

"I'm wound too tight, Erica." His head fell back on the couch and he swallowed, the notch in his throat moving with the action.

I wanted to kiss him there, but I needed to figure out where his head was first. "So?"

He squeezed his eyes shut and his body tensed beneath my touch.

"Touch me," I begged. I fumbled with the buttons of his shirt, unable to wait any longer for his skin on mine. Running my fingers over his chest, I leaned in to taste his throat, relishing his scent and the saltiness of his skin.

"Wait," he said through clenched teeth.

I pulled back obediently. "Why?"

My heart sank and the sadness crept back as the silence grew between us. After everything I'd shared with him tonight, I'd been foolish to think that we could go on like nothing had happened.

I searched his eyes. A flicker of emotion passed over his features before he looked away. Was it fear?

"I want you, Blake." God, did I ever. I shifted, unable to ignore the uncomfortable ache between my thighs.

"I want you too. I'll probably lose my mind if I can't be inside you tonight." He exhaled a shaky breath. "I just don't want to ... freak you out."

"I'm not a china doll. I promise you won't hurt me."

He closed his eyes again, his hands unmoving on either side of us, as if he could block out the temptation to touch me that way.

Appreciating every hard ripple of his abdomen, I trailed my fingers down his chest, following the soft hairs that disappeared under the band of his pants. I reached for the clasp, but before I could release him, Blake caught my wrists, holding them steady while he breathed hard.

"I want to feel you lose control, Blake." My body pulsed, my self-control hanging on by a thread. I wanted nothing more than for him to take me the way he wanted to, the way I needed him to.

He caught me by the waist and stood, lifting me effortlessly. I wrapped my legs around him as he walked us to his bedroom. The room was dimly lit by two wall sconces, the near darkness enveloping me like the warmth of his body.

He shut the door behind us and pinned me to it with

a growl. I took in a sharp breath when my back hit the hard wood of the door. I bit my lip and tightened around him, wanting everything he could give me. The thin straps of my dress fell down my shoulders, a welcome invitation for him to release my breasts one by one, taunting each peak with his tongue and then his teeth. The sharp edge of the sensation cut through me. I whimpered his name, begging for more.

He lowered my feet to the floor and freed me from the dress, leaving me bare and shameless as he kneeled before me, trailing hot wanton kisses from my ankle to the folds of my wet sex now clenching in anticipation. He draped my leg over his shoulder, opening me to him. The friction from his stubble on my inner thigh almost unraveled me on the spot.

I ran my fingers through his hair and tightened my hold when he took me in his mouth. A fire began to grow in my belly after only a few strokes of his tongue. God, his mouth had talent all its own. He centered his focus on the tiny bundle of nerves that had my whole body tensing, climbing to the edge of release. His strokes came harder and he sucked my clit with a fervor that took my breath away.

My vision went white as I went over the edge, a free fall into a shuddering climax that had me nearly collapsing in his arms.

Before my knees could give out, Blake caught me, my body, soft and yielding against the hard lines of his. He kissed me, slow deep kisses that quelled the tremors of my recent orgasm. My hands splayed over his exposed chest and pushed off his shirt, greedy at the chance to touch him freely, the way I'd wanted to for days. His skin was on fire, stretched tight over every taut muscle that seemed to struggle with impressive restraint. I ached to have him completely. Unrestrained. Raw.

"Blake, if you don't fuck me soon, I'm going to lose it, I swear."

His lips curved under mine and he brought us to the bed. He undressed quickly, his muscles flexing with each effort, each motion a promise of the power he could wield. I waited, not so patiently, as he retrieved a condom from his pants and slid it onto his admirable length. I cursed myself for making us wait, for keeping us from this place where we both fiercely wanted to be.

Right when I expected him to join me, he caught my thighs and pulled me to the edge of the bed, spreading my legs around his waist and notching himself at the slick flesh between my legs. His eyes were dark. His breath hissed as he thrust into me in one hard, singular motion, digging his fingers into my hips.

I gasped at his depth, letting my body acclimate to being so completely overtaken by his. I closed my eyes for a minute to absorb it all, the perfection of how he felt inside me.

When he didn't move, I opened my eyes. His expression was tense, the line of his jaw rigid. He ran his hand from my hip to my knee and pushed away a fraction.

I made a small whimper of protest. I hooked my ankles and pulled him closer, deeper. "This is how I want you."

"Erica—"

"I don't want you to hold back. I want all of you, Blake." Desperate, I arched into him. The need to feel him moving inside me, ravaging me, was relentless. Whatever he thought I couldn't take was exactly what I needed. "Please," I begged.

He released a shaky breath and pulled back slowly. Then he drove into me, hard and deep. I cried out. My back bowed off the bed.

Just like that.

I met his rapid thrusts, now fierce and unapologetic, as my cunt tightened around him. My entire body trembled in a seemingly perpetual state of climax. I reveled as he pushed deeper and deeper, hitting a tender spot inside me that I never knew existed until he created it.

I gripped the edge of the bed, adding even more leverage to his efforts. Just when I thought I couldn't take any more, he lifted my hips off the bed, bringing the contact to a new level. I fisted my hands in the sheets.

"Blake, oh God. Yes." Unintelligible cries poured out of me as I melted around him, pleasure rippling out from my core.

Blake tensed. Every plane of his body turned to stone, his breath ragged as he came in a rush.

"Erica, fuck." He threw his head back, his fingers marking my skin.

He stilled inside me while my body quaked with the aftershocks of his sheet-clawing brand of sex.

Wasted from the release, I lay boneless and satisfied. After a moment Blake climbed in the bed, pulling me up against his side. He curled his arms around me and nuzzled into my neck.

"Erica?"

I hummed, huddled against his chest.

"Are you okay?" he murmured.

I looked up into his eyes, dilated from our passion but filled with concern. My heart twisted, and I struggled to fill my lungs on my next breath.

"I'm more than okay." I swallowed over the knot in my throat. "I've never been with anyone like you Blake. I—"

The next words caught. He touched his fingertips to my lips and pressed a soft kiss there, stealing the unspoken words. I was falling for Blake, harder and faster than I'd ever fallen for anyone.

He kissed along my jaw and then found my mouth, soothing me with long and deep strokes of his tongue. While gentle, the act lit the fire in me again. My hands roamed his body, appreciating every breathtaking curve of his anatomy. I couldn't get enough of him, whether it was looking at him or sleeping with him. The need to claim him overwhelmed me. My caresses became more urgent. I tugged him closer and he shifted over me, bringing the weight of his body above me.

"You're insatiable," he murmured between kisses, teasing my lower lip between his teeth.

"I'm sorry. I don't know what's wrong with me." I arched into him. The more he gave me, the more I needed.

"Why the hell would you be sorry?"

"It's too soon," I said, feeling him harden between us as the words left me.

"I can go all night, if you can." Stretching my arms above me, he interlaced our fingers together. He held me captive, a state that heightened my senses and had me tingling again from head to toe.

Being with Blake intoxicated me in every way, and my addiction to him solidified with every toe-curling orgasm he delivered. I wrapped my legs around him, my arms powerless, and urged him to me.

"Is that a challenge?" I teased, tempted to put him to the test.

"Yes," he said. His voice was raw with lust as his lips crashed down onto me.

CHAPTER ELEVEN

I woke in the morning, wrapped in Blake's soft down comforter and the memories of the night. I stretched out onto Blake's empty side of the bed. Sunshine poured into the room, and I smelled coffee brewing. I got up and picked out a plain white T-shirt from one of Blake's closets to cover myself. In the bathroom, Blake had laid out some toiletries for me. I smiled. Most girls had to work their way up to that.

I finished cleaning up and made my way through the apartment, following the sounds from the kitchen. I found Blake cracking eggs into a bowl. He was shirtless, wearing only a pair of flannel pajama pants that hugged his hips. His hair was still thoroughly mussed and he wore a pair of dark rimmed glasses that amplified the sexiness of this early morning look. They made him look older and somehow more human, a Clark Kent quality.

I leaned against the granite island and appraised his progress. He had cut up some fruit and laid bacon in a pan while he figured out the egg thing. My stomach did a little leap at the thought that he was doing this for me.

He dropped what he was doing to wash his hands and turned to me. He smirked and traced the hem of my T-shirt.

"I like this."

"I wasn't trying to make a fashion statement, but I'm glad you approve." I leaned back into the counter and tilted my head to the side. "I didn't know you wore glasses."

"I don't usually, but you kept me busy last night, so I forgot to take my contacts out."

"I'm sorry."

"Don't be. I'm not."

He lifted me onto the countertop and leaned into the space between my legs. His hands traveled up my thighs and under the shirt to my back where he stroked my skin, leaving trails of heat everywhere in his wake. I moaned when he found my breast and thumbed my nipple until it beaded under his touch. As he kissed me, his tongue delivered soft measured strokes that reminded me of the sweet, dull ache between my legs from last night's marathon.

"You're turning me into a wanton harlot," I said, feeling my entire body come alive with a different kind of awakening.

"Mmm, I like the sound of that."

He growled into my neck where he kissed and sucked, the vibration rippling through me. With one hand he caught my ankle and wrapped my leg around his waist, and with his other, massaged the tender flesh between my legs.

"God, you're already soaked."

"I can't help it, Blake. You do this to me." I leaned into the strokes of his hand.

"I'm just getting started, baby."

He took my mouth as he pressed two fingers inside me, mimicking the motion of his fingers with his tongue, reducing me to a quivering mess. I clung to him desperately, my nails digging into his shoulder. My breath ragged and my heart pounding wildly, I held on as an orgasm ripped through me.

His fingers slipped from me, and he adjusted the now

sizeable erection tenting his pants. "I need to get a condom. I wasn't expecting to fuck you for breakfast."

I giggled a little at the expression, delusional and hungry for more of him all at once. "We don't need to, if you don't want."

"Trust me, I want to fuck you for breakfast."

"No, the condom, I mean. I'm on the pill."

His silence sobered me momentarily. I tried to backtrack. "I'm sorry, it's fine, I just assumed." *Shit, way to kill the moment.*

He shook his head. "No, it's not that. I trust you. I just haven't ever *not* used one."

"Forget it, I'm sorry." Most guys complained about wearing them, but I felt even safer knowing he always did.

"Stop apologizing to me, Erica," he said harshly.

I bit my lip, waiting to see where this would take us.

"Good girl," he said in a low predatory tone.

He divested me of his T-shirt, revealing my bare chest. His eyes darkened. Before I knew it, he'd moved us to the living room, setting me on his lap so I straddled him naked on the long cream couch. I gave him a slow, lazy kiss, taking his glasses off and placing them safely on the table behind us.

Blake lowered the band of his pants below his hips, freeing his cock, which in the bright daylight of the room looked more impressive than ever, thick and virile, waiting for me.

Wanting to taste him, I slid onto my knees and closed my lips around the lush head. I fluttered tiny licks over the sensitive tip before taking him farther into my mouth. I sucked him greedily, forgetting myself as I worshipped him, until Blake's grip on my hair tightened, stilling me.

"Get on top of me," he ordered.

I shivered and my skin grew warm. The physical reaction I had to the demand was unmistakable. Slick with anticipation, I obeyed and climbed up.

"Now slide down onto my cock. Nice and slow."

Aflame with anticipation, I lowered onto him with painstaking restraint, wanting to appreciate this new state. Nothing between us, he stretched me inch by delicious inch until he rooted inside me.

I closed my eyes as a small whimper left my lips.

"Look at me," he whispered.

I opened my eyes to see the raw hunger in his. He caught my face in his hands and kissed me hard. I moaned, steadying myself with my hands on his shoulders. He broke away, his breathing rough. He slid a finger down my cheek and over my collarbone, grazing my over-sensitive nipple and finally resting on my hip where he held me possessively. He looked up and held me in his gaze.

"You're beautiful."

The intensity in his eyes leveled me. My chest tightened. I was in too deep with Blake, but I didn't care, not when he was inside me, touching me, looking at me this way. I couldn't escape how he made me feel.

I answered with a subtle swivel of my hips. With one arm he circled them, holding me in place as he changed his angle and thrust upwards, ramming hard giving me more of himself. I sucked in a sharp breath at the jolt of pain that came when he hit the end of me. The slight discomfort quickly gave way to pleasure when he massaged tiny circles over my clit.

A fine mist swept over my skin as he pumped into me—steady and determined motions that made me momentarily forget my advantage in our present position. I met his movements, rolled into them until Blake loosened his hold, gradually giving me control. His hands flexed anxiously at my hips.

"Trust me," I whispered. Tightening around him, I scored my nails lightly down his chest and kissed him feverishly, sharing every breath that brought us to the brink, where we fell apart, together, never looking away from each other.

★ ★ ★

I had fallen asleep on the couch after breakfast when we finally ate. Between last night and this morning's exertions, I was exhausted. When I woke hours later, Blake was sitting on the other couch, his shiny black laptop resting on his thighs. He was a different Blake from this morning, fully dressed and looking intensely at the screen, typing with expert speed.

"I thought you didn't work at home," I said, stretching out.

"Just doing a little research." He didn't look up.

"What kind of research?"

He closed the laptop and set it to the side, his expression softening when our eyes met. "I think I found him," he said quietly.

"Who?"

He folded his hands in his lap.

Oh God. My stomach turned, threatening my breakfast. My thoughts were still foggy from sleep and now reeled as I processed what Blake had just told me.

"How?" I sat up straight and tried to shake the cobwebs.

"I pulled the transaction records from the restaurant.

Specifically the bar. I narrowed it down pretty easily from there based on his age and alma mater."

"I don't even want to know how you did that." This was too much. He'd gone too far.

"Well, I wasn't planning on telling you anyway. How I found the information is far less important than the actual information, don't you think?"

"Why would you do this? It doesn't even matter."

"You don't think that identifying the man who raped you matters?" He raised his eyebrows.

"At this point in my life, no. Why do I need a name for a face I'd rather forget?"

"You could still press charges against him. You're well within the statute of limitations."

"And what would I say? Hello, Officer, I was eighteen and drunk at a frat house when this asshole had his way with me. I bet they've never heard that one before."

"What if he's still doing this?"

My throat became thick and tight at the thought. What if I wasn't the only one? As much as I blamed myself for getting into such a perilous situation, deep down I knew no one deserved to go through what I did. I would have done almost anything to erase the painful memory from my past.

Still, I wasn't ready to face it. These memories, or him. The man who did this to me. Here Blake was forcing them onto me, shining a light on the details I'd given up hope of ever knowing. Now I didn't want to know. I wanted nothing to do with any of it.

I stood up quickly, but the sudden movement made me dizzy, nearly throwing me off balance as I made my way down the hall to the bedroom.

"Where are you going?"

Ignoring him, I disappeared into the bedroom. A teal sundress lay on the bed, which Blake must have collected from my place while I was sleeping. On top of it lay the lacy white panties that had gone missing in Blake's Vegas hotel room.

Damn it. I screwed my eyes shut, overwhelmed in every way. The past day with Blake had been amazing and intense. Being with him was conjuring feelings that I still wasn't sure what to make of. I didn't want to hurt him, but I couldn't think straight right now.

I dressed quickly and grabbed the rest of my things. He met me in the doorway, blocking my way out.

"Erica, don't go."

"You had no right."

He frowned, lowering his hands from the doorway. "You're telling me I had no right to find the man who hurt you?"

"I don't want to know who he is. Don't you get that?" I tensed my jaw, blinking away the burn of the tears welling behind my eyes. I wished I could stay angry with him. When I looked into his eyes, all I saw was confusion, but I couldn't expect him to understand.

With trembling hands, I pushed past him. I hurried out and down the stairs. I paused at my door, listening for his footsteps, but I heard nothing. I entered my apartment and latched the chain. I closed my eyes and swallowed hard, but nothing could stop the tears and the memories from coming. I slid down to the floor and sobbed until everything didn't hurt so damn bad.

★ ★ ★

I arrived in New York later that week. Somehow I had managed to avoid Blake and was grateful when he didn't seek me out. Thanks to our living situation, simply knowing his proximity was distracting enough, and I needed time to think. The past few days had been intense. I decided now was as good a time as ever to see Alli and clear my head.

I cabbed a short ride from JFK to an address Alli gave me in Brooklyn Heights. The driver pulled up to a stone multi-story building with an ornate overhang. I entered the expansive lobby and greeted the doorman who smiled politely.

"I'm Erica Hathaway. I'm here to see Alli Malloy."

"Certainly, you're expected. She's in Mr. Landon's suite, number forty-two."

"Thanks," I said, trying to hide my surprise. So much for my grand plan of staying under the radar for a few days in New York.

I knocked once and waited a few seconds. I knocked again more loudly—still nothing. I tried the doorknob. Just as I did, Alli opened it, her eyes bright and her skin flushed, looking like...well, I knew that look. She reached for me and pulled me into a tight hug.

"You're here!"

I hugged her back. I had missed her terribly. She felt small and warm in my arms. Had she lost weight? Before I could mention it, she pulled back and appraised me. New York was beastly hot today, so I had dressed in cut off denim shorts and some layered tanks, topped with a white fedora, just for fun.

"You look so cute," she said.

"Yeah, um, you too." I wished I meant it.

"Oh God, no, I'm a mess. I just got up from a nap."

"Some nap," I said, noting the just-fucked hairdo she was trying to smooth out as we walked into the enormous open layout of the condo with unobstructed views of the Manhattan skyline.

She laughed a little and blushed. I looked around, expecting to see Heath right around the corner, but he was nowhere in sight.

"Nice place," I said.

"I know, right?"

The condo itself was nothing short of impressive, everything and more than I expected from someone in the Landon family. The ceilings were high, characterized by exposed dark wood beams and matching hardwood floors. The furniture and décor were muted with periodic pops of color. The decor reminded me of Blake's place in Boston.

"Can I get you a drink?" Alli asked.

"Sure, anything with ice."

She busied herself in the kitchen while I settled at one of the bar stools at the island.

"So when were you going to tell me you were staying with Heath?"

She leaned into the counter. "I'm sorry, Erica. I just figured it might be easier to explain in person."

"You can stay wherever you want, Alli. It would have been nice to know though. Blake doesn't know I'm here."

She frowned, and I heard a door open down the hallway. Heath emerged, freshly showered and dressed, a content smile on his face. He looked more like Blake than I remembered. I couldn't shake the sense that something lay hidden beneath all of his charm though. Sure, Blake had layers. Many in fact, but he didn't seem to mask them as conspicuously.

"Erica, long time no see." He gave me a quick hug before joining Alli in the kitchen. He kissed her and I looked away.

Heath and Alli were adorable together, and energy radiated off them in a very familiar way. I'd only been here ten minutes and I already felt like I was horning in on their privacy.

My chest tightened, and my thoughts went to Blake. What lengths would I go to, to have him here kissing me that way? Still, I knew better. Whether or not he agreed, I needed some space to make sense of what had happened. The way Blake had pried into my life was completely unacceptable, and illegal. The violation had left me raw and vulnerable.

I swiveled on the stool, stood, and walked to the massive windows overlooking the park below. I wondered how much of this was a result of Blake's support, or if Heath actually contributed to his lifestyle in any way. Maybe I was being too hard on him. He was obviously sweeping Alli off her feet, which I'd never seen happen in the three years I'd known her. I hoped it wasn't too good to be true, for her sake.

"Are you hungry? I was thinking we could get lunch," Alli said.

"That'd be great."

"Let me show you your room." Alli reached for my bag.

Heath took it from her swiftly and led us both down a hall opposite to the one he'd previously emerged from.

I peeked into a nice-sized bedroom decorated with the same muted off-white tones and a deep red bedspread. I regretted I wouldn't be sharing it with Blake. The vision of him spread out under me, or vice versa, was more than appealing. The memory of our last time together washed over me, and my eyes misted. I shook my head. I needed to get Blake out of my system.

CHAPTER TWELVE

Alli and I devoured our appetizers between sips of Prosecco as we waited for the main course, which for me was a pile of carbs. Going through Blake withdrawal had involved a serious lack of appetite, but being around Alli made me feel relaxed again and comfortable enough that my hunger had returned with a fury.

"How do you like the new job?" I asked.

"I love it, most of the time, anyway. It's crazy, fast-paced, and can be stressful running around after everyone, but I feel like it's a major step toward where I want to be."

I smiled. "That's exciting."

"It really is. And I'm totally making connections for you, by the way. Heath hooked me up with someone who's getting us into an opening at a gallery tomorrow night."

"An art show?" I said, wondering what that had to do with fashion and me.

"Yes. It'll be very chic and a lot of super important people will be there."

"Chic, eh? I suppose." I eyeballed the plate of steaming pasta that the server set in front of me. I took my first bite. *Heaven*, I thought. I could replace sex with food, surely.

"What's going on with Blake?"

An unexpected wave of emotion surged through me. I told her about the last day I'd spent with Blake. From meeting with Max to getting screwed to the door by Blake. The good, bad, and the ugly.

"Do you love him?" she asked.

"Are you kidding me?" My voice was shrill, the very mention of the L word launching me out of my longing and headlong into panic and fear.

"Is that such a crazy thing to ask?"

"Are you in love with Heath?" I spat out, desperate to change the subject but scared of what she might say.

She turned her focus back on her lunch wordlessly.

"There." I countered, vindicated.

"I am," she whispered, almost too quietly for me to hear.

We ate in silence for a while. I wasn't sure why, but the news saddened me. I'd had Alli all to myself for three years. We shared everything, looked out for each other, and together helped build the business that gave me purpose today. In a matter of weeks she had eyes for no one but Heath. Feeling jealous was irrational, because above everything, I wanted her to be happy, even at the expense of our friendship.

"Is he good for you?" I asked.

"We fit," she said simply. "Things aren't always perfect, but somehow they always seem right. We're figuring it out."

"Well I'm happy for you. I want you to know that."

Her features relaxed and she reached over and grabbed my hand across the table.

"Thank you."

I knew then that she had been waiting for my approval all this time.

"I'm so glad you're here. I miss you," she said.

"I miss you too. Sometimes it feels like we're a million miles away."

"We're not though. I'm always here for you."

I smiled and nodded, not wanting to bring up the fact that she'd been largely unreachable since moving to New York. Still, I felt better hearing her say it. With Blake out of my world at the moment, rekindling life back into my friendship with Alli was more than welcome, even if I had to share her with Heath.

★ ★ ★

With Alli at work, I spent most of the next day catching up on my own. I took a few breaks and meandered around the park to collect my thoughts and people watch. As dozens of tiny figures walked across the bridge to Manhattan, I tried to imagine what it might be like to be a New Yorker.

Maybe it was time for a change. Alli was so blissed out here, due in large part to Heath jumping her bones expertly and frequently it seemed, based on the very little sleep I'd gotten the previous night. But maybe I could be happy here too.

I pulled up Blake's text thread in my phone more than once, tempted to write to him. I missed him, but after days of silence, maybe I'd lost my chance. Obviously being with me wasn't going to be easy. I'd left him in the heat of the moment, not knowing how to react to the bomb he'd dropped on me, and hadn't even given him a chance to explain or talk about it. I groaned, frustrated in more ways than one. *Fuck*, maybe I did love him, though I had no idea what that really felt like.

I loved Marie. I loved Alli. In my youth, before I knew anything about anything, I loved my mother deeply, with every ounce of my being. Yet I didn't know how to love someone I was sleeping with. With other guys I'd dated, keeping a comfortable distance had always been easy. Ideal, really. When they wanted to move on, I mostly felt relief that I wouldn't have to deal with negotiating a more serious commitment that I couldn't ever see myself fulfilling.

None of the men I dated knew me, really. Not about my past anyway. Now, not only was Blake blowing my mind in bed, he was systematically stripping away the emotional barriers I'd so carefully built around myself over the years. I couldn't keep up the façade much longer at this rate. I prided myself on portraying an impenetrable image of success, of having it all together, but he broke that down with a few strokes of his fingers and his persistence. His goddamn persistence—which was why I was in this situation to begin with.

I miss you.

I typed the short message into my phone, regretting it the moment I sent it. Every moment that went by, I wondered if he'd received it.

With no word from Blake, I finished up work and dressed for the gallery opening. I had an image in my mind of mingling with a crowd of snobs in turtlenecks, quietly assessing a collection of art that I might have a hard time appreciating at all. I scolded myself for being so negative, blaming my text to Blake for throwing me off.

I scoured Alli's closet, appreciating some of her newer additions. Eventually I decided on a pair of tight black crop pants and a bold fuchsia and black lace tunic and pulled my hair back into a tight bun. Unfortunately when I arrived, the motif at the event was strictly black and white, matching the starkness of the artist's photography.

I spotted Alli chatting with another woman on the other side of the gallery. I slipped through the crowd, drawing attention as I went. I pushed away my self-consciousness. If I was here to network, the last thing I wanted to be was forgettable.

I joined the two women, nodding to Alli before I introduced myself to her long-legged friend. She looked oddly familiar. Maybe she was a model. She was tall and incredibly beautiful, with long dark brown hair.

"Erica, this is Sophia Devereaux. She's friends with Blake—well, Heath too actually."

Blake's name in the presence of this Amazonian made my throat tighten. So *this* was Sophia.

Alli went on to explain Clozpin and our role in it, saving me from the task of tooting my own horn. Sophia looked mildly interested, but Alli didn't stop there.

"Sophia actually runs her own modeling agency here in New York." Her eyebrow arched toward me. "She works with a ton of brands for their shoots," she continued, spoon feeding me talking points now.

"Impressive," I said, meaning it, though I had a difficult time pushing thoughts of what she might mean to Blake out of my mind. There was only one way to find out. People invariably loved talking about themselves, and over the space of a few minutes, I learned just how well Sophia was connected. She had worked with every major designer I knew, dozens I didn't, and casually spoke of them on a first name basis. Yet it seemed strange to me that someone so young would be running an agency versus working for one. She was the picture of physical perfection, at least when it came to high fashion and the type of look it demanded.

In the midst of our small talk, Alli briefly excused herself, winking at me, silently letting me know she would come rescue me soon. I hoped that's what the wink meant anyway.

"So how do you know Blake?" Sophia asked, her voice low, deliberate, and laced with a hint of bitchiness that had been previously absent from our conversation.

I stared hard at her, trying to gauge her intent, my adrenaline spiking. "We're seeing each other," I said evenly. Sure, we'd spent the past few days enduring what, at least to me, felt like a devastating separation, but she didn't need to know that.

Her head cocked. "Interesting."

"And how do you know Blake?" I asked, burning with curiosity.

She smiled, catching a few strands of shiny perfect hair between her fingertips. "We catch up from time to time."

"Interesting," I said, mimicking her sneer, praying she was bluffing. Based on her tone, there was no doubt in my mind that *catching up* in this case meant fucking. And the thought of Blake fucking her filled me with a blind jealousy. I garnered every ounce of self-control not to show it just then.

"A little advice, from one woman to another. If you're after his money, or his connections for that matter, he won't keep you around for long. He protects what's his."

"You would know, I suppose?" My teeth gritted with restraint. This woman definitely had a dark side, devious almost. I barely recognized her the moment Alli left us, and just as quickly, her expression changed again when we were joined by a young man holding out two glasses of red wine.

"You two look entirely too sober for this event," he said, his eyes lighting up with humor.

"Darling," Sophia purred, taking her glass from him and air kissing him from cheek to cheek.

I took the glass of wine he offered with no care of its origin or vintage. This bitch was winding me up.

"Isaac. This is Erica Hathaway. She runs a fashion website. The details escape me," Sophia said with a careless wave. "Would you two excuse me? I am running late for another engagement. It was delightful to meet you, Erica. Please stay in touch?"

I forced a smile and reached out to shake her hand. I reveled a bit at the opportunity to crush it. She winced at the contact. For being so imposing in height, she was a wet noodle when it came to handshakes.

"I'm Isaac Perry," he said as soon as she left.

"What brings you here tonight, Isaac?" I asked with blithe interest.

"The art, I suppose. Definitely not the people, though I have to say I'm rather interested in you." He grinned.

Not only was Isaac in a great mood, he wasn't hard on the eyes. Tall and lean, with pale blue eyes and a mop of sandy blond hair, he was dressed in black slacks and a V-neck sweater. His entire persona came across as casual and boyish, making him seem less pretentious than most of the people around us.

"And what do you think of the art?" I asked, skipping right over the bait he offered for me to talk about myself. I was already strung too tight missing Blake. I couldn't quite handle meaningless flirting at this point.

Isaac breathed out a whistle and stared at the piece in front of us. "I think I like it, which is good since we'll be doing a write up on it."

"Are you a writer?"

"Publisher. I own Perry Media Group."

I recognized the name, which had somehow penetrated my tech bubble somewhere over the course of my time at school. The write-up he spoke of could belong to any number of quality international publications. I coughed a little on my last sip of wine and caught him smirk as he surveyed the room.

"Tell me more about what you do. I have to admit, I don't know as much as I should about the social space these days, but it's fascinating, isn't it?"

"It is," I agreed. "There's nothing quite like it. I'm sure publishing moves quickly, but technology sort of blows your hair back sometimes. It's a challenge to stay current, but that's what I really love about it."

"You're so young to be doing this."

He was buttering me up, but coming off of my time with Sophia, I couldn't argue with some praise and thoughtful appreciation.

"I guess so."

"On top of being a woman, that seems rare."

"That's true. I guess I'm a bit of an endangered species in the high tech department." I would have enjoyed having a peer group with a little more gender diversity, but I figured that would change eventually. All in good time.

"I'm on the flip side. In publishing, I'm surrounded by women. They're just so damn good at it."

He shot me a disarming smile. He was officially enchanting, though I couldn't imagine why on earth he would be seen air kissing the diabolical Sophia.

"So, fashion, huh? You must be tapped into the fashion bloggers in the city then?" he said.

"Not really, no."

"Oh wow, you should be. They're like the grass roots effort that gets all of the cream rising to the top. If you can get into their good graces, you'll be everywhere."

"I'll definitely look into it. Thanks for the tip," I said, clinking our plastic glasses together, my jovial mood beginning to match his. I wasn't sure if it was the wine or just his sheer force of positive energy, but I felt better than I had all day.

"What are you doing for dinner Saturday?" he asked. His voice was markedly lower.

I chilled at the suggestive tone. I didn't want to be wanted, but he didn't know that yet. "I'm sorry, I can't."

"Brunch on Sunday then. I'd love to learn more about your business. Maybe we can figure out a way to work together."

I hesitated. The publisher of Perry Media Group wanted to discuss working together. I couldn't turn that down, no matter how he was looking at me. Dinner meant too much, implied too much, but brunch I could do.

"That sounds doable," I said.

We shared contact info, digitally penciling each other in.

Alli joined us shortly thereafter and excused us so we

could meet Heath for dinner. We decided to walk, and Alli wasted no time grilling me for details.

"Who was he?"

"That was Isaac Perry."

"Holy shit, good find, Erica. He couldn't keep his eyes off you."

"Whatever." I shrugged. "I guess Sophia knows him too," I added, hoping to prompt Alli. I was eager to know more about her even though she'd already put me in a pretty foul mood.

We turned into our destination, an Asian fusion restaurant that emitted some fantastic smells as we passed through the doors. Alli spotted Heath and immediately changed. Her countenance, her body language, all her energies focused on him. I groaned quietly, knowing neither would notice.

We settled in and ordered.

"Alli says you know Sophia," I said, interrupting Alli and Heath's canoodling.

Heath straightened himself as if he were all business now. "I do. We're invested in her agency, actually."

"Blake too?"

"Yes, Blake knows her too."

I looked to Alli, who appeared conveniently distracted by something at the other end of the restaurant.

"Sounds like he more than knows her." I took a sip of my water.

Heath looked to Alli, drumming his fingers on the table. Like Blake, he was always cool and calm, with an added layer of carefree charm that set the two brothers apart. Why did talking about Sophia ruffle him? She must mean something to Blake. It was the only logical explanation, considering he probably already knew more about my relationship with Blake than I wanted him to.

"I think they dated on and off, when he was in town, you know. But they've just been friends for years."

If I didn't know better, I would have thought someone punched me in the gut. Jealousy pulsed through me as I absorbed his words. He emphasized *years*, but nothing he could say diluted the devastating fact that they had history.

The question was whether they had a present, or a future. I checked my phone. Still nothing. The rejection implied in his silence tore a hole in my heart, and tears threatened suddenly. *Get it together*, I told myself.

Heath's phone went off and his eyes widened a bit, darting to me and back to the phone. "Excuse me, I've got to take this," he said and left us alone at the table.

"Well this is awkward," I said.

"What?"

"I hate to be the one to tell you this, but you've done a complete one-eighty since moving here. First you move in with Heath and don't bother telling me, and now you're introducing me to Blake's ex-girlfriends without any warning? You could have given me a heads up, you know."

"I'm sorry. I didn't realize it would come up. Like he said, they're just friends."

"That's a shitty reason for not telling me, and you know it. I realize you're serious about Heath, but what the hell, Alli? This isn't you."

"I'm the same person I was a few weeks ago. It's just…things are more complicated than you realize."

"No doubt, because you don't tell me anything."

She sighed and twisted her hair. "I said I was sorry,

okay? I admit it. I should have told you about Sophia. If you introduced me to someone Heath had history with, I'd want to know."

I relaxed a little. Alli shielding me from the truth wasn't doing me any favors. I was falling hard for Blake, and I needed to know if that was a reckless effort. She had loyalty to Heath now, but protecting him, and Blake, at my expense wasn't going to work.

CHAPTER THIRTEEN

I slept in the next morning, nearly as drained and confused as I had when my head hit the pillow the night before. I checked the clock and forced myself up. I assumed Alli had made it to work all right. She and Heath had gone out for drinks after dinner while I headed back to the condo. We'd made plans to go out on the town the following night, but maybe they needed alone time. Restless, I tossed and turned for what seemed like hours but finally fell asleep, never hearing their return. How she kept up like this I would never know.

I made myself at home in the kitchen, brewing coffee and frying up an omelet. I looked up some local yoga studios on my phone and found a class I could walk into just before lunch. As I devoured my breakfast, Heath came from the adjacent bedroom, looking more than tired. The long night had left heavy bags under his eyes, and for the first time, I noticed he actually looked older than Blake, fine lines fanning out from his dark hazel eyes.

He had the same toned chest and intense eyes as Blake, but while I could appreciate his obviously quality looks, I felt no attraction to him. Blake's appearance had sparked my attraction from the start, but so much more kept that flame alive. Other men had become invisible to me.

Shirtless, Heath shuffled to the coffee maker. He filled

an oversized mug to the brim and emptied it to a halfway point before he finally acknowledged me with a nod.

"Morning," he said, looking into his cup.

"Long night?"

"Yeah." He rubbed his face and sighed.

"How was Alli this morning?"

"Uh, fine. She—" He paused. "She came home earlier than I did."

Something wasn't right.

"Is everything all right?" I asked gently, tiptoeing since I was prying into his personal life, though everyone seemed to think that was all right when it came to mine.

"Yeah, definitely. You know how it goes." He shrugged.

A tired and overused smirk that I had started to peg as bullshit marked his face. He was obviously trying to downplay something.

"Do you love her?" I blurted it out, surprising myself even as I said it. It was a bold enough question, let alone one to ask someone in as bad a shape as he was.

His gaze shot to mine, burning with an emotion I couldn't name, all trace of the bullshit smile gone.

"Obviously."

He set his mug down hard on the counter. He sounded bitter about it, though. As if the reality of it stung him. The tone spurred me, my protectiveness kicking in.

"I hope so. Because she's hopeless over you. I've never seen her like this."

A tell tale twitch in his jaw appeared. The same one that tipped me off when Blake was on the edge.

"If you hurt her, Heath..." I lifted my chin, ready to make a point, but my empty threat fizzled as I delivered it. How could I hurt him back? Shielded by his billionaire brother and the lifestyle he afforded, he was sheltered. Threatening him was beyond pointless.

"I won't," he said, his voice clipped with fatigue and irritation.

When our eyes met briefly, I recognized a flash of pain behind them before he turned to go. I finished my breakfast and retreated to the bedroom to change while Heath slept off whatever had him looking so harrowed.

Hours later, the yoga studio was filling up quickly. The instructor wasted no time warming us up, mentally and physically. I needed this. I needed to burn off all the decadent New York meals I'd been treated to, but what I needed more was clarity, to be centered. I could never seem to empty my mind of the constant chaos that Blake created within me.

By the end of the half hour, I was straining for perfection in a wheel pose, my torso bending up toward the sky. I breathed through the discomfort. I was sorely out of practice. The challenging movements drained me but awakened me at the same time, as each muscle activated to keep me in good form. In an audience of a dozen or so other attendees, I refused to falter.

The class ended just as I was ready to give up. We lay in relaxation and my thoughts floated to Blake. So much for emptying my mind. When we devoted our practice, I sent love and light to him. I missed him terribly. No sooner had I rolled up my mat, when my phone vibrated next to me, a quiet intrusion into my hard-earned calm. I fumbled for it, too eager. I hurried out into the hallway for some privacy.

"Erica, it's Max."

"Hi, how are you doing?"

"Great," he said.

"Is everything okay? I mean, with the deal?"

"Absolutely. That's why I called, actually. I wanted to let you know the legal prep is taking a little longer than expected, but everything is still on track."

I let out a breath I didn't realize I was holding. "That's great. Thanks for letting me know."

"No problem. How's everything with the site?"

"Going great. I'm actually in New York doing some networking. It's going really well."

"Excellent, that's what I like to hear." Someone was talking to him in the background. "I've got to go, Erica, but I'll keep you posted, all right?"

"Wonderful, thanks again."

"See you soon." He hung up.

We were so close to hitting this milestone, I could taste it, but even with his reassurances, I would worry until everything was absolutely finalized. I tried to ignore all the ways it could fall through, but knowing about the rivalry between Blake and Max now added exponentially more possibilities to the list.

★ ★ ★

That evening, as I stood at the edge of the rooftop deck of the club, a warm breeze danced over my exposed skin. Alli had fussed over me to the point of ridiculousness before heading out together. The cut out dress we decided on was scarce in the fabric department, but the evenings were hot and the club below was even hotter.

City lights decorated the darkening sky, reminding me of the last night I'd enjoyed a view like this. I closed my eyes and Blake was behind them. A smile that left no doubt that he'd always get exactly what he wanted from me. The body that drove me wild whenever he did.

Behind me, Alli and Heath laughed quietly, their limbs tangled on one of the outdoor couches decorating this exclusive part of the nightclub. I sighed inwardly and sipped on my third martini, hoping this would be the one to make me forget Blake's silence today.

Maybe my text had come too late. Maybe he'd written me off as too much trouble. Maybe he'd be right. I never asked for a relationship, but now that I was losing it, I couldn't fight the crushing feeling that I was losing something precious. I'd never met someone like Blake, and no one had ever made me feel the way he did.

The intense throb of house music came and went as the deck door opened and closed behind me. I leaned forward on the metal railing overlooking the traffic below us. Car horns sounded in the distance, mingling with the quiet jazz that hummed around me.

I needed to get Blake out of my head and make the most of my time here, even as heartbroken as I'd felt these past few days. I polished off the last of my drink and decided to find Alli. Maybe she could detach from Heath for a little while and hit the dance floor with me.

I turned and froze, unable to take another step forward. Blinking, I reassured myself that the person in front of me was Blake and not the memory of the man I'd been tearing myself up over for hours.

"Erica."

Blake's voice slid over me, confident and full of meaning. The intensity in his eyes had me paralyzed. I took him in slowly, my fingers gripping the railing behind me as if it might anchor me down when I wanted to fly to him.

I harnessed all my willpower not to. The mere sight of him had my heart racing. A slow heat rushed over my skin, inflaming my senses as I raked him in. He was dressed head to toe in a black suit, his dark shirt casually unbuttoned at the top. Jesus, why couldn't he be wearing one of those stupid T-shirts when he dropped in on me like this? He was a smoking hot slice of heaven, and as much as I loved him in those clothes, I could think of nothing else but taking them off.

"What are you doing here?" My voice was breathy and unsteady, betraying the riotous emotions pulsing through me right now. Maybe Alli or Heath had tipped him off. As much as I wanted to care, I didn't. My whole body came alive knowing he was close enough to touch me, to set me off in ways that no one else ever had.

The corner of his mouth lifted as he cocked his head slightly. "I thought you missed me?"

"I—yes," I admitted. There was no point in denying it now. "I wasn't expecting to see you here."

He took a step forward, closing the distance between us. Taking his hands from his pockets, he placed them on either side of me on the railing.

"You're lucky I'm here. If I found out you were wearing this in public without me, I'd have to punish you."

His hand left my side, roaming, touching my skin where the dress didn't cover it. My grip on the railing tightened and my chest heaved with my rapid breathing. A heat built in my belly at the promise in his threat.

"You like it?"

His smirk faded as he lowered, kissing my jaw. "If we had some privacy, I could show you just how much," he murmured, licking the rim of my ear before biting gently on my earlobe.

I exhaled sharply, trying not to moan when a sweet sharp pain speared right to my groin.

"I've been hard since I saw you standing here."

I sighed and leaned into him, the evidence of his desire hard against my belly. I loved that I could do that to him. Relief washed over me knowing that he still wanted me as much as I wanted him.

"Blake…I'm sorry," I whispered.

He leaned back silently, his gaze locking with mine.

"I'm sorry for the other day. I shouldn't have left like that." I took a deep breath, wishing we could erase that part of the past, but knowing that I had to face it and make him understand as best I could. "I was…scared."

He frowned. "Of me?"

"No. Of him…being real. And that you found him so easily. I can't explain it. I guess a part of me wished that you would have asked me first."

"A part of me wanted to, but a much more protective part of me needed to know, no matter what you would have said." He traced a fingertip over my cheek. "I couldn't sit there and do nothing. I can't stand the idea of someone hurting you the way he did."

"Knowing who he is doesn't change what happened."

"Maybe not. But how you choose to use the information is up to you now. Don't you want to know who—"

"No," I rushed. "Please, I don't. You can't possibly understand, Blake."

"Okay." He hushed me and brushed his lips over mine softly. "I didn't come all this way to upset you."

I kissed him back and wrapped my arms around him, wanting to feel him close. "I'm glad you came."

He nuzzled into my neck, trailing his lips over the sensitive skin there.

"I was going to come back, you know. You didn't have to come all the way to New York for me," I said, grateful that he had.

"I knew you'd be back. But I have business here too, occasionally, so I thought I'd drop in on you. Call me crazy, but I missed you too."

I melted a bit, until an unpleasant thought invaded the moment. *Sophia*. Could she be his reason for business? I chilled at the vision of them together, him seeing her for any reason, platonic or otherwise. She was toxic and spiteful.

"I met Sophia," I said, trying to sound casual. I lifted my chin to catch his reaction, my gaze fixed on him. What did she mean to him? If he were planning to see her here, or God forbid, if he already had, I couldn't take it. He had to be here for me. "She's a real gem," I said, unable to disguise my utter distaste for her.

I wondered if he could see past her perfect features. His jaw twitched and he stared past me out over the horizon, saying nothing.

My insides writhed with the jealousy that had been haunting me since I met Sophia. The way she waved her relationship with Blake around in front of me and that snide fucking smile. I wanted to believe Heath's version of the story, but I couldn't shake the worry that she meant more to him than he'd let on.

I moved sideways, feeling trapped between him and the railing, at the mercy of his hands and circumstances that were well beyond my control. Before I could get past him, he caught my wrist.

"Where are you going?"

His voice was hard and sent a shiver through me. I swallowed. As much as I wanted him, I wondered if I could stomach sharing him with someone else. I squeezed my eyes closed, feeling the drinks take hold of my better judgment.

I didn't care. Not tonight. I'd wished for him for hours and here he was. We'd sort it out later.

"Let's dance," I said, opening my eyes to find his filled with concern.

No more talk. I wanted to lose myself in the music and in his arms. I wanted to pretend that he was mine before I could find out that he wasn't.

His features softened for a second, along with his grasp. He laced our fingers together and took me downstairs.

CHAPTER FOURTEEN

We descended into the smoky darkness of the top floor of the club. I embraced the noise, hoping to drown out the thoughts reeling through my mind.

I led us out to the dance floor, bringing us deep into the crowd through throngs of people gyrating to an especially popular Rihanna remix. I stopped and moved to face him, but he stilled me. His strong hand gripped my hip and pulled me back slightly until our bodies were flush with each other. The motion was so fluid and effortless, as if he was simply reuniting us to where we should have been all night. Together.

In an instant, my body melted into his. Everything felt right in his arms. The pounding base guided my movements as I began to sway to the beat of the music reverberating through my body. My muscles relaxed, and I got lost in the moment, in Blake.

The crowd was tight, but I didn't care. All I could feel was Blake's hands on me. In sync with the song, I pressed back into him, feeling a wild frenzy to be close to him, to feel that physical contact I'd been craving for days now. The song came to a close and merged into the next, slightly changing our rhythm and bringing us even closer. His erection became more pronounced, pressing against my ass, silently demanding what we both wanted. Arousal prickled my skin and my head fell back. His arm circled my waist and he kissed my neck. A hot, open-mouthed kiss that had my head spinning. Alcohol maybe, but more likely that drug that was Blake was taking over.

He spun me around to face him. Before he could speak, I grabbed him by the jacket and pulled him to me. Crushing my mouth onto his, I kissed him with a wild hunger. He met me full force. Our tongues tangled and I pulled him closer. He slipped his hand under the tight elastic of my dress, cupping my ass and grazing the edge of my panties. I moaned into his mouth, forgetting myself and our surroundings. I wanted to climb him right there among the hundreds of other hot, sweaty, and sexually charged people.

He growled a little as he pulled away. The lack of connection was abrupt, leaving me bereft, but the discomfort of not being connected was soon derailed by the knowledge that I was being led from the dance floor and down a hallway away from the chaos that once surrounded us.

We traveled farther until the hallway split. On the left, a tall thickly-built man stood guard near a door. Blake approached the bouncer and pressed some bills into his hand, who nodded toward the door. We entered what appeared to be another private VIP area. An ambient light filled the room, which was quite large and entirely unoccupied. Dark red leather couches lined the walls along two sides, and along another, a private bar lit up with everything a good party might need.

"What is this?"

Blake closed the door behind us and wasted no time pinning me to it.

"This is where I'm going to fuck you without interruptions."

He hitched my leg over his hip and pressed against me. I gasped as he ground into me, connecting with my clit through my panties in just the right way.

I slid my hands into his hair and tugged him down, kissing him hard. His hands were everywhere, massaging my breasts through the tight thin fabric before freeing them easily from the strapless top. I spilled out of the dress and he caught my nipple in his mouth, palming my other breast with his hand. A violent craving burned inside me, so potent I would have done nearly anything with him in that moment if not for the niggling doubt that lingered.

One last time, I thought. *But…*

"Wait. We shouldn't do this."

Blake's hand slammed against the door beside me. "Christ, Erica. Wait for what?"

I covered myself with my arms, suddenly feeling too exposed. The anger combined with the sexual energy coming off of him scared me. I'd seen him wound tight before, but not like this.

"I want you, Blake. More than anything else right now or possibly ever. But I can't share you with someone else."

"What?" He shoved his hands through his hair and stepped back.

"I don't know what's between you and Sophia, and I'm not about to tell you how to live your life. I know you must have your pick of women. I get it, but the way I feel about you…I just don't think I can do it." I winced at the tightness in my chest.

Blake wasn't like the other guys I'd been with. In fact he was nowhere close to them, and being with him had turned my entire philosophy on sex and relationships upside down. Now I was falling hard for him, and the idea of him being with Sophia, now or ever, was more than I could bear. An infidelity with Blake would break me.

"You think I'm fucking Sophia?"

I stared at him. "She implied that you were—I just assumed..."

He grimaced, as if he'd just tasted something unpleasant. "I'll be speaking with her then. But you need to know that there is absolutely *nothing* between us. There hasn't been for years."

"Yes, Heath corroborated your story already," I said, cutting him short.

"It's not a story. It's the truth. What the hell do I have to do for you to believe me?"

"I don't know," I said, wilting against the door, wishing my conscience could just shut up and let us be.

Blake closed the distance between us, holding my shoulders and stroking the tops of my arms with his thumbs, sending waves of relief over me.

"Erica—" He tipped my face to meet his.

Our eyes met and my heart stopped.

"You are the one I'm here for."

He kissed me deeply and slowly, exploring every opportunity to tantalize me with his tongue, making my knees impossibly weaker. He broke away and our gazes locked.

"The only one."

"You're mine," I breathed back into him, drunk on his taste and scent.

"If you could stop running away from me for five goddamn minutes, I could have told you that."

My lips lifted and I kissed him again, licking and teasing.

He growled in response, lifting me up and coaxing my legs around him.

"Now let me show you."

I nodded. I couldn't speak for tomorrow or the day after that, but nothing else would come between us tonight. He slid his hands under my skirt, and with a sudden jerk, he ripped the delicate fabric of my panties. He tossed them to the side, carried me to one of the long leather couches, and laid me down. He lowered himself above me, caging me with his arms. I arched toward him, knowing it wouldn't be long now before he was inside me again, where I'd wanted him ever since I left him days ago. He pinned me with his hips, rocking into me, a promise of what was to surely come. I unbuttoned his shirt quickly and my nipples dragged across the soft hairs of his chest.

He fingered me gently, gliding through my wet folds and curling up to reach the sensitive spot inside of me while kneading the hard knot of my clit with the heel of his hand. I quivered on the edge of release. He slowed and made his way south, trailing kisses along my inner thigh.

I tried to urge him back up to me with little success. "Please, Blake, don't make me wait."

"I want to taste you, baby," he said, pumping into me with this fingers.

I cried out, nearly insane with desire. "I need you inside me. Now!"

My nerves were raw, and the promise of his merciless style of fucking only spurred my craving. With that, his fingers left me and he undid the clasp on his trousers, lowering them only enough to free his cock. I caught his hard length in my hands, circling his hot skin with my own and appreciating what I knew he could do for me as I positioned him at my sex and guided him inside. Slow and deep, he rooted himself fully. The sensation was searing and intense.

Complete.

I fought the surge of emotion that came over me with the connection. My chest felt heavy, like my heart was about to burst. Desperate to distract myself from what that meant, I kissed him frantically, our tongues tangled in the heat of the moment. *I need this. I need you.*

I shifted restlessly beneath him, wild for the friction of his cock moving inside me. I wanted to own him and be owned, and this was the only way I knew how to make sure he couldn't think about anyone but me. "Fuck me, Blake."

"My pleasure."

He drove into me, hard and deep, again and again. I came quickly with his name on my lips, tears sliding down my face as the waves crashed over me. I tried wiping them away before he could see them, but he intercepted them with his mouth. He kissed them away, his touch salve on the intensity of my release and the pain of our separation these past few days. He slowed momentarily before changing the angle and increasing the depth of his punishing strokes. I clung to the precipice of another orgasm.

"More," I whimpered, throwing my head back, overwhelmed by every sensation yet needing more.

"More?"

"Deeper."

He stopped suddenly and my breath hitched. He flipped me onto my belly and lifted my knees beneath me, slapping me on the ass so hard I yelped, the pain of it stunning me back into reality. Before I could protest, he shoved his cock back inside of me with a force that took my breath away.

He pulled out completely and bent over me, leaving me empty and aching. "No more running away from me, Erica. I mean it." His voice was hoarse and his breath hot against my neck.

"Blake, please," I moaned, rocking back into him.

"Promise me."

"Yes. I promise."

He straightened and his palm made sharp contact in the same place, the sting sizzling under the sensation of his cock ruthlessly powering into me. He withdrew again. I pressed back into him, the need to orgasm with him inside me destroying my inhibitions. He answered my plea, steadily pumping into me, and when his hand made contact with my ass again, I clenched around him uncontrollably, crushing his cock with the walls of my pussy.

"More," I cried.

He picked up the pace, never breaking the connection and shattering me with every measured slap. My body shuddered, every muscle tensing beyond my will as he brought me to the very edge. I moaned into the couch, my fingernails clawing at the expensive fabric, and I came with a scream that the bouncer very likely heard. Blake ground out his own release, emptying himself into me with a shuddery sigh, his breath gusting on my neck as he bent over me. He stilled, then circled my waist and turned me to face him, meeting me with a gentle breathy kiss.

"That was different," I murmured, boneless and punch—well, slap-drunk.

"You liked it," he said.

I moaned and tightened my legs around him.

He smirked. "For being such a bossy little minx, you make a great submissive."

My eyes went wide. "I would hardly describe myself as *submissive*."

He laughed. "You say that like it's a dirty word."

"It is to me. I don't—"

"Wait, before you start, let me just ask you this. Do you want me to do that again sometime?"

I blinked, suddenly embarrassed that he was going to make me admit it. Getting spanked in the heat of the moment felt very different from negotiating it face to face. "I don't know. Maybe."

"Good, because I plan to." His face left no doubt that he was serious, his voice harder than it had been. My skin prickled, hot and anxious anew.

I wanted to argue, to tell him to fuck off and get lost, but I was getting turned on by the very thought of it.

"You're making me want things I'm not sure I want."

"You're allowed to want different things in bed than you do in your normal everyday life. And I promise not to spank you in public." His face softened with a smile as he moved down my body. "Unless you're a very bad girl." He took my nipple in his mouth and took the hardened tip between his teeth.

Oh, I love that. I tightened at the sensation and panted softly. "I'll be good," I promised deliriously.

He chuckled softly. "I highly doubt it."

"Am I that bad?"

His eyes darkened, the slight curve of his lip softening

an otherwise dangerous countenance. "You might want to get comfortable with the idea of punishment."

Blake gave my nipple another hard suck and rolled the other between his fingertips, twisting the flesh just enough to inflict the perfect measure of pain.

I gasped, but he didn't relent. "How do I know this isn't just the next phase of you dominating every part of my life? First the apartment, now this..." I breathed, barely able to string the thought together.

"That's a compelling idea, but I hardly think you'd let me get away with it." He moved higher, brushing his lips along my collarbone. Suckling my neck, he continued to taunt my nipples.

I bowed my chest into his palm, and a satisfied smile spread across his face as he pulled away and stood. He was still hard, a thrilling show of his stamina. I scowled when he tucked himself back into his pants.

"Don't pout. Let me take you home," he said, the promise of more twinkling in his eyes.

Less than twenty minutes later, we barreled through the doors of the condo. I had Blake flat beneath me on the crimson bedspread of the guest bed in a matter of seconds, exactly where I'd wanted him for days. After his earlier punishments and our little conversation on being his submissive, I was still wild with lust for him. Frenzied, I removed his shirt, licking and nipping at the skin leading to his pants, tugging him free. He sat up and stripped me out of my dress. Naked and filled with longing, I let my hands roam over his fevered skin while he traced the contours of my torso with his mouth, worshiping me inch by inch. His soft breath warmed my oversensitive skin and piqued my craving.

"Erica, God, your body is amazing," he whispered, his voice low.

I could almost taste his fervor, the determination to possess me in every way. He slid his hands from my shoulders to my wrists, binding them in his one hand behind me. I bit my lip and moaned, pleasuring myself with the little movement he allowed me by rubbing myself on his cock, back and forth over my clit until I quickened with need.

He tightened his hold around my wrists, and an irrational fear sliced through me. I stilled, my breasts jutting out shamelessly toward him. My heartbeat was frantic as I warred with instincts that would never let me give any man this much control.

"Blake, I don't know," I said, my voice quivering with a confusing mix of fear and desire as he held me captive.

He silenced me with a tender kiss. "I'm going to take care of you, baby."

His voice left no doubt, and his face was calm and reassuring, more controlled than I could ever hope to be under the circumstances. I looked into his eyes and my heart ached for what I felt for this man.

"I'll never hurt you." He traced my lips with the pad of his thumb.

I trusted Blake with my body. With him, I had never felt safer, or more vulnerable.

The tension in my muscles that had me on edge, ready to fight, released.

Ready to give myself to whatever he had planned, I kissed him back. My heart raced, anticipation overtaking the fear.

Blake banded an arm around my hips, lifting them

slightly before we connected, and I slid carefully onto the scorching heat of his erection. He took my hardened nipple into his mouth, flicking the tip with his tongue and his teeth like he had in the club. The dual sensations overwhelmed me, but also held me captive. I couldn't release any of the energy that coursed through me by touching him or hastening our movements. Instead, it lingered inside me, built up like a ball of fire dying for oxygen, waiting to explode and enflame everything around me.

He arched his pelvis, pumping into me over and over and rendering my own undulations unnecessary. He circled my clit with his thumb, taking control of every movement with expert skill until I idled perilously on the brink of rapture. My muscles tensed against the bonds of his strong warm hands bending me to his will.

"You can feel everything now, can't you, baby?"

As he said the words, an acute awareness of everywhere our bodies met shot through me. His big cock rooting inside me, his fingers, playing the notes of my desire like a song he knew so well. I trembled, losing my mind with every passing moment.

"Yes...you feel amazing."

"You were right, Erica. I'm going to make you want things you never knew you wanted."

He left my clit to leverage my hips again, shoving himself deeper. A small, helpless cry escaped me as I felt myself unraveling around him.

"You're going to want me to hold you down and fuck you hard. To take control of your body."

"Blake, please...oh, God."

"You want it right now, don't you?"

"Yes. Now. All of you." I spasmed uncontrollably around him, his words spurring my gnawing hunger.

He released me then and flipped me to my back, covering my body with his own. He lunged into me with powerful thrusts that carried us up the bed and drove me straight into a heart-pounding orgasm that shot through me like lightning, a blinding white heat. I sobbed his name and raked my fingers down his back, steeling myself at his shoulder as the fire in me exploded around us.

"Blake!"

"You have me, Erica," he said, desire thick in his voice as he pinned my hips to the bed with the force of his last growling thrust.

We lay there for several minutes, tangled in each other, tied together by the experience, while relief and waves of sheer bliss rushed over me. I sifted a hand through the damp strands of his hair as he traced my face with his fingertips. His eyes never left mine, transfixed with an almost reverent intensity.

Physically and emotionally, I'd never felt more connected to another person. No one could ever make me feel this way. So stripped, so raw.

The reeling in my mind slowed as he pressed petal-soft kisses on my swollen lips, whispering adorations in my ear until I fell asleep in his arms.

I awoke a few hours later. The day was dawning and Blake's arms had me firmly tucked next to him, preventing any remote thoughts I might have had about escaping. I turned slightly to look at him, but when I moved, his arm tightened around my waist. His face was relaxed and peaceful. I smiled. I was right where I wanted to be. I draped my arm over his, holding him closer to me as I tried to fall back to sleep.

Suddenly Blake's phone rang from his pants on the floor. After a few rings he stirred and rolled off the bed to retrieve it.

"What's wrong?" he said.

An odd way to start a conversation.

"Where are you?" he continued, pressing the phone to his shoulder as he reached for his clothes on the floor. "Okay, I'll be there in ten."

He ended the call and finished dressing, seemingly forgetting that I was there.

"What's going on?" I asked.

He paused and looked over to me, his face lined with concern. What the hell could be going so wrong that he had to walk out on us this very second?

"I'm sorry. I have to take care of something. I shouldn't be too long."

"Can I come with you?"

"No, just pack up. I'll drive you back to Boston when I get back."

"I can't leave. I have a meeting tomorrow," I said, glancing at the clock. "Today actually."

"With who?"

"I'm having brunch with Isaac Perry."

"Reschedule it," he ordered without hesitation. "I'm getting you out of here."

"Blake, what the fuck is going on?" I crossed my arms defensively, a little insecure that I was still completely naked while he wasn't.

He sighed heavily. "I can't explain right now."

"Forget it. I'm staying here. I'll meet you back in Boston when I'm done today." I marched over to my bags, wrapped in our sheet.

"Trust me, we're getting out of here," he said. His jaw was set in that familiar uncompromising line. "I'll explain everything when I get back, I promise."

I gauged his expression, wishing I could believe him. He bridged the distance between us and made my decision for me with a kiss that had me wishing we had ten more minutes together.

"I'll be back soon," he said, and then rushed out the door.

Showered and dutifully packed, I cursed myself for letting Blake talk me into blowing off my meeting. I eventually fell asleep again waiting for him. Hours later, he sat next to me on the bed, nudging me awake.

"Time to go, baby," he said, his voice quiet and tender.

"Is everything okay?" I asked, shaking off the cobwebs.

"Come on, let's talk in the car." He stood and grabbed my packed bags. I did a quick inventory of all my things and followed him out.

I bid a silent farewell as we headed north out of the city, realizing I hadn't had a chance to say goodbye to Alli. I'd call later, much later when she and Heath had a chance to sleep off what was undoubtedly a late night for them.

"Are you going to enlighten me?" I finally asked.

Blake tightened his grip on the wheel.

"Who called you earlier?"

"Alli."

I frowned, curious why she even had Blake's number. My mind juggled the possibilities, but there just wasn't enough to go on.

"Why would she be calling you?"

"I'm sure Alli didn't tell you this, for obvious reasons, but Heath has something of a drug problem. I thought he was clean, but he's relapsed."

I blew out my breath, absorbing the shock of this news. My mind sped up, connecting all the dots. Everything added up. His strung out look the other morning, the late nights, and an undercurrent of distrust that I couldn't shake when I was around him.

"What kind of drugs?"

"Cocaine mostly."

"Alli," I whispered, covering my mouth with a shaky hand. How she could be with him under these circumstances? This was serious. What if Alli were involved with drugs now too, because of him? This would explain her being out of touch, and the weight loss that, though subtle, was still noticeable to me.

"Alli's not using with him," he said, as if reading my mind.

I frowned. "How do you know?"

"I believe her. After years of dealing with Heath, my bullshit meter is pretty well honed. She's clean."

I nodded, relieved and feeling suddenly sorry for Blake. How long had he been dealing with this? Cleaning up Heath's messes?

"What happened tonight?"

"He got into a fight at the club. They called the cops, and they found drugs on him. Same old story."

"So now what?"

"They've kept him overnight. I already arranged to

have him bailed out, then I'll have to get him into rehab so he can avoid jail time again."

Again? "Where will he go?"

"I'm thinking about getting him out of New York. Coke, models, and clubs. You can't have one without the other two apparently, and he just can't shake the club scene."

I tried to digest everything, fitting the pieces together like a puzzle. I hated that I'd been in the dark for so long. How long had Alli known and kept this from me? First Sophia and now this. In a matter of weeks there were so many secrets between us. Maybe she wasn't blatantly lying to me, but she was keeping the truth from me, which felt like the same thing.

"Is that how you met Sophia?" I asked, hesitant to suggest her involvement, but unable to resist.

He was silent a long moment. "I met her through Heath, yes."

I stared at him, watching him decide whether to share more.

"I guess you could say she was in his entourage, or he was in hers. I don't know. We started seeing each other off and on, until she hooked up with Heath while I was away."

"She slept with him?"

"Neither of them would admit to it. I didn't even realize either of them had a problem until I crashed one of their parties at the condo. They were all over each other. I decided not to ask and just assumed the worst."

"What did you do?"

"I sent them off to rehab. Threatened to cut them both off until they got clean. When Sophia ended the program, I broke it off with her. She didn't take it well, but I agreed to help her start fresh."

"That's why you invested in her business."

A fleeting look of surprise crossed his face. He was probably willing to do anything to keep her clean, knowing the breakup would send her into a tailspin. Did he love her?

"Yes, but the relationship ends there." He took his eyes off the road for a moment to meet mine.

"I believe you," I said. As much as I enjoyed looking into his eyes, I wanted them on the road right now.

"Good."

"What's Alli supposed to do now?"

"She can stay at the condo as long as she needs to, obviously."

"But, their relationship? I mean..." I'd never seen Alli like this, so in love. But could I really support a relationship with Heath when he had so many issues? Serious issues. Billionaire brother or not, he was trouble, and the thought of her being tied to him in any way was disconcerting.

"She needs to figure it out, but I don't want you involved," Blake said, a note of resolve in his voice.

I frowned. "What does that mean exactly?"

"That means I don't want you anywhere near Heath or his circle of friends until he's been clean for a very long time. And that includes Alli."

"Are you telling me I can't see her?" I bristled at the suggestion.

"If Alli decides to stay with him, that's her choice, but I won't have you anywhere near it."

My anger bubbled to the surface and I stewed, trying

to come up with a way to win the argument. I needed my coffee.

I pouted on the far edge of my seat, trying to gain as much distance from him as the car would allow.

"Breakfast?" he asked.

I stared out the window, refusing to answer him.

After a few tense minutes, he exited the highway and parked in front of a quaint diner down the road. He powered off the car, stepped out, and circled to open my door for me.

When I stepped out, he caged me with his arms, leaning me into the car and bringing our bodies too close for how angry I was with him.

"I need you to understand," he said.

"Understand what? Your sick need to control everything and everyone around you?"

"Have you ever known someone with an addiction?"

I tightened my arms around my chest and looked past him to the highway and the cars speeding by. He was going to try to convince me that controlling my life was somehow acceptable, I knew it. "No," I admitted.

"Good. I don't want you to."

"You can't tell me who to have in my life. You said you weren't interested in dominating me that way."

"I never said that, and secondly, this is different."

"Great." I shivered, chilled by the idea that deep down Blake really wanted to, maybe needed to, control me—an expectation that seemed to root itself further into our relationship with every passing second.

"Erica, stop."

"Stop what? I've never had to answer to anyone, and I'm sure as hell not answering to you. So stick that in your fucking dominant pipe and smoke it."

I moved to leave but he didn't budge, trapping me.

"Erica..."

"Don't *Erica* me—"

He groaned and shoved his hands through his hair, giving us the smallest separation. I glared at him, but when I met his eyes, they were tired, storming with emotion, pleading with me without words.

"I care about you. I'm falling in love with you, and I'm going to do whatever I need to do to protect you. Do you understand?"

My heart slammed in my chest. *Shit. Shit. Shit.* His words couldn't have hit me any harder. My palms prickled with heat and became damp. I rubbed them nervously on my jeans as the silence grew between us.

"Heath has ripped our family apart with this. My parents worry every day about what they did wrong and I'm trying everything I can to set him straight again, praying something will work before he kills himself one day."

I relaxed a little, grateful that he'd spoken. I was nowhere close to making sense of the emotions rioting through me.

I needed coffee, or sleep. Mainly I needed to be somewhere outside of Blake's bubble of earth-shattering sex and emotional intensity. I was fucked up enough without all of that. I shook my head, trying to focus on the argument I was determined to win.

He'd thrown me a curve ball, but somehow we needed to find a middle ground, though I worried that Blake wasn't used to negotiating middle ground much when he wasn't with me. I took a deep breath and placed my hands on his chest. His heartbeat quickened, mimicking my own.

"Blake, Alli is my best friend. If she's going to stick this out with Heath, I need to be there to support her, the same way I'll support you."

For a split second, he looked lost. His expression changed again and he straightened. "I don't need support, Erica. I'm used to dealing with this. I just don't want you getting hurt. I couldn't bear it."

My anger faded into an overwhelming desire to take the pain away, to help him fix this mess. "Listen to me. You can't play master of the universe and refuse help from the people who care about you."

Blake covered my hands with his own, squeezed them slightly.

"Listen, it's been a long night. Let's talk about this later...when we're not so wiped out."

I sighed and nodded, accepting that we were agreeing to disagree for the moment.

CHAPTER FIFTEEN

The buzzing wouldn't stop. I hid under the covers, clinging to sleep and wishing Alli would answer the goddamn door.

Oh shit. My eyes shot open and I sat up straight. I was back at my own apartment. I jumped up to answer the intercom by the door, seeing no signs of Sid.

"Hello?"

"Hey, baby girl," the voice sang through the speaker.

I smiled. "Come on up, Marie." I buzzed her in and opened the door. I set to making coffee, glancing at the clock on the stove. I had missed lunch along with most of the afternoon. My stomach grumbled. *Coffee first.* Marie joined me a few minutes later, looking fresh in a floral dress, the bright colors contrasting with her enviable skin tone.

"Wow, nice place." She surveyed the main living area, which now looked a lot less empty since the furniture had arrived. Sid had assembled everything while I'd been away, which I hadn't been able to thank him for yet. Soon though. We were probably on the same schedule for once.

"Thanks, I'm loving it," I said. "Coffee?"

"Water's fine." She hopped up on a stool by the counter and dropped her purse and a shopping bag to the floor.

She seemed to study me a moment, her brow wrinkled. "You look like hell, Erica. Is everything all right?"

I sighed, feeling as haggard as I probably looked. "Long night and long story. I'll spare you the details," I said, willing the coffee to drip faster. I needed a few extra minutes to wake up and figure out my current reality before I could even think about talking about it. "What's new? Any updates with Richard?"

"Oh, I don't know." She shrugged, taking the water glass from me. "He's got his life, I've got mine. We'll see how it goes, I suppose."

"I'm not hearing wedding bells." I leaned back against the counter to face her. Marie had spent years on the dating circuit, and I was used to hearing about every new beau's husband potential. She had a kind heart, but couldn't ever seem to find Mr. Right. Heaven knew she was a hopeless romantic and deserved a good relationship more than anyone.

"Doubtful. We're both used to having our freedom. I guess when you get older, it's harder to change your life for someone." She sighed a little and twisted her glass on the countertop. "Sometimes I miss the days when I could lose myself in someone completely, and he'd do the same."

"That doesn't exactly sound healthy."

"Maybe not always, but it's intoxicating. There's nothing quite like it. You should try it sometime." She winked at me.

"Unfortunately, I think I'm knee deep in it at the moment."

"Mystery man?"

I blew out a breath, realizing she didn't know half of my recent history with Blake. "Yeah. Mystery man. Blake is his name. He lives upstairs, actually."

She cocked an eyebrow. "Did I miss something?"

"It's complicated, but he seems to want to be with me. I want that too, I think." I trailed off, not knowing how to put into words how I truly felt about Blake.

"So what's the problem?"

I grabbed a mug, filled my cup before the pot brewed completely, and took a cautious sip. She had a point. Even I questioned why I'd fought so hard to temper my feelings for Blake.

"It's…frightening," I said. "First of all, he's very intense, and secondly, I've never needed anyone, but the more we're together… It's like I can't think about anything else. It's so distracting."

I closed my eyes, trying to clear my thoughts of him, an impossible task. He was everywhere, even when we weren't together. And when we weren't together, I yearned to be with him. Obviously the sex was unmatched, but when we weren't ravaging each other, being with him always felt right. I had nothing to compare it to other than my string of lackluster flings with guys who were killing time with me until their parents forced them to marry a senator's daughter or something. There was no comparison.

"You're in deep, baby girl," Marie said.

"I know. But I don't want to lose myself, Marie. I've come this far, and this is who I am. I like my life and my independence, just like you. Why would I want to change all that and lose myself for someone I barely know?"

"You lose yourself, Erica, because with the right person, who you become together is something so much greater, more than you could even realize right now."

Her words rang through me, rattling me to the core. My lip trembled a little, and I blinked away the tears that stung my eyes.

"I think I love him," I whispered. "And it's scaring the hell out of me."

Marie hopped off the stool and came around to hug me tight. I hugged her back, so thankful to have her in my life. How could I surrender my heart to someone like Blake though? He had so many secrets, not to mention serious control issues. I couldn't imagine how we could make it in the long run with all these hurdles. If we didn't make it, how could I survive it with everything else I'd been through?

"I have something for you." She interrupted up my troubled thoughts and stepped away to retrieve her shopping bag from the floor.

She pulled out an old shoebox and handed it to me. I brought it over to the counter and opened it. Inside were stacks of photos of my mother from their college days, early on when Marie was just beginning to dabble with photography.

"I was going through some things and found them. You should have them."

I sifted through the stacks and studied each photo. My mother's face and her smile warmed me. At times like these, I missed her more than ever. I tried hard to remember what she sounded like, her voice and her laugh. So much time had gone by, but the memory of her love echoed through me, a wordless melody that held my heart through time and distance.

Marie leaned over my shoulder as if she were seeing the photos for the first time in a long time, making comments about where they were around campus in some of them. I stopped on one that showed a group of five friends with arms linked, dressed in light jackets for a cool fall day judging from the foliage behind them. Something about the photo gave me pause. My mother was laughing, her long blond hair whipping around her face. She was turned to the man next to her. Unlike the others, their expressions revealed more than the frivolity of the moment—a fleeting look of adoration that I only recently had come to know.

"Who is that?" I pointed to the man who had short sandy brown hair and blue eyes that I recognized.

When Marie fell silent, I turned to find her shaking her head.

"An old friend, I guess. I can't remember."

"It looks like my mother knew him though."

"Patty had a lot of friends. She was very charismatic. Half the campus was in love with her, I swear."

"Marie—"

"Erica, I don't know who that man is. I wish I could tell you." She collected her purse and touched up her makeup in her compact mirror.

Marie was carefree and energetic, even a little immature at times, but she wasn't much of a liar. She wasn't telling me something. I had a niggling suspicion as to why, but I didn't push her.

"Sweetie, I'm off. Keep me posted on Mystery Blake, okay?" She smiled as if the past five minutes hadn't happened.

"I will. Good luck with Richard too."

She responded with a weak laugh that didn't give me much hope for Richard. She opened the door and shrieked when Blake met her at the entrance. He looked as surprised as she did.

I laughed and joined them at the threshold. "Marie, this is Blake. Blake, this is my friend, Marie."

"It's a pleasure, Marie," he said, greeting her with a heart-stopping smile.

She mumbled something unintelligible before leaving, waving me off with a knowing grin.

Blake leaned on the doorway, freshly showered and barefoot, his hands tucked into a pair of board shorts paired with a plain white T-shirt. Only he could make something so casual look so impossibly sexy.

"Can I interest you in take out?" he asked.

"Actually that sounds perfect. I'm still feeling pretty wiped out."

"Me too. Thai?"

"Sure. I'll meet you upstairs. I need to change." I gestured to my pajamas.

"You don't need to. Clothes are optional, you know."

He smirked, and I rolled my eyes and smacked his shoulder, trying to hide my smile before heading back to my room.

★ ★ ★

"Oh my God," I moaned. "I don't think I'll ever cook again."

"I can't allow that," Blake said between his bites, eating noodles out of a tin container.

He thought I was joking, but this had to be the best Thai food I'd ever had. We settled back into the couch, exhausted and full.

"Do you want to watch a movie?" he asked.

"You mean, go out?"

"No, we can stay in, unless you want to go out?"

"What about your no electronics rule?"

"It's more like a guideline." He opened a drawer in the

coffee table in front of us and reached for one of several remotes. Whatever he pressed pulled a large flat panel television out of a hidden pocket of the mantle.

"Sounds good to me. Pick something out and I'll go clean up." I collected our mess and took it to the kitchen. My eyes lighted on a square black velvet box, if only because it was solitary in its place on the counter. I tried to ignore it and focused on putting away the leftovers.

"That's for you," Blake said, leaning his hip against the counter on the other end of the kitchen.

My eyes widened in surprise. "That?" I pointed to the box.

"I wanted to give it to you in New York, but we rushed out of there before I had a chance."

Oh.

"Open it," he said, his voice low with that sexy rasp that made me forget myself.

I tentatively reached for the box as he crossed the space between us. I held it in my hands, unable to open it. After a few awkward seconds, he popped the lid open for me, revealing two diamond bangle bracelets, each with a tiny charm hanging from the clasp. I lifted one out and identified its charm as a miniature roulette wheel in solid matching platinum.

"For being my good luck charm," he murmured.

I smiled at the memory. That was pretty lucky, I had to agree.

I lifted the second out. On it hung a delicate woven heart. My own heart started to beat wildly, my nerves suddenly on edge.

"Every charm has a meaning," he said quietly, setting

the box to the side and clasping both bracelets around my left wrist before pressing a soft kiss into my palm.

"Thank you." My voice wavered. I admired the bracelets, which were simple and elegant. Knowing Blake, they had no doubt cost a small fortune, but the meaning behind the gift was what took my breath away. I had been running his words from this morning over in my head all afternoon, wondering if he'd said he loved me on a whim, or just to make his point in the heat of the argument. But the gift solidified the sentiment. He'd known it before he'd said it.

Words caught in my throat. I wanted to say more. I loved Blake too. Trying to convince myself that I didn't was beyond ridiculous. The words, and everything they meant, were tearing me up inside. I wanted him to know it too, but something kept me silent.

I toyed with the bracelets—the cool metal on my skin and the faint clinking of the charms that would always remind me of him, even when we were apart. Before I could try to say anything, he cupped my cheek and bent to kiss me. I ran my fingers through his hair and kissed him back with every ounce of passion I felt, telling him the only way I knew how. He met my intensity, holding me tight and lifting me to him with his strong arms.

"Erica—"

"Shh." I pressed my fingertips to his lips before he could say more. I couldn't bear hearing the words again, knowing I couldn't say them back right now. Instead I kissed him gently, closing my eyes to avoid his.

He stepped back before we could go further, holding my hand and leading me back to the living room. Relieved, I got comfortable in the nook of his arm as the movie started. We settled in and I relished the moment. I couldn't remember feeling so completely content with anyone else. No words, no expectations—we spent the next two hours unwinding together, forgetting the drama that had surrounded us the past few days until I fell asleep in his arms.

The apartment was quiet and dark when I woke. Blake carried me into the bedroom as if I weighed nothing. He sat me down on the bed and helped me out of my clothes. Feeling rested from my recent slumber, a quiet energy stirred in me. My skin came alive under his touch.

"I thought you'd be tired."

"I'm not anymore," I murmured. I pulled off my tank top and bra, undressing myself from where he'd stopped. I shimmied back onto the bed where I waited for him.

He pulled off his t-shirt, revealing his naked chest. "I can see you'll be keeping me busy."

I smiled. "You were the one who said relationships could be distracting."

"I was only hoping to be that distraction."

Pushing down his shorts, he revealed his thick arousal. In the soft light of the room, he looked beautiful. Shadows played against the sculpted angles of his toned body. I bit my lip hard at the sight of him.

"Then by all means, distract me."

He crawled onto the bed, the mattress dipping as he crept closer.

"Lie back and I'll do more than distract you."

I leaned back. He slid my panties down and went right for the tender flesh between my legs, licking me with expert finesse. He moaned, vibrating the sensitive tissues as he teased them lightly with his tongue.

"I fucking love it down here," he said, his breath gusting on my wet flesh. "I could lick your sweet little cunt all day long."

His words set my nerves on edge. I quickened, the promise of release brewing like a storm inside me. He dug his fingers into my hips to keep me still as I bucked against him. I held on, gripping the sheets beneath me, as the orgasm crept closer. I cried out, my body reacting beyond my control, but before I could ride out the last of the aftershocks, he'd nestled his hips between my legs and pushed into me, angling my hips to hit the deepest part of me on his first thrust.

My breath caught as I stretched to accommodate him, my body exquisitely tight.

"It's so good," I breathed.

He moved slowly, easing into a rhythm that I eagerly met. Slow and intense. Nothing felt so right. Like coming home. This was where I wanted to be every night, in his arms where I could savor the pressure of his body over me, around me, inside me, filling me completely and fucking me tirelessly until we disappeared into each other—until we felt that magic together.

"God, Erica. You're so tight," he murmured into my neck. "Perfect."

I pulled in a sharp breath and a blinding love rushed in with it. Chills erupted on my skin. I was crazy to think I could go on without him, without this. I was his, in every conceivable way. I'd never wanted him so badly, and I never wanted this moment to end.

We made slow love, though it was no less profound for its lack of kink. Wrapped in his smell and his lingering caresses, I clung to the rigid curves of his muscle-bound body and to the promise that he would sate the burning hunger that consumed me every time our bodies met. He held me tight as another orgasm built inside me, slow and steady, pleasure taking me over. Overwhelmed by the emotions ripping through me, I closed my eyes, but Blake stilled.

"Look at me," he whispered.

My body responded to the smallest of his commands. I opened my eyes into his, and the passion and love I found within them made my chest ache. There was no denying that I loved this man.

CHAPTER SIXTEEN

When I woke, the sun was up. Blake was gone, but he'd left a note.

Morning, boss,

Made you fruit salad for breakfast, in the fridge. See you tonight.

Love, B

My tummy did a little flip, like the bottom had dropped out on one of those theme park rides. I shuffled into the kitchen and found a single serving of chopped up fruit in the fridge. I smiled and brought it downstairs with me, along with the note, which I stuck on the corkboard in my bedroom. I showered and dressed, trying to focus on the mountain of work I had to do.

A few hours went by, and I was finally beginning to make some progress, when Sid walked into the apartment unexpectedly. He stopped when he saw me.

"You're back."

"I am. Where were you?" I peeked over the screen of my laptop.

His hair was mussed and his big brown eyes looked tired. "There's this girl, Cady. She lives downstairs."

"Shut up!"

"Uh, okay," he said, frowning.

"I'm sorry, that's code for 'please continue.'"

"She's got the new *Call of Duty* game, so we were up late with that. I crashed down there."

"Do you like her?" I asked, not caring if I was getting way ahead of myself. This was real progress, and Cady seemed unconventional and geeky enough that this could possibly work.

"She's nice, yes," he said, shoving his hands into his pockets nervously.

"That's cool." I tried to temper my excitement. "Hey, thanks for putting the furniture together."

"No worries. It's kind of fun actually."

I grinned. "Only you would think so."

He shrugged. "Probably. How was your trip?"

I hesitated for a second. How could I censor the sequence of events that comprised my rather short stay? Blake's ex-girlfriend threatening me, an unexpected reunion with Blake, and the crescendo of discovering Heath's criminal drug problem, which had unknown consequences on Alli. She still hadn't returned my calls or texts.

"I made a few connections," I said and left it at that. Alli and Sid had never been especially close, and his energies were better spent on the business rather than mulling over or even hearing about her drama.

"Sounds good." He signaled his retreat back to the cave with a tap on his forehead.

I stopped him. "Hey, I might need your help with something."

He pivoted back in my direction. "What's that?"

"Wait here."

I went to the bedroom and retrieved the photo from

the box. When I returned, I placed it on the counter in front of him.

"Who's that?"

"That's my mother. And *that*," I said, pointing to the man next to her, "could very well be my father."

His eyes shot up, traveling between the photo and me a few times. "What does this have to do with me?"

"I need you to help me find out who he is."

"From this photo?"

"He was at Harvard with my mom in 1991. That and this photo is all I've got."

Sid picked up the photo. He frowned and pursed his lips, a common expression when he was calculating and a good sign that he could and would help me.

"What's your plan?" I asked tentatively.

"Unless Harvard keeps some sort of public digital database of former students, which I doubt they do, I'll need to figure out how to access it privately. Then I'll try to run some decent face recognition software and go from there."

"Are you okay with that?" What I was asking of him probably required blatantly illegal access. Guilt consumed me already. I could always scour the yearbooks in the library and find the same information, but Sid's method was surely faster and more accurate.

He cocked his head. "Is this guy really your dad?"

"I wish I knew."

"All right, I'll let you know what I find," he said. He returned to his room, taking the photo with him.

I turned my focus back to my laptop. I still had a hundred things to do, including sorting through the pile of resumes I'd accumulated since posting for Alli's empty position before the trip. Now I couldn't concentrate worth a damn. How long would this search take? What if Sid found him in a matter of hours? What if he couldn't find him at all? I chewed my fingernail.

My phone rang, nearly launching me out of my chair. I had the number saved to my phone and recognized it immediately.

I took a deep breath and answered cheerfully. "Hi, Isaac." I was grateful to have any distraction right now.

"What are you doing for dinner tonight?" he asked in a smooth voice that reminded me how charming he'd been in person.

I hesitated. "I'm not sure. Why?"

"I'm flying into Boston this afternoon. I figured we could touch base while I'm in town."

"Oh, sure." I still felt guilty for canceling on him at the last minute without a genuinely believable excuse. For all he knew, something had come up with the business that took me away abruptly at the crack of dawn on a Sunday morning.

"Great, can you meet me at the Park Plaza, around six?"

"Perfect, I'll see you then."

I hung up. Any excitement about meeting up with Isaac wilted knowing I'd be missing a quiet dinner with Blake at his place. I missed him too much already. I was falling hopelessly in love with Blake. *So what?* I was going to stop beating myself up over every step that took me further into our relationship. If I was going to be falling hopelessly in love, I would do it wholeheartedly and without regrets.

I glanced at the clock, debating for only a second before sending Blake a text.

E: Can I visit you at the office?

B: Please do.

I changed into a beige pencil skirt and white button up blouse and straightened my hair, making it smooth and sleek. I checked myself in the mirror, satisfied that I looked professional enough for dinner with Isaac and sexy enough to give Blake something to think about while I was gone.

Blake wasn't in the bullpen when I arrived. No one seemed to notice me, so I walked back to his office. He was camped in front of his triple monitor set-up. The televisions were silently broadcasting stock feeds and news channels on the other side of the room, reminding me why his no electronics at home rule was in place.

I shut the door behind me.

He swiveled in his chair. "And to what do I owe this pleasure?" He leaned back with a wicked grin on his face.

"I have a dinner meeting tonight." I walked over to the opposite desk where he was forced to work with lowly paper and pens and propped myself up on it. "So I wanted to come see you for a little bit first."

"Who's the meeting with?"

"Perry."

He scowled. "That fucking guy is relentless."

"Do you know him?"

"I know him well enough to know he's attracted to you."

I laughed at his blatant assumption. While his suspicions might not be totally off, he had no way of knowing that. "Do you know how crazy you sound right now?"

He ignored me and cupped his hands behind my knees, rolling himself closer to me. "Why don't you let me come with you? I can be your business partner."

My smile faded. "I don't think that's a good idea, Blake."

"Why? He'll stick to business, and I won't have to worry about you."

"First off, you aren't my business partner, and secondly I really don't think you have anything to worry about. He seems very professional, and I'd rather he be able to speak freely. You know, one on one."

He gave me a hard stare. "You're set on this?"

I kicked off my heels and slid off the desk, straddling him on the chair. "You're overreacting," I whispered. I kissed his neck, already intoxicated with his scent. He smelled clean and uniquely Blake. I took his earlobe between my teeth and gave it a gentle bite.

He took in a sharp breath.

I hooked my fingers in his belt loops and tugged myself closer, sliding my hand under his shirt. His muscles were hard and unforgiving, not unlike his present mood.

"What can we do to cheer you up, Blake?" I said, worrying the top button of his pants.

He caught my hand before I could go farther.

"None of that."

I met his gaze. He was serious, but I had a feeling I could win this battle.

"Oh, I forgot, you have a reputation to uphold. No nookie in the office, or your minions will mutiny?" I tried to tease him out of his mood by keeping mine light.

A ghost of a smile crossed his face. "What am I going to do with your smart mouth?"

I lined his jaw with soft kisses. "I could think of a few things."

I brushed my lips over his as he bunched my skirt

higher up my thighs. My breath came in short pants, my desire for him already at a fever pitch. He slipped his hand between my legs and teased me through my panties.

I moaned, pressing into his hand, my clit already throbbing for his touch. He pushed the fabric to the side, parting me and gliding through my folds.

"You're ready for me," he murmured.

"Always." I circled my hips slightly, coaxing his movements.

He slid down my center with two fingers, grazing my clit between them, and then dipped them into my pussy and thumbed my clit again. He traveled that path over and over until my entire body was taut from the pressure, rocking precariously on the precipice of release.

"Come, Erica. Now. I want to feel your greedy little cunt get nice and tight."

I dug into his shoulders. I muffled a scream and convulsed against his body, my sex clenching almost painfully without his cock inside me. With trembling hands, I fumbled with his fly, determined to change that fact. His erection struggled beneath the denim, the only barrier between us. He caught me by the wrists again, turning my palms up to press a slow wet kiss into each one.

"Blake," I whimpered.

"You have to go to your meeting." His voice was even as he released my hands. He held my gaze and dipped his fingertips into his mouth, sucking the moistened tips that I'd been riding only moments ago.

Fuck me. My heart skipped a beat.

"We have plenty of time," I said, heading back for his fly. After all, I'd calculated my arrival time with this in mind.

"Get up," he ordered, slapping my ass lightly.

Reluctantly I stood and leaned against his desk while he disappeared into the bathroom that connected with his office. He came back with a damp hand cloth and cleaned me, an act both tender and arousing.

"Am I being punished?" I asked, confused why he was being so steadfast, especially since he clearly wanted me too.

"No."

"You want me." I massaged his cock through his pants.

He shifted out of my reach. "I do. You'll just have to hurry back from your meeting to find out how much." He turned away and returned to the bathroom.

Resigned that this would be the end of our rendezvous, I straightened. I smoothed out the faint wrinkles in my skirt and tried to put myself back together, physically and emotionally. Out of fucking Blake mode and back into work mode—not an easy transition when all I could think about was how amazing I'd feel if he pounded me on his desk instead. I ran my fingertips over the surface, the charms on my wrist clinking against it.

Blake came up behind me and pressed his warm body into mine. He kissed my shoulder.

"I have to go," I said. The statement caught somewhere between frustration and desperation.

"Hurry back." The depth of his voice reverberated through me. "The longer I have to the wait, the harder I'm going to fuck you."

I gasped. My breasts felt swollen and heavy, aching for his touch. I pressed back into him and he let out a low growl. He grabbed my hip and released me just as quickly.

Then he was gone. I turned to find him at the mini bar. He poured himself a scotch and looked out the window.

I had too much pride to beg, and I didn't feel like psychoanalyzing why he insisted on torturing us. We'd finish this later, but I was on fire now. I'd be counting down the minutes until my meeting was over. Of course that was exactly what Blake wanted. What else could I expect from a control freak hacker? He fought dirty.

★ ★ ★

Between the restored antiquities of the hotel, the chandeliers, gold crown molding, and the Frank Sinatra music pouring through the lobby, I might have stepped into a Rat Pack film. Isaac rose from a club chair on the other side of the room. I went to meet him, my heels clicking on the marble floors. He wore an expensive suit, but his shirt was unbuttoned at the top. That, with his winning smile, made him look casual and approachable.

When we met, he leaned in to air kiss me on the cheek, a gesture that reminded me too much of Sophia.

"Where to?" I asked, eager to get the meeting underway.

"Let's go to Maggiano's. It's right next door."

We crossed the street and stepped into the sprawling Italian restaurant. Settling into a booth, sitting the booth across from me, Isaac ordered a bottle of wine from the server who greeted us.

"How'd everything go today?" I asked after she'd gone.

"It went well, nothing notable. To be honest, I probably wouldn't have made the trip if I couldn't meet with you."

"Oh. I guess that worked out then." I straightened my napkin on my lap, gliding my fingers absently over my still-wrinkled skirt.

"So tell me, why are you running the business in Boston?"

I lifted my eyebrows and searched for the right response. "This has been my home for years now. I don't really want to leave unless I have to."

"There are so many more opportunities for you in New York."

"Not enough for me to leave, I guess."

He leaned in with a slanted grin. "There must be someone keeping you here then."

I sat back and drummed my fingers on the checkered tablecloth. I tried to keep my expression cool. Why did he insist on making the conversation so personal? My small talk skills had never been great. Maybe I needed to give a little before diving into the logistics of how he envisioned us working together.

"There is someone keeping me here, yes." A glimmer of an idea formed as I said the words.

"And he gave you these." He brushed his fingers along my forearm to touch the diamond bangles that sparkled impressively in the dim light of the restaurant. "Beautiful."

The contact shot through me, and not in a good way. I pulled my arm back and tucked my hair behind my ear nervously. I chilled, wishing I'd brought a sweater, something to keep me warm and hidden from his suggestive looks. I regretted the blouse now. I'd dropped a button for Blake's sake and there was no going back without being awkward now.

"Thank you." I kept my eyes low and focused on the food that had arrived.

"Who's the lucky man?"

"Blake Landon. I think you might know him." Blake had a reputation of his own, so perhaps the name would deter him.

He grimaced slightly. "No kidding. I suppose Sophia gave you fair warning on that one. He has a reputation for discarding his hobbies."

I let the comment roll off me. Blake's version of the events with Sophia were in line with what someone could expect from that kind of relationship and situation. He didn't always tell me the whole truth, but I hadn't yet caught him in a lie. Beyond that, I had a hard time imagining someone as cold and calculating as Sophia stealing anyone's heart.

"How do you know Sophia?" I asked, figuring I'd snatch the opportunity to learn more about her.

"We use her models for various shoots for the publications, and of course she's a savvy businesswoman, like yourself. You're wise to connect with her."

I bristled and the colors of the room became momentarily more vivid as I pictured her in my mind. If she ever touched Blake, I'd definitely connect with her.

Isaac was pissing me off with all of this personal banter. I needed to get us back on track. Maybe Blake had been right. Having him there would have kept Isaac to the point, though the conversation could have become incredibly awkward too.

I took a steadying breath and tried to steer us back to business. "You mentioned that we might find ways to work together. I wondered what you had in mind."

He smiled. "Well, you're the social expert. What did *you* have in mind?"

The tension backed off a little as I was able to concentrate on talking business. I questioned him on the mechanics of his marketing strategy, the details of which he knew very little, but overall I had a better sense of how his departments were structured under each publication. I could think of a few ways we could work together.

We spent the next hour or so discussing the logistics of cross promoting between his publications using Clozpin's tools. The plan sounded promising, and Isaac seemed receptive. I agreed to put together a proposal outlining the options we discussed.

Once my personal life was off the table, the conversation was productive, enjoyable even. We polished off the Pinot Grigio and I recommended some other spots in Boston for him to try next time he was in town. A silence fell over the table as we waited for the check to come. I checked my phone for the time. Nearly three hours had passed. Blake would be furious.

By the time we left the restaurant, the sun had gone down and I was more relaxed, thanks to the wine. The air was warm as I stepped out onto the street. I twisted back to Isaac to ask him which way he was headed. With the movement, I lost my balance and tumbled. Isaac grabbed me and pulled me tight to his chest.

"I had a great time with you tonight, Erica." His voice was low and gravelly.

The sound might have melted another woman but it raked over me like nails on a chalkboard. Nothing felt right about it, even after ending the dinner on such a positive note.

"Thanks, Isaac, but I—"

He muffled my protest, pressing an unexpected kiss to my lips. I froze as he plunged his tongue into my mouth and grabbed my ass, grinding his hips into me. I shrieked into his mouth as I tried to find my footing and push him away, but he held me firmly in place.

I tried to twist away, alarms going off everywhere. Adrenaline surged through me in a potent rush. My body buzzed with the impulse to fight, to get him off me as quickly as possible. My mind shouted commands, but against every instinct, I hesitated, hoping he'd just leave me be.

"Why don't we go back up to the hotel?"

"Let me go, Isaac." *Please. I can't do this again. Please.*

He laughed, a wicked sound that sliced through me. "You think Landon gives a shit about you, don't you?"

I seethed with anger and prepared to knee him in the balls when he froze.

"Perry."

The deep voice emerged from behind me. Isaac let me go, immediately creating space between us. He backed away toward the stone wall of the building. In a flash, Blake was on him, pinning him by the throat to the building.

Isaac sputtered out a string of apologies. "She tripped, I just caught her. It was nothing, I swear."

"It didn't look like nothing."

I glanced up and down the street. Night had fallen and we were alone. I struggled to breathe as the aftermath of the panic raced through me, but I kept reminding myself we were safe. Blake was here, and by the looks of it, Isaac didn't have a chance. In a matter of seconds, he'd been reduced to a pathetic puddle of apologies while Blake squeezed him tighter, threatening him to make one wrong move.

"She's mine, Perry. And if you lay another hand on her, you won't have hands. Is this clear?"

"Yes. Yes, definitely." He loosened his grip just enough to slam him back, causing Isaac to cough, clawing at Blake's hand around his throat.

I'd never seen him so angry, not like this.

Blake finally released him. "Leave," he ordered.

Isaac disappeared down the street toward the Plaza. Blake turned to me, his face cold as stone.

CHAPTER SEVENTEEN

I followed Blake down the street to where his sleek sports car was parked. How long had he been stalking me? How had he even known where we were meeting? His uncanny knowledge about my whereabouts was unsettling, but I wasn't about to bring it up now.

He opened the door for me, a mere gesture I guessed because he didn't say a word to me as he joined me in the car and sped the few blocks back to the apartment. We stepped out and I stopped him at the entryway.

"Are you angry with me?"

"I'm not happy about finding you in a lip lock with that fucking guy, if that's what you mean."

"He just—I *didn't* want that."

"I know that, but you wouldn't have been in that situation if you'd listened to me."

I cringed, hating that he was right. The whole situation embarrassed me. "He caught me off guard. I could have handled it if you'd let me."

"Would you have had Max go with you, as an investor?"

I tapped my toe on the pavement. This was a trick question. "Blake, it's not realistic for you to be with me for every business meeting. Let's not go there."

"Answer me."

I hesitated. "Maybe."

"That's what I thought. I'll fund the business. I'll call

Max and let him know the deal is off." He dug into his pocket.

"No, stop right there. This is *my* business. I have to make these decisions." I'd barely stopped shaking from Isaac's advances. Now the threat of Blake calling Max under these extreme circumstances had ratcheted my panic to a whole different level. My mind raced, frantically trying to stay ahead of wherever Blake was going with this.

"Right. And you need two million dollars to continue running it and maintaining the lifestyle which you currently enjoy," he said.

I stilled. "Are you threatening me with the apartment? Say the word, and I'll pack my things right now. You're the one who forced me into it."

He ran his hands through his already tousled hair, his breath whistling through clenched teeth. "Just take the money and we can forget about all this."

"Blake, we have a relationship, or at least we did twenty minutes ago, which I think you can agree is complicated enough. I'm not taking your money."

He paused, holding me in a penetrating stare. "You don't trust me."

The words cut me to the core. Not because he felt that way, but because they were true. I trusted Blake on many levels, but keeping the business on my terms was imperative.

Unable to formulate a convincing response, I pushed through the doors of the building and nearly ran into Cady and Sid walking into her apartment. Blake barreled in after me.

I offered a quick hello and goodbye before climbing the stairs up to the apartment. Blake followed me all the way to the bedroom. I didn't argue.

"Clothes, off," I ordered, directing him with my index finger.

My mind was an epic jumble. I could think of no better cure than to fuck Blake straight to oblivion. As it was, I'd thought of little else for the better part of the day.

His eyebrows arched. "Shouldn't we talk about this?"

"Did I stutter? Clothes. Off." I cocked my head, daring him to argue.

He paused another minute, then undressed completely. As the last garment hit the floor, I stared in awe at the specimen at my mercy in front of me. Every sliver of flesh stretched tight over the sculpted muscles beneath. My fingers itched to run all over them, to feel them flex beneath me, above me, inside me. My anger slipped away, rapidly replaced with the craving I'd been staving off for hours.

The longer I looked at him, the harder he got. His expression was calm, but the longing that simmered behind his eyes reflected my own. I stepped closer and gave him a little shove onto the bed. He reached for me but I stepped back. Stripping down, I took extra time removing my white lacy bra and panties that I had chosen just for him.

I climbed him leisurely, systematically kissing his throat, his chest, nibbling the dark disks of nipples as they hardened under my touch. I finally turned my attention to his cock, tonguing his length and licking off the drop of pre-cum at its tip, savoring his flavor before gliding him into my mouth, deeper until he hit the back of my throat.

"Christ, Erica." He sucked in a sharp breath.

I reveled at the small victory. He was much better at the self-control game, never letting on that I was tormenting him with my touches until now. His thighs were taut with restraint when I released him, sliding him out of my mouth with slow retreat.

"How do you feel?" I asked.

"Come here, and I'll show you." His eyes were half-lidded and dark with lust.

My body hummed. I positioned myself above his cock and inched onto him slowly, giving my body time to adjust to his length.

A wave of heat rolled over me as I sheathed him completely. I rose, and he grabbed my hips, slamming me down onto him, reminding me of the place inside me that only he could satisfy. I threw my head back and cursed. I stilled, overcome with how well we fit, how no one else had ever come close to this.

He grasped my hips and tried to flip me, but I angled away so he couldn't.

"No," I said firmly.

He stilled and loosened his hold. "We should probably talk about safewords."

"That *is* my safeword. When I say no, trust me, I mean it."

"Okay," he said quietly.

"I'm going to fuck you until my legs turn to jelly and I can't remember my name. And then you can be in charge, all right?"

"Whatever you say, boss." He swallowed hard and laced his fingers behind his head—a self-imposed restraint.

I circled my hips, rising and dropping down with measured impact until I found a rhythm. My breasts were heavy and tender. I tugged on my nipples to quell the deep ache to be touched. Blake's hands never strayed and his eyes never left me. His hips lifted, meeting my strokes and hitting me deeper with each one. The climax coiled inside me. I quivered, biting my lip until it was numb, trapped in an orgasm that kept climbing to its peak.

"I want to hear you," he said. "Now, Erica."

The damn broke and a strangled cry left me as I came hard. Breathless and losing steam, I fell forward, threaded my fingers with his, and kissed him.

Blake sat up with me, took one nipple in his mouth and then the other, and drove himself deeper into me. I whimpered. He cupped my face with one palm and circled my waist with the other, bringing me tight against him and kissing me—a deep, penetrating kiss that spoke volumes. I could taste the need on his lips. I was more than ready to let him take control.

"It's okay," I said.

He turned us over with measured control, covering my body with his before lunging hard. I arched, welcoming everything he had to give me. With each thrust I unraveled, hours of wanting him coming to a peak, to this pinnacle of a moment where I could lose myself in him.

I kissed him frantically, caught between anger and love and passion. My nails scratched down his back as we climaxed together, slick with sweat.

Blake buried his face in my neck. "You're mine," he whispered.

I squeezed my eyes shut and held him close. He had no idea how true that was.

We lay, breathless and sated, on the bed, side by side. I admired Blake's amazing body stretched out before me. I trailed my fingers lightly over the raised flesh on his back where I'd dug into him harder than I'd meant to.

"I got you," I whispered.

"If you keep touching me like that, I'm going to get *you*."

I giggled and rolled onto my back, mesmerized by the moment and unable to take my eyes off the beautiful man in my bed. He propped himself up and stared at me.

"That was incredible, by the way," he said. He tucked my hair behind my ear, tracing my curves, as if he were committing them to memory. "Why is it that you can trust me with your body, after everything you've been through? And while I've built and sold dozens of businesses, you won't trust me with yours?"

I groaned and closed my eyes. He wasn't going to let a little fucking get in his way. He'd likely use it to his advantage.

"The business is everything to me." I cringed as the words left me, but in so many ways, it was true. "I mean, the business represents years of effort. Not just the time I spent building it, but the years I spent putting myself through school and becoming who I am."

"Yes, and..."

"When we're together it means something to both of us. I do trust you, more than I've ever trusted anyone. But what about when something happens between us, or you get tired of my little business venture? What if it becomes a drain on you, or fails?"

"The amount of money you're asking for is inconsequential to me," he said. "It's unlikely, if not impossible, that it could ever become a drain. Plus, I wouldn't let a business I was involved with fail."

"Then why didn't you just invest when you had the chance? What's the difference now, other than you flying into a rage every time I get within five feet of another man?"

"I was more interested in figuring you out than writing you a check. I knew if I passed, Max would pick it up. I was right. Now ... things are different. I care about you, and I want to care about the things that matter to you."

The proclamation settled over me, and a little part of me even wanted to give in. I'd spent weeks harboring doubts about the business because he'd passed so easily. To know that he'd seen value from the start was reassuring, but this didn't change the fact that mixing business with pleasure, at least to this degree, was a terrible idea.

"I appreciate that, but it's not a good reason to invest. It's bad enough that you and Max have issues, but I can't put the business at risk if you and I have tension. It's just too much."

He was silent, but I sensed that the conversation was far from over. He drew me closer and tucked me against his chest where I fell asleep, warm and safe.

★ ★ ★

I checked my email in the morning, still worn out from the previous night. Blake had woken me more than once, possibly attempting to screw me into surrender on the investment issue. I didn't argue, but I didn't surrender, at least when it came to the business.

I fished through the mail until I hit a message from Sid titled "Results." My stomach dropped as I reread it.

Erica,

Wasn't as hard as I thought. Daniel Fitzgerald, Class of 1992, Economics major. Google "Daniel Fitzgerald Boston."

Sid.

★ ★ ★

I opened a new tab and typed in the search. The first result showed attorney biographies at a law firm where his name was listed first as a partner. The second result was an official website for Daniel Fitzgerald's run for governor of Massachusetts, featuring a stylish red, white, and blue logo and a catchy campaign slogan. Beneath was a photo of an aged version of the man in the photo. *Oh God.* I scrambled for my phone and called Marie.

"Hey, baby girl," she answered happily.

"Daniel Fitzgerald," I said.

"What?"

"That's the man in the photo."

"Oh." She sounded more resigned than surprised.

"I know Mom didn't tell me for a reason, but I need to know."

"Erica, I—"

"Marie, I have a *right* to know. You were her best friend. If anyone would know who my father is, it's you."

She was silent for a long stretch before speaking. "Yes."

"Yes, what?"

"He's your father."

"Oh, God." My face dropped into my palm, my head suddenly spinning. I'd had my suspicions, of course, but I'd half expected her to say no. To lie or to tell me I was crazy thinking up something so far-fetched. Now, faced with the truth, I didn't know what to feel.

I'd spent my whole life accepting the shadow of his absence, ignorant to the other half of who I was. But had I ever truly accepted it? By the time I was old enough to really demand the truth, my mother had been gone. Knowing that no one could ever hope to fill that place in my heart, I never bothered to seriously wonder who he could be.

Now, I had a thousand questions and no answers. Did he even know I existed? Did he love my mother? What was he like?

"Honey, are you all right?" Marie interrupted my reeling thoughts.

"Did you know he's running for governor?" The one thing I did know about him was the one thing that could keep us apart. I had no idea how I'd get through the layers of people that surrounded him.

She laughed quietly. "No, but I can't say I'm surprised."

"It's not going to be easy connecting with him," I said.

"Just be careful, honey."

My brows knit together. "What do you mean?"

"You don't know what you're walking into with him."

"Should I be worried? You obviously know more about him than I do."

"You're a smart girl. Just pay attention and don't let your guard down," she said quietly.

"Okay." I paused, trying to collect my thoughts. "Thank you."

"For what?"

"For telling me the truth. Even if it was a little late."

She sighed. "I hope you don't regret that I did."

I shook my head, unable to comprehend how I could. "I can't explain what this means…to finally know who he is. But with Mom being gone…"

"I know, baby," she said quietly. "I'm sorry. I was only following her wishes."

I blew out a breath, wishing this news brought me more relief than it did. I didn't like the idea that Marie had kept my father's identity hidden from me, or that my mother had wanted it that way. But I wasn't a little girl anymore. As scary as it seemed, I needed to know more about the man and what he meant to my mother.

"I should go. I need to think through all this. I'll talk to you soon though."

"Sure thing. Call me anytime. And Erica?"

I paused. "What?"

"Be careful, okay?"

"I will. I promise."

I hung up and stared at the photo on the website, wishing I knew the man on the other side. Not the lawyer or the politician, but the man.

I clicked around and learned as much as I could about him, which only reinforced how difficult it would be to get a meeting with him. I couldn't simply walk into his office and announce myself. The idea of Blake as a connection crossed my mind, but I squashed that idea. I didn't want to associate him with any of this, for my sake and his.

I scrolled through my phone and called Alli. We still hadn't spoken, and I was shocked when she picked up.

"I've been trying to reach you," I said, trying not to sound as concerned as I was.

"I know, I'm really sorry. I've been flat out with work, and dealing with all this crap with Heath doesn't help either."

"Are you all right?"

The phone was silent a moment. "Yeah, I think so."

"How's Heath?"

"He seems good…better. He's in L.A., so I can't go see him right now with work."

"Right…I can't imagine what this has been like for you."

She laughed listlessly. "I'm thinking I should have majored in psychology instead, because being with him has been like dating two completely different people."

"Except you're in love with one of them."

She sighed on the other end. "Trust me, I know."

"Alli, I know I haven't always been the most supportive friend when it comes to Heath, but I hope you know you can talk to me about this. This came as a shock to me, but I want to be here for you. You're still my best friend. I don't want this to keep us apart."

"Thank you," she said. "That means a lot. Obviously, I can't talk to my parents about any of this. They would completely freak out."

"Hopefully Heath can get straightened out before you have to."

"Hopefully."

I tapped my fingers on the counter. "So I have some interesting news."

"What's that?"

"I think I found my father."

"What? Are you serious?"

"I need your help though. He's some big-wig lawyer, and he also happens to be running for governor, so I have no idea how I'm going to get in touch with him, you know, discreetly. I was hoping you had some ideas."

"Wow, okay. Let me see what I can do. I know some people at the Review. We might be able to request an interview."

Alli's mood had shifted. She was suddenly peppy with a new mission. The girl was born for marketing.

"Thanks."

"No problem. But how are you handling this?"

I chewed my lip and stared at nothing. How was I handling this?

"It's hard to put into words. I'm excited, I guess. But nervous. I have no idea what kind of person he is. Regardless, I feel like I have to reach out to him. I can't just sit here knowing who he is without trying to see if he might want to know me too."

"I'm sure he does."

I shrugged. "Maybe. I guess we'll see."

"I'll see what I do with this interview. Let me know if anything comes up."

"I will. Thanks, Alli."

"No problem. I'll call you later."

CHAPTER EIGHTEEN

Nervous, I flipped through a magazine until Daniel Fitzgerald's beautiful blond receptionist gave me the go ahead to enter. The offices of Fitzgerald & Quinn were nestled in the heart of Boston's financial district, and the large corner office I stepped into left little doubt that the man in front of me was one of the most important executives in the city's corporate landscape. Dressed in an imposing three-piece suit, he pored over the paperwork on his double pedestal desk, his reading glasses resting on the ridge of his nose. He was no longer the carefree young man I'd seen in the photo.

"Mr. Fitzgerald." My voice faltered at the simple greeting.

He looked up at me, a mirror of my own cool blue eyes. His hair was graying and his face was lined, but he was still very handsome. The essence of the man in the photo was recognizable.

"I'm Erica Hathaway." I reached out to shake his hand.

He rose to greet me and motioned me to the chairs in front of his desk with a pleasant smile. "Erica, please have a seat."

I settled into one and breathed in the rich aroma of well-loved leather.

"Let's see. You're with the Harvard Review?" He arched a brow at me.

"Well, about that—" Alli had gotten me the interview

under the guise of being with the well-known publication, and if this didn't go well, someone would probably get kicked off the staff because of the favor she'd pulled.

He looked at me expectantly.

I swallowed hard and took a deep breath. *Here goes nothing.*

"Does the name Patricia Hathaway mean anything to you?" I asked finally, watching him intently as I spoke the words.

If the mention of her name meant anything to him, he didn't show it, his face frozen, void of emotion. His blue eyes bore into me, giving nothing away.

He glanced to his watch casually. "I'm not sure it does. How does this pertain to the interview, young lady?" His voice was even and incredibly composed.

I swallowed hard, fighting the sudden urge to throw up. Was I crazy for doing this? What if I was wrong? What if Marie had misinformation?

I shoved the doubt out of my mind and focused on the present. I looked down at my hands that were twisted anxiously in my lap. "I'm Patricia Hathaway's daughter. I was hoping I could speak to you about that."

A long silence fell between us, and within it, the truth hit me. My body felt numb at the realization.

Rising abruptly, he crossed the office with fluid grace, shut the door, and sank back down into his seat. He whipped his glasses off and tossed them onto the desk, revealing a hardened stare. "Where are you going with this?"

Oh my God. My doubts gave way to the unmistakable truth that this man really was my father. I could feel it. I gripped the edge of the seat, my palms sweating profusely. I offered up a silent prayer he didn't kick me out on the spot after I said what I was about to say.

"I'm—" I tried to imagine myself saying the words, but they caught in my throat. They sounded crazy and presumptuous. But they were true. I knew it. What if he didn't believe me? I shut my eyes tight and blurted it out before I lost my resolve. "Mr. Fitzgerald, I believe I'm your daughter."

He leaned back in the chair, his jaw tight, his eyes penetrating mine. We stayed like that for what felt like an eternity. My heart pounded in my chest, the anticipation of what he might say or do hung in the air between us.

He exhaled slowly and leaned forward into his desk. "So let's get down to it. Is this about money? If so, just let me know how much we're talking about."

I struggled to speak, but his words had cut through me. He thought I was extorting cash from him? *No, no, no. Shit.* I shook my head frantically and rubbed the space between my brows. This was going all wrong. "It's not like that. I just wanted to meet you. That's all." I didn't need anything from him. At least nothing like that.

He hesitated for a moment before he leaned forward on his desk again, pinching the bridge of his nose with a sigh. "I can't say I was expecting this."

"Neither was I, to be honest. I never thought I would meet you."

"Likewise. Listen, Erica." He cleared his throat and rearranged some papers on his desk. "This isn't really the time or the place to delve into this, I'm afraid."

I nodded. "I know. I'm sorry—"

"I'm in the middle of this campaign. They schedule me fifteen minutes at a time here so I have another meeting shortly."

I stilled as I caught his meaning. If I wasn't a threat, he didn't have time for me. My throat thickened and my eyes burned with unshed tears. *What a waste of time.* The part of me that had held out so much hope for this meeting now flooded with painful regret. I should have known better. This was stupid, foolish. If only Marie hadn't shown me that goddamn photo...

"I understand." I reached for my purse, hoping I didn't appear as hurt as I felt. "It was a pleasure meeting you, in any case. Good luck with the campaign."

I rose to shake his hand and glanced down, avoiding his eyes. I wouldn't give him the satisfaction of knowing how I was hurting. He caught my hand and held it a moment longer.

"Tell Patty I said hello, all right?"

"She's dead." My voice was flat, emotionless. Of course he would assume she was still alive. She'd been taken from me too soon.

He exhaled in a rush, his hand dropping from mine. I caught a shadow of emotion pass over his eyes. He rubbed at his chest, wincing with the motion. "I had no idea."

I nodded. "She passed away when I was twelve. Pancreatic cancer. But she didn't suffer long." My voice was quiet as I spoke the words, steady and objective. As if I were talking about someone I barely knew, I detached myself from the emotions as soon as they threatened to show up. Today was not the day to revisit my grief. I was hanging on by an emotional thread as it was.

"I'm so sorry."

"Thank you. You couldn't have known." *Right?*

I turned to go and he stopped me, placing a powerful hand on my shoulder to still me. "Erica, wait."

My eyebrows shot up and my heart raced from the roller coaster of emotions rushing through me the past few moments.

"My family and I are spending some time on the Cape this weekend. Maybe we could…catch up? Talk through this a bit more."

"Sure," I said quickly. I took a deep breath, feeling a weight lift from my body at the offer. *Did he mean it?*

"Wonderful." His smile met the small one that formed on my lips.

"Mr. Fitzgerald—"

"Please, call me Daniel—I guess." He shrugged nervously. He looked more human, less formidable now than before.

I relaxed, and a seedling of hope grew within me. "Daniel, I'm sorry about this approach. I don't suppose there's ever really a good way to do this."

"Probably not." He turned back to his desk, scribbled an address on a monogrammed notepad, and handed a sheet of paper to me. "Here's the address of the house. Let's plan for dinner on Friday then. You can stay as long as you'd like."

"I look forward to it."

He showed me to the door. "Me too."

I gave him an awkward wave goodbye. We were nowhere close to being on hugging terms.

★ ★ ★

Back at the apartment, wine in hand, I took a long soak in the claw foot tub that stood in the center of my adjoining bathroom. Sure, it was midday, but today was no ordinary day. Today had been possibly the most emotionally intense of my adult life, and it most certainly could have been worse.

The phone rang beside me, shattering through my moment of peace.

"Hello?"

"Erica, it's Max."

"Oh, hi." I pushed myself up in the tub and glanced around for anything I could write on if I needed to.

"Is this a good time?"

"Sure," I lied, embarrassed that I was about to have a business conversation in the tub.

"So good news. The deal is all set. I'm reviewing it for any final edits right now, and we should be ready to sign off tomorrow."

"That's perfect. I can be there in the morning, if that works for you." My nerves would be shot if we scheduled it any later.

"Great. I'm really looking forward to working with you, Erica."

"I can't thank you enough."

"You can actually. Thank me with a return on the investment."

A little pang of fear shot through me. "I'll do my best," I promised.

"Oh, and dinner tonight. I'd like to celebrate with my new business partner."

I smiled, but my excitement was dampened by the very recent memory of my last business dinner going horribly wrong. What were the chances I could get through another one without Blake delivering death threats and choke holds?

"I actually have plans in the evening, but how about a celebratory lunch, my treat?"

"Sounds good. I'll see you tomorrow."

We hung up and I sank back in the warm water of the tub, enlivened by the sudden reality that with these funds, my entire existence was about to change. I'd been lying low for the past few weeks, waiting for this big break. Now, in a matter of hours, we'd be funded and we could begin operating on a much larger scale. I'd have employees, payroll, paperwork, and problems that I couldn't possibly anticipate right now.

The future was uncertain and scary as hell, but a little flutter of excitement grew within me. I'd never felt more ready for the challenge. I sent up a little prayer to the universe that I wouldn't screw it up.

I was very relaxed and a little buzzed when Blake came in.

"Hard day at the office?" He sat on the lip of the tub where my feet were propped up out of the bubbles.

"I need a down day before my life gets busy."

"After tomorrow, I'm sure it will."

"What do you mean?" I asked, hoping against hope that somehow he didn't know about a deal going through his own firm.

"Yes, I know you're finalizing everything with Max tomorrow," he said. "Can we talk about alternatives?"

"No, we can't, Blake, because we've already discussed this and the answer is no." I sounded as resolute as I could.

"You don't even know Max, and you're willing to hand

over ownership of your company to him," he continued. I could tell he was digging in to win this.

Fuck. "That's what I'd be doing with you. What's the difference?"

"I never said I wanted ownership. You could give me common stock, or we could call it a loan. It doesn't really matter to me."

"Exactly."

He rolled his eyes. "That's not what I meant, Erica."

I rose from the tub, wet and covered in bubbles. "Can you hand me my towel?"

"Not until we talk about this." He didn't budge.

He stared at me, his arms folded resolutely across his chest, seeming only slightly distracted by my nakedness. Fortunately, I could live without the towel.

"You need to stop this," I snapped.

"You need to trust me," he said quietly.

Something about the way he said it gave me pause. Why was this suddenly so important to him? What had changed between us over these few weeks that made the possibility of investing with Max so unbearable to him? I would have asked if I thought he'd give me a straight answer. Regardless, nothing he could say would change my mind. I had made my decision. He would know once and for all that I was not his to own and control.

I stepped out onto the tile floor, nearly slipping on the soapy water I'd brought with me from the tub. He moved to help me, but I yanked away from his reach.

"This conversation is over," I said. "You have serious control issues and I recommend you seek therapy to work through them, because clearly I can't help you."

"Okay, I have control issues, and you have serious trust issues, Erica. We could probably both use some therapy."

I glared at him. At least my trust issues were rooted in legitimate experiences. Blake's control issues no doubt came from his success, which, as far as I knew, was hardly traumatic. Beyond that, I'd always hated therapy. His insinuation that I needed it, throwing my words back at me, made me feel small. Flawed.

I gritted my teeth and wrapped a towel around me. "Go to hell."

"Erica, this is who I am. I'm hardwired this way. And if I'm trying to take control over the situation, please understand that I have very solid reasoning for it."

I took a deep breath, determined not to turn this into a bigger disaster. "It's simple, Blake. I need checks and balances in my life. I'm not about to go all in on you, mind, body and business, and then have you ordering me around like your little submissive puppet. It would break me. It would break *us*."

"You've made your decision then?" His calm voice sent an unexpected shiver of fear through me.

"It's final. Deal with it." I retreated to the bedroom to find my comfy sweatpants.

Blake was eerily silent, and when I returned from the closet, he was gone. I sighed with relief until a wave of sadness flooded me, making me weak to the bone. He was gone. I collapsed onto the bed. The line between my loneliness for him and my overwhelming anger blurred as I stared at the ceiling. This was just a fight. Couples had them all the time. We'd work through it.

But what did this mean for our relationship? What if

this was it? The end? How could I go on without him? A little part of me had wanted him to leave, or at least let up on the investment subject. Now that he was gone I couldn't explain the strange emptiness I felt.

I closed my eyes and tried to convince myself that once everything was said and done tomorrow, we could find a way to work through it. I prayed we could.

I tossed and turned all night. I woke in a cold sweat, disoriented when I realized Blake wasn't with me. I ached for him, to have all this upset behind us.

I fantasized about sneaking into his apartment with the key he'd given me, seducing him. Admitting that I loved him. Everything made sense when he was inside me, making love to me, taking us to a place where nothing else mattered. Now nothing made sense. I ran my hands over my misted skin, wishing his hands were on me. If I could just feel him with me, maybe I could know that we weren't through. That he still loved me as much as I loved him, despite his maddening disposition.

I fought the urge to go to him as the night rolled into the dawn. A surge of anger sliced through me, that he could do this to me. He'd possessed me like no one ever had. Exhausted and overwrought, now I was sick with need, literally losing sleep because I couldn't—wouldn't—give him what he wanted.

I wanted to give him what he wanted, but at what price?

The next morning I poked into Sid's room where he slumbered noisily. I didn't bother to whisper knowing he wouldn't rouse easily. "Sid, I need a favor."

He turned over and grumbled, "What?"

"I met with my dad yesterday, and he invited me to his place on the Cape this weekend. I'm not sure if I'm going to stay over, but I was hoping I could borrow your car to get down there?"

He got up, still fully dressed from the previous day. "Here," he said, handing me the keys from his desk. "You don't really know him that well yet. Are you sure this is such a good idea?"

"He's running for public office. I'm pretty sure he's not an axe murderer, Sid. But I appreciate your concern."

He shook his head and fell back onto the futon, disappearing under the blanket.

I threw an overnight bag into the silver Audi and adjusted the seat to accommodate my much smaller frame. Sid lived on next to nothing, but he spared no expense with vehicles. I eased gently out of the space where he was parallel parked. If a knick or ding resulted from my borrowing the car, he'd grieve for weeks.

I found a space close to Max's office. I checked myself in the mirror. Closing the deal wasn't contingent on my presentation anymore, but I wanted to look great for the occasion so I wore a tight white sheath dress, cinched with a thin belt, and nude pumps.

I stepped into the reception area of Angelcom, looking and feeling like the fully-funded CEO I was about to become. The receptionist escorted me into the boardroom where I'd first presented.

I found myself alone in the room again, remembering how Blake had driven me crazy from that first day. I tensed at the thought that what happened today could change us forever.

Max entered the room, and his bright white smile pushed away my doubts.

"Today's the big day!" he said.

A giddy laugh escaped me. Max's enthusiasm was easily contagious. I met him for a polite hug and he kissed me on the cheek again, but I was feeling so jovial I didn't care.

"So where do we begin?" I clapped my hands together, eager to sign something, until I saw the stack of papers he dropped onto the table that rivaled an issue of Italian Vogue. Dozens of multi-colored sticky tabs stuck out from the stack, indicating where signatures were needed. A wave of anxiety seized me. "All of that?" I asked.

"Unfortunately, yes. This is why these things take so damn long to prepare."

"I'm not signing away my first born, am I?" I settled into a chair across from him, worried now that I wouldn't have the time I needed to actually review any of this. What if I found something that could be a deal breaker? What if I had no idea what the hell I was signing?

"I wouldn't put it past him," a voice said from behind me.

I swiveled in my chair as Blake entered the room. Dressed in jeans and a navy V-neck, he looked ruthless despite his casual attire.

"What can I do for you, Landon?" Max's voice was clipped and his lips thinned into a tight line.

"You can give me a moment with Miss Hathaway."

"Certainly. We'll be finished here shortly."

"Now."

"Is there a problem?" Max said through gritted teeth.

"You're the problem."

With that, Max stood. His chair rolled back and hit the glass window with a thud. "Take your time, Erica." He glared at Blake, then left us and shut the door behind him.

My heart beat wildly, a combination of the sheer relief of seeing Blake superseded by a gnawing fear that the deal with Max now hung in the balance. If Blake was going to be this difficult with my affairs, why would Max even want to bother with me now? He'd be signing on for months of irritation.

"What the hell are you doing here?" I snapped.

"I didn't want to do this, but you didn't leave me much choice."

"I told you, I've made my decision. It's basically done."

"Not nearly. You haven't signed anything yet."

"I fully intend to, so I suggest you take your compulsive tendencies and leave us be."

"It's too late for that."

Oh no. I hesitated. A sinking dread crept over me. "Too late for what?"

"I've wired double the funds you need into your business account."

I tried to formulate words, questions that needed to be asked, but instead I stood there, slack-jawed and gaping at his audacity, which true to form, never failed to completely amaze me.

"Don't bother figuring out ways to give it back, because I'll block you from getting investors anywhere else in the city," he continued. "You know I can."

"What if Max still wants to invest?"

"He won't," he said with finality. "No deal goes through here without my authorization, and he won't be getting it."

"Why are you doing this?" My voice quivered. He'd effectively backed me into a corner. I could think of other avenues, but I knew he'd already out-thought them.

"I care about you more than Max ever will, though God knows he'll try to tell you otherwise."

"This isn't about your goddamn pseudo-sibling rivalry with Max. This is my life you're playing with. This is everything I've worked for, and you're ruining it!" I slammed my fists on the table before I stood, facing him.

"This is not nearly close to what you'll achieve. The fact that you think I'd fuck it up for you just shows how completely naïve you are."

I slapped him, hard, the sound slicing through the room the way his words sliced through me. My hand stung with the contact and my breath left me in uneven pants.

Shock registered on his face, but he hesitated only a second before cupping my nape and kissing me, bruising my lips with his. I fisted my hands at my sides. *No.* He wouldn't wear me down. Not this time. I wouldn't let him.

I went to war with myself, fighting how he made me feel as his lips crushed mine, owning me with every plunging kiss. *You're mine.* I heard his voice in my head. A moan escaped me and I realized I was kissing him back, my body responding beyond my control. I trembled with all the love and hate I felt for this man. I hated myself for it. For wanting him the way I did.

He'd worn me down.

He'd won.

CHAPTER NINETEEN

Barely out of the city, I sat in traffic heading south, filled with a rage that had me wanting to go eighty instead of ten, which is where the needle hovered over the speedometer. Hundreds of people were headed to the Cape this Friday afternoon, and while I wasn't exactly in the mood for a family reunion with my newly discovered father, I wanted to be as far away from Blake as I could.

Somehow I'd found the strength to leave Blake in the boardroom. I offered a brief apology to Max but spared him the details, knowing Blake would bring him up to speed. Good riddance to both of them. They could carry on with their inane rivalry until they destroyed each other in a goddamn blaze of glory for all I cared.

Blake hadn't given me any other professional options, but I sure as hell wasn't going to reward him with our relationship. I loved him, madly and with a passion that I would likely never find again, but I wasn't about to be a kept woman. The apartment, and now the business. He'd keep meddling until I was completely under his power, subject to his whims and wants. In the bedroom, I wanted that, I craved it. But in real life, we needed boundaries, and as hard as I tried, I couldn't get him to accept them. My anger bubbled back to the surface and I slammed the steering wheel.

A couple hours later, the traffic finally broke. I wove

through, switching lanes like a speed racer until the GPS directed me to an exit.

I drove the winding back roads toward my destination with a little more care. The shore dotted with mansion after sprawling mansion, each property taking advantage of the beautiful ocean view. Other than a short girls' trip with Alli, I had spent very little time on this prime stretch of the seaside in the eight years since I'd lived in New England.

I pulled into the driveway of a three-story monster of a home next to a Lexus SUV. This was it. I took a few deep breaths and loosened my grip on the steering wheel, trying to purge my anger at Blake from my system. Today was supposed to have been a happy day. Maybe it wasn't too late for that.

I got out and peeked over the fence that separated the driveway from the small yard and the beach below. The house was built on a steep cliff positioned well above its neighbors, offering an impressive view of the sea on three sides.

"Erica!" Daniel's voice rang out from the back door.

He looked different. Casual in khakis and a linen shirt, he smiled when I approached.

"I'm glad you came." He wrapped me in a friendly hug.

The gesture took me by surprise, but I welcomed it. "Me too," I said. Muffled by his shoulder, I hugged him back tightly, wishing I didn't feel so raw right now. If I wasn't careful, I'd be crying at the drop of a hat. He wouldn't think I was after his money, but he'd know I was a complete basket case.

"Come in, I want you to meet Margo."

I nodded, and he took my bag and set it in the enclosed

entryway. We entered an expansive great room where a dining room with weathered whitewashed furniture flowed into a living room. Oversized couches covered in white canvas slip covers and faded blue throw pillows—everything about the home screamed quintessential seaside.

He led me into the kitchen where a tall woman with dark auburn hair busied herself tossing a salad. "Erica, this is Margo."

Margo removed her apron and came toward me with arms outstretched. She was a lithe figure, with freckles sprinkling her tanned skin. Heavy pearl studs hung from her ears, matching the simple string of pearls around her neck. Despite her height, she felt frail in my arms. When she stepped back, I was instantly grateful for my wardrobe choice.

"Aren't you a vision? It's wonderful to meet you, dear. Are you hungry?"

I hadn't thought of eating all day. My nerves had gotten the best of me this morning, and since the meeting, eating had been the last thing on my mind. "I'm famished actually."

"Give me a few more minutes and we'll be ready to eat. Honey, you can put the fish on now." She motioned Daniel to the refrigerator.

He nodded and left my side to retrieve a tray. "Want a beer?"

"Um, sure," I said, though I'd be drunk in a flash unless I got something in my stomach soon. If I got to the bottom of this bottle, they'd know more about me than they probably wanted to. Daniel grabbed two bottles with his free hand and signaled me to follow him.

We stepped out onto the deck, and while he focused

on the grill, I took in the scenery. I'd spent the entire trip fuming about Blake instead of thinking about things Daniel and I could talk about to get to know one another better. I really wanted him to know me, to *want* to know me.

I looked over the horizon and at the calm ocean before us. In the distance, a smattering of black blobs moved along the rocks at the foot of the cliff.

"What are those?" I asked.

Daniel looked up to where I'd pointed. "Seals. They hang out there all day. Loud beasts, they are. They're the first thing we hear in the morning."

I laughed a little at the thought of seals being a rooster of sorts in these parts. "You have a beautiful home."

"Thank you. We love it here. It's a great getaway."

He closed the cover of the grill and joined me at the railing, which separated us from the steep drop off only a few feet away. A tiny collapsible ladder led from the edge of the property down to the beach. The cliffs were beautiful but dangerous, especially if anyone were to get stuck on the beach during high tide.

Daniel interrupted my idle thoughts. "So I Googled you, but I have to admit I'm a little lost about what you do. What's Clozpin?"

I smiled, warmed that he'd made the effort. The little hope I'd felt before fluttered to life. "It's a social network startup, focused on fashion. It helps people find outfits and connect with labels and designers, that sort of thing."

"So you built this while you were still in school?"

"With a couple of my friends. Since I graduated, I've been working to get angel funding, which..." I paused, questioning the words as I said them. "We got our funding today, so hopefully there are some big things to come."

"That's fantastic, Erica." He smiled and tipped his beer toward me.

"How about you? Have you always wanted to be in politics?" I asked.

His nose wrinkled as he stared out into the darkening horizon of the ocean. "In a fashion, yes. My family's been involved in local politics for a few generations, so I suppose going into it has been an inevitable progression of my career."

"Are you feeling positive about the governor's race?"

"Definitely. We have some powerful endorsements, and I think we're running a pretty good campaign. The social media component, though I know next to nothing about the details of it, seems to be garnering results as well. You could probably tell me a thing or two about it."

I nodded and laughed. No doubt we spoke two very different professional languages.

"About the campaign..." He hesitated, as if contemplating what he were about to say. "This will sound awkward, but it's something I have to ask you." He rubbed the fine stubble on his chin. "As I said, you know, meeting you was unexpected. A happy surprise, of course."

"Of course," I agreed.

"I have a lot riding on this campaign, Erica, and I don't know how to say this without sounding completely, I don't know, horrible, I guess."

"You'd rather I not come out publicly as your illegitimate daughter." I blurted it out. Knowing politicians, he could have danced around the subject for several more minutes before he got to the point.

His face softened and a flicker of guilt passed over his features, but I understood where he was coming from. The last thing I wanted to be was a burden or a source of stress for him.

"It's not a problem, really," I said. "I just wanted the chance to get to know you, which I hope can still happen. But I have my own business and my own PR to work on. The last thing I want to do is complicate what you've built here. Honestly I have nothing to gain with your political affiliations."

He nodded and took a long swig from his beer. "I suppose that makes sense. Obviously we know what we know, and I suppose that's the most important thing, right?"

I nodded and ran my hand along the railing, contemplating a question I had been meaning to ask.

"Maybe it was my age, being so young when she passed. But I always wondered why my mother never spoke of you."

He straightened and a frown marred his brow. "We had a complicated relationship. At least, we did when we found out she was pregnant. Neither of our families were going to be happy about the news."

"I can see that." My mother's family had always been distant too. With Daniel's background, I imagined circumstances wouldn't have been much different. A blue blood family like his wouldn't have reacted well to him knocking up a girl out of wedlock, no matter where she'd come from.

"After she went back to Chicago, I assumed she was going to take care of it. I didn't hear from her, and I didn't want to reach out and raise suspicions with her family."

"So you never spoke after graduation?"

He shook his head and stared out at the ocean, as if the answers for how life had changed for him were out there somewhere, just out of sight.

A car door slammed and I looked over, catching a glimpse of a head of brown curly hair that passed the fence and entered the house.

"That would be my stepson. Just about your age too, actually."

Daniel gestured for our return to the house and I braced myself for another introduction.

Margo was setting the table with salad and a steaming bowl of rice. The aroma from the food mingled in the air, and I couldn't wait to stop talking and start eating. The young man came through the door and walked toward her, but he stopped short when he saw me.

Everything stopped moving. The room turned cold and silent. I heard my heart beat, a deafening uneven thud, pulsing an icy pain through my veins, chilling me to the bone. In a room with others, I was alone. Alone with my memories and the shame of what he'd left me with. A sick repulsion twisted through me as I tried to comprehend the horrible nightmare standing in front of me.

I gripped Daniel's arm, uncertain if my legs would hold me. I looked up at him, as if somehow he could know. He only stared back at me and gestured to their new guest.

"Erica, this is my stepson, Mark."

Mark.

After four years, I finally knew his name.

★ ★ ★

I excused myself immediately, finding the nearest bathroom. I locked the door behind me, struggling with the effort while my hands shook uncontrollably. I splashed water on my face and looked into the mirror for help. I was as pale as a ghost. Nausea hit me in relentless waves, and I fought the urge to heave, to purge his poisonous memory from my body.

I needed to get back in control. And I needed a game plan. My phone was in my purse. It was still in the living room.

But who would I call? Beyond that, what would I say? *The man who raped me in college is my fucking stepbrother.* Hell, how was I going to get through this? I could barely look at the man without having a full-blown nervous breakdown. Now I needed to sit through a dinner with him, as if none of that history existed, an entire chapter of my life blurred out.

This was a personal emergency, but not an actual emergency, I told myself. We'd get through dinner and I'd find a reason to leave. I'd have to figure out how to deal with Daniel later, though the prospect of building a relationship with him seemed completely impossible now. I dried my face and tried to pull myself together before stepping out into the hallway. I could do this.

I stepped out and the second I shut the door behind me, Mark was there.

"Everything all right?" he murmured.

His eyes were dark, almost black as he stalked closer. I stepped back, pressing my palms against the wall behind me. Panic shot through me. Every nerve stood on edge, ready to fight.

"Stay away from me." My voice was small, betraying the

fear that threatened to take me over. I was a puddle of fucking anxiety, not the fierce intimidating woman I needed to be to scare him off.

"Or what?" He came close enough for me to feel his breath. "This is perfect, really. I've always wanted a sister."

He ran a finger from my knee to the hem of my dress lifting it a fraction. Every cell in my body came alive and adrenaline coursed through me like a lightning bolt. God help me, I wouldn't be his victim again. I pushed him off with every ounce of my strength, shoving him into the opposite wall of the hallway.

"Don't ever fucking touch me again. Do you hear me?"

An amused grin appeared on his face. I hurried to the dining room, no less flustered than when I'd left. *This is the part where Daniel will think I'm a basket case.*

"Erica, are you sure you're okay?" Daniel asked as I took a seat beside him.

"I'm sorry, I haven't eaten all day. I'm not feeling so well."

"Oh no, sweetheart, please eat!" Margo assembled a plate for me with all of the wonderful things I'd smelled earlier.

Mark joined us, sitting across from me with the same smug smile on his face, looking undeterred. I stabbed some lettuce with my fork and forced the food into my mouth. My body was in panic mode, my appetite completely gone now.

"Mark, Erica runs her own Internet company. Isn't that impressive?" Daniel said.

He regurgitated the details from our earlier conversation for Margo and Mark's benefit, though I cringed knowing that he was simultaneously revealing critical details that

Mark might use to reach out to me again. With his identity revealed, my own anonymity—maybe the only thing that had kept me safe from him—was gone.

"And what do you do, Mark?" I asked. Two could play this game, though I couldn't imagine wanting to seek him out for anything other than putting a hit on him.

"I work at the firm with Daniel."

"Of course," I said, smiling politely. How lucky for him, to rape and pillage his college years away and subsequently walk into a prime position at one of the largest firms in the city. Somehow I hated him more than I already did.

"What part of the city do you live in?" he asked.

I stared at my plate, popping a bite of lightly seasoned haddock in my mouth while I weighed a sampling of false answers I could give him.

Just then the doorbell rang, chiming through the house. I startled at the sound, nearly jumping out of my chair.

"I'll get it, darling," Margo said as Daniel moved to get up. She rose with economical grace and disappeared into the entryway that shielded my view of the door.

"You two should get together sometime," Daniel suggested.

I fought the urge to roll my eyes. He was quick to divert my attention to Mark, I thought. I kept filling my mouth to keep words from spilling out and silently planned my escape. They'd want me to stay longer, I suspected, but I needed to get back home. Someplace safe.

Home. Yes, I finally had a home, and there was no place I'd rather be.

I closed my eyes against a vision of Blake. I'd give anything to be with Blake now, but I couldn't go running to him every time I felt vulnerable. Maybe I could stay with Marie.

"Erica," Margo's sing-songy voice floated through the air. "You have a guest. He's at the door waiting for you."

My head shot up. Only one person could find me here.

Blake stood in the doorway, looking casual and perfect as usual.

I tried to conjure the anger I'd felt earlier. All I could feel was relief, gratitude, love. I fought the urge to run into his arms and let him take me away from this horrible situation. "Blake..."

He stepped into the house and pulled me into his arms, holding me so tight it was almost painful. I buried my face in his neck, breathing him in. My body relaxed. Everything would be all right now that he was here. I was safe.

"Is he here?" He cupped my face and searched my eyes.

"Who?"

"Mark."

"Yes. Wait, how did you know?"

"Forget about that, let's get you out of here." He grabbed my hand and turned to leave.

"No, I can't." I pulled him back, keeping his hand tight in my own.

"Erica, I'm getting you away from here. We're leaving now."

"Wait, I just need to say goodbye. To Daniel."

He frowned.

"He's my father, Blake. We're trying to get to know each other. I don't want to throw this all away." We'd never have anything close to a normal father-daughter connection, but I'd only just found him. I couldn't lose him again now, so soon.

"Fine," he relented. "Introduce us and we'll leave."

"Be good," I said gently, before guiding him into the main room where the family of three waited for our return.

As soon as we entered, his gaze darted to Mark. His posture changed and the tension seemed to radiate off of him. I tightened my hold on his hand slightly, reminding him not to go postal.

"Daniel, Margo, Mark… This is Blake." I tucked my hair nervously. How ironic that I was introducing my lover to my only living parent days after our first meeting. And of all the emotions rushing through me now, I still felt an inkling of anticipation hoping Daniel would approve. He'd seemed to take pride in my achievements earlier. Certainly he'd approve of Blake.

"Blake Landon. You're with Angelcom, right?" Daniel rose and shook Blake's hand.

"Correct. I believe you negotiate many of our term sheets for us," Blake said.

"Right. It's a small world, isn't it?" He paused, his gaze traveling between us and then down at Blake's fingers interlaced with mine. His face fell. He looked back to me, as if a terrible thought had gripped him in that moment.

He knew that Blake knew. For all Daniel's careful composure, I could read his face like a book. Our embarrassing little secret was spreading in circles he wasn't anticipating.

Margo jumped up and gave Blake a kiss on the cheek. "Blake, let me go get you a plate. Please, sit down and join us."

"Actually, there's a situation that came up with the deal

we've been working on. Unfortunately, it's imperative that I head back so we can resolve it. But thank you so much for your hospitality."

"Oh." Margo pouted a little. I could tell she was looking forward to getting to know Blake.

I gave Daniel, and then Margo, a quick kiss on the cheek and waved goodbye. Blake grabbed my bag on the way out.

Blake held out his hand to me and nodded to the Tesla. "Let's go."

I stared at him, the details of our morning returning to me. "Blake, I'm not going home with you."

"No, you're not. We're going to go somewhere so we can talk, and if you still want to go home, or wherever, you can."

"Where are we going?"

He didn't answer.

CHAPTER TWENTY

"I'm really not in the mood to be stuck on an island with you right now, Blake."

We were at the ferry station and Blake was begging me not to leave. He'd locked the doors and driven us onto the big boat, and now he was doing everything in his power to keep me there.

"I promise, we can turn around and take the next ferry back if you don't like what I have to say."

"You're being insane right now, you know that? This is like kidnapping."

"Promise me you won't get off."

I groaned. "I promise, now let me out."

He released the locks, and I walked up the ramp to the upper level of the ferry where we'd spend the rest of the ride to Martha's Vineyard. If Blake thought he could romance his way out of the doghouse, he was dead wrong.

I walked through to the front of the boat, stepping out onto the deck. I picked a table for two near the end, knowing Blake was on my heels. I sat, and he joined me a second later. I finally met his stare. His eyes glittered from the setting sun reflecting against the water. God help me, he was as beautiful as he was maddening. We sat in silence for a few moments while a few of the other tables filled around us.

"Are you going to tell me how you found me? You don't have a tracking device planted in my stuff do you?" If I was going to be subjected to this odyssey, he needed to start filling in the gaps quickly.

"Sid told me you were going to visit with your father."

"You asked, and he just told you?" I sincerely hoped Blake hadn't terrorized Sid the way he had a habit of doing with almost everyone else I came into contact with lately.

"Actually, yes. He wasn't wild about you staying with a complete stranger either."

"Fine. What about Mark? How did you know he'd be there?"

"I dug up every possible affiliation he had when I tracked down his identity. His step-father and employer were notable. When I found out where you were staying, I figured there was a good chance Mark would be there too."

Of course he would. He'd known Mark's identity for a couple weeks now, so heaven knows what else he'd cooked up. If he'd meddled at all though, Mark didn't seem the wiser.

"And you managed to track down his house on the Cape."

"Erica, don't insult me, please." He drummed his fingers on the table.

"How did you learn how to do all this?"

"What do you mean?"

"You're a hacker. It seems like a strange descriptor for someone with as much money and resources as you have, but clearly you still do it."

He flashed me a wicked smile. "I only use my powers for good."

"Has that always been the case?"

His smile slipped. "Listen, let's talk about the deal with Max. I need to explain some things."

"We'll get there. Tell me how you became a hacker."

He rolled his eyes. "Countless hours on the computer and a propensity for math. Satisfied?"

"Listen, if you're not going to be honest with me, I don't need to be here." I stood to leave.

He caught my hand. "Please, don't leave."

The look he gave me made my chest ache, but I was determined to hold my ground.

I sat back down. "Talk."

He sighed. "I was a bored antisocial adolescent. I begrudged society. Hacking became a creative outlet, gave me options, made life seem a little less insignificant."

I tried to imagine the beautiful man in front of me as an angry teenager, shaking his fists at the world for whatever reason. "How had society wronged you so horribly? Weren't your parents teachers?"

"Yes, and they were grossly underpaid. Anyway, they had nothing to do with me being that way, trust me. They tried like hell to get me out of the house, to be normal, I guess. I think I was just too ... intellectual, maybe, for my own good. The news, politics, the economy. Basically everything that's still wrong with the world today felt overwhelmingly wrong to me at that age. I had a hard time justifying living a normal, happy life and sticking my head in the sand while atrocities were happening everywhere."

"So you thought you could save the world from your computer."

"Not really. I don't know ..."

"How did you end up working with Max's father?"

He blew out a slow breath. I glanced over my shoulder.

They were just beginning to untie the ropes from the dock. I still had time.

"Now or never, Blake."

"Fuck, fine." He leaned in on the table, lowering his voice so only I could hear him. "I hooked up with a hacker group called M89. A handful of other pissed off kids like me. We came up with a plan to deplete the bank accounts of some top executives on Wall Street."

"Why?"

"They were getting rich off some Ponzi scheme and trying to take down the whistle blowers who threatened to expose them."

"So what happened?"

"We got caught," he said. "I narrowly avoided jail time, and in the process somehow I caught Michael's attention. He took me under his wing, figured out how to get through to me. I guess it took a hard-nosed capitalist to paint a view of the world that made sense."

Wow. Blake was so measured, so in control of every area of his life now. To think of him being so reckless frightened me. How we'd both made our way to this point in our lives could not have been more different.

"We both wanted to do something big, so I pulled all-nighters to graduate with honors and you hacked people's bank accounts."

"And here we are, together." He pressed his lips to my knuckles, barely grazing them with his tongue.

My belly quickened, but I forced myself to focus on the matter at hand. "How did you avoid jail for what you did?"

He leaned back, his lips lifting mischievously.

"What?"

"Time's up."

I turned in my seat and saw that we were already several feet away from the dock, fully on our way.

About an hour later, Blake drove us across the island, out of one neighborhood into the next until we sped past a barren landscape where the houses were sparse. I gripped the seat, certain we'd be pulled over at any moment, which would have been the perfect finish to this unbelievable day. Then again, the island probably only had a handful of cops, and we seemed to be getting farther away from civilization, if that were even possible.

We pulled up to a large single family home, distinguishable from any of the other cedar-shingled homes only by its sheer size and that it appeared to be the last home on this point of the island. We stepped onto the wraparound porch, and instead of taking us inside, Blake led me around and down to the beach. We passed through the dunes to where two whitewashed Adirondack chairs were perched on the sandy beach facing the soft waves of the ocean.

I kicked off my shoes and sat in one of them. After a mostly sleepless night and everything that had gone down today, I could barely hold myself up. Blake pulled out a bottle of chilled white wine from a bucket of ice nestled in the sand.

"How do you plan these things, Blake, honestly?"

He smirked. "Don't think I'm telling you all my secrets tonight."

"I could make you," I threatened. I had an increasingly keen sense of his weaknesses lately.

His eyes darkened. "That's a tempting thought," he said, missing the glass he was pouring into.

He corrected his aim and handed me the glass. I took a welcome taste of the cool, fruity liquid.

"Don't be so sure. I'm still angry with you. Like, super, extremely angry."

"The proverbial doghouse?"

"The literal doghouse, and that doesn't even begin to capture how much making up you have to do."

"I like making up. Where shall I start?"

He settled at my feet, tracing tiny circles over my knee and up my thigh, pressing warm, soft kisses in their wake. I tried in vain to suppress the physical reaction that his touch elicited.

"You can't fix this with sex," I said, and damn it, I meant it.

"No? Tell me then. How can I fix this?" He kept up his feather-light touches.

"I honestly don't know. I thought you had a plan for that when I agreed to come out here with you." I wasn't going to make this easy for him. I was beyond drained, but I had just enough fire left to make this point.

He slowed his caresses and settled back on his knees. "I love you, Erica."

Shit, I thought. He had to lead with that? I swallowed back tears. "That doesn't change what you did to me today."

"I know it probably doesn't mean much, but I didn't want to. You didn't leave me many options."

"Well that's not enough of a reason," I said, staring past him.

"Taking on investors is like getting into bed with

someone, Erica. It doesn't always work, and to be honest, you're not really the type for this kind of partnership. I completely understand how you feel about the business. One of the reasons why I didn't bid right away is because you're strong-willed as hell. I knew working with you wouldn't be easy, and you'd fight me every step of the way. I didn't fully appreciate the consequences of you working with Max until recently, and I couldn't bear losing you to him."

"He doesn't want me that way," I insisted, only half believing it. Max, like so many others, didn't entirely respect my personal space, but he hadn't made any overt comments leading me to believe that he wanted me sexually. Even if he did, I could hold my own.

"He does, trust me. Whether or not you want to believe it, he'd stop at nothing to have you if it meant getting back at me. After seeing what you went through with Isaac, I couldn't take that risk again."

I shook my head. Isaac had caught me off guard, but if Blake had given me a minute longer, I could have gotten him to back off without help.

"I can't say exactly how or when Max would make his play, but I can promise you he would have. He'd make you do things you'd never do just to keep the business, knowing how much it meant to you, knowing how much you mean to me."

"How can you know that?"

"Jesus, Erica, I'd walk through fire to make sure you were safe. Can you just believe me, that I could see this coming, that I wouldn't let anything happen to you?"

I closed my eyes. The waves crashed on the beach, and a soft breeze blew over us. I sensed Blake, his magnetic pull willing me closer to him. He was the only man I'd ever loved, and here he was, professing his love for me, promising to protect me from harm, almost too chivalric to be taken seriously, but when I opened my eyes and looked into his, there was no doubt about his intentions.

Everything had become too much. My eyes misted, but I refused to surrender. I wrapped my arms across my chest, holding myself together.

"You're killing me, Blake."

"Do you know how many women have pitched me in that boardroom?" he asked.

"How many?"

"One."

The word lingered in the air, an unbelievable truth that pronounced how perilous my position in this industry could be. If that was true, coming this far was nothing short of a miracle. It also explained why their receptionist looked at me like I had three heads every time I showed up for a meeting.

"Wow." I shook my head.

"Max and I both wanted you that day, for different reasons. I wasn't about to let you go without a fight."

Even with the risks that came with working with Blake, my business was probably safer than it had ever been. Now we just had to figure out how to work together without driving each other completely crazy.

"So now what?" I said, hoping he had some insights.

"Whatever you want, as long as it doesn't involve Max. Or Isaac."

"So we're partners."

He nodded.

"I'm in charge, Blake. You start telling me how to run my business, and we're finished." I meant it. I wouldn't relent on this point, and fortunately he wasn't in much of a position to argue since he had funded the project with no legal claim to it.

He rose on his knees and took my glass from me, sinking his and mine into the sand beside us. "You're the boss, baby."

He tugged me down on the chair, bunching up my dress and pressing hot kisses up my inner thigh. He removed my panties with expert ease and covered my pussy with his mouth.

"Oh, God." I gripped the chair at the sensation.

He parted me with his fingers and his velvet tongue followed. The dueling pressures had me clenching uncontrollably. He slid his slender finger into me and sucked hard, flicking his tongue just so. My head fell back. *Yes.*

I arched, pressing into his mouth, and he delivered the final blow, stretching me with a second finger. His teeth grazed my clit, taunting me with perfect amount of restraint and just enough pressure to push me over the edge.

"Blake..." I cried out into the dusky air and fought to catch my breath. The breeze cooled my skin, washing over the fine mist of sweat that covered me, but Blake kept on. I came again and again, clenching against his fingers until I was boneless and out of my mind with the hunger to have his cock pounding inside me.

I whimpered his name and begged him to stop, unsure how much more I could take.

He stood, and my lips parted when I recognized the hard outline of his jeans. He pulled me up and into his embrace.

"Let's go in," he whispered before I could start undressing him on the spot.

I tasted myself on his kiss, his erection pressed into my belly. Always too much and yet never enough, the fierceness of my craving for him still took my breath away.

I followed Blake into the house and he led us to the bedroom, an enormous room with vaulted ceilings and whitewashed walls. The house put the Fitzgerald summer home to shame in size and elegance. They were old money, but the reality was that Blake could probably buy and sell Daniel.

The bed, covered with a fluffy white down comforter, was the centerpiece of the room, and became my sole focus as I counted the seconds until we could be naked on it. Blake unzipped my dress slowly, taking his time and taunting me with light touches. I slipped out of my dress and walked to the bed. I climbed up and sat on my knees, waiting patiently as Blake stripped down. He crawled onto the bed with the lithe grace of a predator stalking his prey, and I was in just the mood to be hunted.

He shifted me until I was under him, spread around his legs as they parted me. Taking my breast into his mouth with a hard suck, he teased the tip with his tongue. I arched into him and hooked my leg around his in a feeble attempt to urge him closer. He didn't move an inch.

"You are a squirmy little thing," he teased, trailing his hands along my inner thigh, inches from where I throbbed and craved his touch so much more.

"Touch me, please, Blake."

His lips curled up. "Put your arms up."

Eager to please if it meant he'd stop taunting me, I obeyed. He stretched them higher and unclasped one of my bracelets, hooking it onto my other wrist and linking them together, creating a rather expensive pair of handcuffs.

"Blake, no, you'll break them."

"Not if you don't move."

"How am I supposed to do that? You're driving me crazy." Controlling myself when he held me was one thing, but I had no idea how I was going to behave myself without any help.

"Self control," he said simply. "Hold on here."

He guided my hands to the headboard. I swallowed hard and circled my fingers around the metal rails, my mind hyper aware of every sensation stirring through my body and the physical reactions that I now had to keep in check so as not to ruin Blake's beautiful gift. He was barely touching me as it was, and I was already writhing with anticipation.

He started low, nipping at the tip of my toe. A jolt of desire arrowed right to my sex. Jesus, he knew every trick in the book. I tightened, knowing he was miles from being there at this rate. He trailed wet kisses up my thigh, over my stomach, diving into the cleft of my belly button with his tongue. He languished over my breasts and my collarbone, blowing warm breaths onto my neck that gave me goose-flesh in a very good way.

"How do you feel?" He grazed my lips with his, a knowing smile lifting them slightly.

Every nerve stood at attention, every cell in my body lurched toward his, as far as these constraints would allow. "Alive," I whispered, holding on by a mere thread.

"Good."

He held his cock, lubricating me with my own moisture, sliding between my folds. I tightened my hold on the headboard at the friction over my clit. Then he was inside me in one swift motion. I cried out, fisting my hands around the rail, not wanting to struggle against the metal of my bonds.

His lips were on mine then, kissing me frantically. I moaned into his mouth as he drove into me again and again, with a depth that had me spasming around him uncontrollably. I could barely breathe in anticipation of the promised release. I dug my heels into his thighs, urging him deeper.

My emotions were raw and I was desperate for him. Blake reached up and replaced the second bracelet to its rightful place. Freed from my restraints, I fisted my hands in his hair and kissed him hard. I needed more, the rest of him. Whether he knew it or not, I wasn't about to let him go.

I met his dark gaze. "I love you," I whispered. I needed him to know, after everything we'd been through.

He pulled away a fraction, his expression almost pained, as if those three little words cut him to the core.

"Make love to me. Please, Blake, I don't want to feel anything else but you right now."

And for the rest of the night, he did. He loved me with every masterful thrust, reminding me that our bodies were made for this and for each other. We were wasted, physically and emotionally, but Blake never tired. When we slowed, my lazy caresses turned into hungry demands, and he took me again, each time no less earth shattering than the last, until we'd both collapsed in each other's arms.

★ ★ ★

I woke in the morning to the sound of the ocean. Seagulls sailed through the air just beyond our bedroom window. I crept out of bed quietly to let Blake sleep.

Dressed in his T-shirt, I let his scent wash over me. I padded through the house and helped myself to a banana from the bowl of fruit in the kitchen. I took out my laptop and set up at the dining room table overlooking the water. I started an email to Professor Quinlan, addressing him as such. No matter how much time went by, I'd probably never be able to call him Brendan.

I struggled for the right words to describe the current situation. He knew Max's history better than most, but I hoped this turn of events wouldn't reflect poorly on the professor. I felt compelled to bring him up to speed in case it would. I drafted the message and reread it, feeling overwhelmed anew by the breakneck pace my life had taken over the past forty-eight hours.

And I'd thought college was stressful.

I hit send and clicked around a few sites, landing on Clozpin. The browser's loading graphic spun indefinitely. The site was down again.

Shit. I called Sid. No answer. I called again and he didn't pick up. I hurried back into the bedroom, hating to wake Blake, but I couldn't shake the worry.

I sidled up next to him, draped my leg over his, and peppered him with tiny soft kisses. If I was going to wake him up, at least I'd do it pleasantly. He finally stirred, rousing with a smile and a fantastic case of morning wood. As tempting as that was, I needed him for something else right now.

"Baby, the site's down again. I can't get hold of Sid."

He got up, slipped on his jeans, and followed me out to the dining room. He glanced at my screen and fished out his own laptop from his overnight bag, settled on the couch, and powered on.

"Coffee?" I asked.

"Please."

Already he looked incredibly focused, though barely awake, his hair an adorable mess. I figured out the coffee, and while I waited for it to brew, I refreshed the site again. This time it came up instantly, with a large singular logo overlaying the site beneath it. The logo text read clear. *M89*.

Blake was typing furiously. I didn't dare ask, but I had a sinking feeling that being targeted wasn't random anymore. I filled a mug and took it to him. He took it wordlessly, working as if I wasn't there. I stared patiently, waiting for him to come back to me.

"Can you tell me what's going on? For real this time?" I said, my voice quiet.

He looked up at me with tired eyes.

"The photo of us at the conference. It went viral. You probably saw a spike in traffic. Most of that was legit, but they took notice."

"They?"

He hesitated.

"So this isn't random."

"Not anymore," he said, his eyes dark with regret.

"Why are they after you, Blake?"

He shook his head and raked his hands through his hair. "I'm sorry, Erica, but I'm going to fix this. I promise."

I nodded, trusting he would.

BLAKE AND ERICA'S STORY CONTINUES
IN THE HACKER SERIES SEQUEL

HARDPRESSED

HERE'S A SNEAK PEEK...

CHAPTER ONE

"I can't believe I'm doing this again," I said.

Blake slid his arm around my shoulders. He pulled me close and I relaxed into his familiar warmth. We stepped out of his office building and headed a few blocks down the street. He leaned down and gave me a reassuring kiss on the cheek.

"No funny business this time, I promise."

I laughed and rolled my eyes. "Very reassuring."

I almost believed him. The past few weeks had been intense, but something had changed between us. I could joke, but he had my trust now. After all my fervent protests and desperate attempts to fight the way I felt about him, I'd finally let him in. At least more than I'd ever let anyone else in, and nothing had ever felt more right.

He flashed me a mischievous smile. "Don't worry. There was no way I could get Fiona to pull a stunt like that again."

Dressed in white capris and a navy chiffon shell, Blake's sister, Fiona, waited ahead of us near the entryway of a quaint café. We stopped directly in front of the entrance. The engraved sign above read *Mocha*. A young patron swung the door open and the deep aroma of freshly ground coffee and chocolate wafted out, setting off happy signals all over my body. I'd nearly forgotten about our original mission when

Fiona motioned us toward an unmarked door next to the café.

"We're upstairs." She ushered us up a narrow staircase to the second floor.

"Who owns the building, Fiona?" I tried to make it sound like small talk, but who was I kidding? The fact that we were a few short strides from a steady caffeine source was already a major selling point, but Fiona knew my position on renting from Blake or any of his subsidiaries. I trusted Blake, but that didn't mean he wasn't still committed to becoming intricately involved in my business dealings at every possible opportunity.

Blake had plenty of his own contradictions. He could be sweet and heart-wrenchingly tender one moment and be driving me into a fiery rage with his compulsive controlling tendencies the next. He could micro-manage the hell out of my growing business during the day and fuck me straight out of my mind the second we walked through the door every night. Granted, sometimes I needed both, but I still wasn't sure how I felt about all this dominance in my life. Letting him in scared me, but I was learning to be more open to it, to trust him as much as I could.

Today, a part of me, the part of me that needed separation and independence from Blake, wanted to make absolutely sure he wasn't pulling a fast one on me again.

"I can assure you that Blake has no ownership stake in the property," Fiona reassured me.

That was all well and good, but not so long ago she'd sold me on a beautifully updated apartment within the same Comm Ave brownstone that Blake not only owned, but also lived in. The tenuous line between our personal lives and businesses was already too blurred. I was holding firm on this one.

"I'm glad to hear it."

Fiona dug into her purse. Despite my misgivings, my anticipation grew. She unlocked the door and we filed into the space. The long room was small, at least compared to Blake's. Though musty and in dire need of a cleaning crew, the space held promise. Behind me Blake sighed.

"Fiona, seriously. This is the best you could do?"

She shot him an annoyed look.

"We—Erica and I—discussed her budget, and for the location and size, this is a fair option. Obviously the space could use some TLC, but you have to admit it has potential."

I took a long look around, envisioning the many possibilities. I had been so busy keeping things running out of my apartment, all while hiring, that I hadn't had a chance to get excited about this move. But this would be fun.

"I love the wood floors."

"They're filthy." Blake scuffed the sole of his shoe on the floor, drawing a faint line through the dust.

"Have a little vision, Blake. We just need to clean it up, and with a few enhancements, this could definitely have a cool design studio feel."

"Exactly. Exposed brick never goes out," Fiona added.

"Pretty old." Blake wrinkled his nose.

I laughed and slapped him on the shoulder. "Show me a building in Boston that isn't old."

The space was a far cry from the Landon Group's

renovated modern offices, but I had modest and realistic expectations. The current state of the space left much to be desired, but with some elbow grease and a few additions, we could make this work.

We stopped in front of the large windows facing the street. A flutter of excitement coursed through me. Giving the business its own address would be a major milestone and make everything we'd accomplished so far seem much more real.

I turned to gauge Fiona's reaction. "I think I like it. What do you think?"

Fiona pursed her lips and looked around. "The price is fair and the lease term gives you options for growth. All things considered, I would say this is a safe bet. Can you see yourself here?"

"I can." I smiled, having renewed faith in Fiona's brokering skills. At the end of the day, we needed a comfortable, affordable working space for the new team members of Clozpin, the fashion social network I'd spent the past year growing.

"Let me make some calls and see if I can get the price down for you. Because Blake's right, this place is kind of dirty. Plus, if you plan on fixing it up, that gives us a bargaining chip." Fiona pulled out her phone and exited toward the hallway, leaving us alone again.

"You didn't ask me what I think." Blake gave me a crooked grin.

"That's because I already know what you think."

"I could give you twice the square footage and you wouldn't even need to leave the building to come visit me.

Plus you'd get the girlfriend rate, which I think you'll find is unmatched in this part of town."

Blake's uninvited assistance in all matters was a lost cause. Sure, he was controlling, compulsive, and persistent as all hell, but he was ultimately a fixer. When the people he cared about ran into problems or wanted for anything, he came to the rescue, sparing no expense in the process.

"I appreciate the offer. I really do. But you can't put a price on independence, Blake." We'd had this conversation before, and I was standing my ground. He needed to trust me to make things work on my own. This trust thing went both ways.

"You can be independent. We'll put it all in writing."

"In my experience, putting it in writing only commits me to being dependent on your ample resources for a minimum length of time." Blake already had me bound to a year-long lease with my apartment, though he'd yet to cash any of my rent checks.

"Call it rent control. You could lock in the girlfriend rate for, say, a twenty-year lease, and then we could negotiate from there." He encircled me in his arms, pressing me firmly against his chest, his lips inches from mine.

My heart pounded. This went beyond our usual banter of trying to outwit each other. We had only been together a matter of weeks and he was already thinking about the long-term? My lips parted slightly as I struggled to take a full breath. Blake's words and his proximity made my world spin, time and again. No one had ever affected me like this, and I was gradually learning to enjoy the roller coaster.

"Nice try," I whispered.

He growled and closed his mouth over mine. He claimed me with gentle urgency, teasing me with tiny licks of his tongue.

"You drive me crazy, Erica."

"Oh?" I breathed, trying not to moan as the air left me.

"Yes, in every conceivable way. Let's get out of here. Fiona can wrap up the paperwork if you're intent on renting this dump."

He grabbed my hips and sandwiched me between his rock hard body and the wall behind me. I didn't know what it was about him pinning me to hard surfaces, but I fucking loved it. I slid my hands through his hair and kissed him back helplessly, so easily forgetting myself in his embrace. What time was it? Where did I need to be later? I mentally ran through every possible obstacle between me and being naked with Blake. His thigh found the space between my legs, exerting the perfect amount of pressure so the crease of my jeans rubbed me through my panties.

"Oh, God."

"I swear, if there was a clean surface in this place, I'd fuck you on it right now."

I giggled. "You're bad."

His eyes went dark. "You have no idea."

"Ahem."

Fiona leaned into the doorway, wide-eyed.

Blake stepped back abruptly, leaving me dizzy and momentarily confused. For the first time ever, I witnessed him flush as he ran his fingers through his hair, seemingly embarrassed at having been caught making out in front of his little sister.

"If you two are finished, I got the price down another

couple hundred. Can we make a decision on this, or do you want to see some more places in different parts of town?"

I straightened and stepped away from Blake to join her, knowing the farther away I was, the more clearly I could think.

"Decision's made. Let's do this."

DISCUSSION QUESTIONS

1. Blake is determined to learn more about Erica and goes to great lengths to achieve this. What are the qualities in Erica that you think capture Blake? Why is she so different than any other person that he's met before?

2. Blake is the first to pursue Erica and to declare how he feels about her. Why do you think after being the one to initiate everything, he still continues to keep his past hidden after Erica has finally opened herself up to him?

3. This book is told from Erica's perspective only. Are there certain points in the story in which you wish you could know what Blake is thinking? Which scenes or moments would you pick, and why?

4. It's important to Erica to maintain autonomy with her business, despite Blake's offers to be more involved. If you were in her position would you choose to be the same way, or would you choose to handle it a different way?

5. Blake thrives on control, in both his professional and personal life. Were there instances in the story where you felt he had or wanted too much control either professionally or personally?

6. How do you think Erica's past affects how she handles Blake's need for control in the many aspects of their relationship? Does she need the control in their personal relationship because of what she's endured in her past? Can she ask for that control in their personal relationship, while fighting against that same control in their professional relationship?

7. Blake is very protective of Erica within their relationship and with her business. Do you think his protectiveness in her business solely stems from his protectiveness in their relationship?

8. Blake and Erica have strong chemistry, and they can't help but be drawn to one another both physically and emotionally. What do you think draws them to one another to make their connection so powerful?

9. There are many outside influences on Blake and Erica's relationship. How do you think people like Max, Alli, Heath, and Sophia affect the Erica and Blake's relationship? Do you think these outside influences change how Erica and Blake want to build their relationship?

10. Both Erica and Blake come from different and complicated family situations. How do you think their respective family lives shaped them in the present tense? How do you think their family situations affect their relationship together?

ACKNOWLEDGEMENTS

The process of rediscovering myself as a writer through this book has been a powerful one. I am forever in debt to those who have made the experience possible.

Hardwired could have never come to fruition without the steadfast and fanatical support of my husband. Thank you for cheering me on every step of the way and for letting me disappear for hours and sometimes days at a time in order to tell this story.

Special thanks to my spectacular editor, Helen Hardt, for whipping my dangling participles into shape and for pushing me to create a sexy and emotional story that I could be proud to share with the world.

Thanks to the writing community on Twitter. This book was written one #1k1hr and #5hourenergy at a time, and having writing buddies has made a remarkable difference.

Thanks to Kurt and Luc for your friendship, loyalty, and wicked programming skills. May your eyes only ever grace this page of the book.

Last, but certainly not least, many thanks to all the fans who have expressed their enthusiasm and support for *Hardwired*. You gave crossing the finish line new meaning. I can't wait to share the next part of Blake and Erica's journey with you!

ABOUT THE AUTHOR

Meredith Wild is a #1 *New York Times*, *USA Today*, and international bestselling author of romance. Living in the White Mountains of New Hampshire with her husband and three children, she refers to herself as a techie, whiskey-appreciator, and hopeless romantic. When she isn't living in the fantasy world of her characters, she can usually be found at:
www.facebook.com/meredithwild

You can find out more about her writing projects at www.meredithwild.com